Sarah's Story

Sarah's Story

AN HISTORICAL NOVEL

Polly Hobson

JOHN MURRAY

© Polly Hobson 1983

First published 1983
by John Murray (Publishers) Ltd
50 Albemarle Street, London WIX 4BD

Reprinted 1984

Typeset by Inforum Ltd, Portsmouth
Printed and bound in Great Britain
at The Pitman Press, Bath

British Library Cataloguing in Publication Data
Hobson, Polly
Sarah's story.
I. Title
823'.914[F]   PR6058.o/
ISBN 0-7195-4079-8

Contents

The following manuscript was found together with a gold ring in the secret drawer of a seventeenth century writing cabinet at Morbury House.

I write to ease my heart and mind and in my great happiness in some sort do penance if only by confessing to these dumb pages. For even in contentment, past sin can lie heavy on the soul. By writing all down that has befallen me I hope to shed this burden, and in seeing myself plain lose the bitterness of guilt. As well I pray that in acknowledging what I am I may secure myself from future follies. Already, as my pen touches the paper I breathe with greater ease.

But I beg you who find, faithfully, having read, to destroy.

CHAPTER ONE

Childhood

I was born on April 6th 1645, at the manor of Bradstock in Shropshire, on the edge of the great Wyre forest. My father's was an ancient family and had held the manor with all its farms and forest rights for as long as anyone could remember. My mother had brought lands with her as well; but by the time of my birth these properties were already much diminished. In the rebellion against the King the countryside was fought over and both armies pillaged as they pleased, carrying off corn and cattle so that our tenants had nothing with which to pay their rents. My father was a loyal supporter of the Crown; he fought as a colonel in the army of the blessed martyr Charles I, and not only did this take him from home to the detriment of his estates, but, after the King's defeat, he was forced to sell lands and pay fines in order to compound with the Commonwealth and avoid losing all. Nonetheless, when Charles II returned to fight at Worcester my father at once joined him. And for this too he suffered.

My first clear recollection is of his returning home from the battle. I was woken from sleep by the commotion in the house; my nurse rising from bed and lighting the candle, doors opening and shutting and my father's voice in the hall below, sounding strange. Frightened to be alone, I crept downstairs in my nightclothes, the polished boards cold to my bare feet. My mother cried out "You are hurt!" My father answered "No. It is another's."

Only one candle was burning in the hall. Not even my nurse noticed me come in. I stood petrified, my heart thumping inside my chest. I had never seen my father in such disarray; his eyes were wild, his clothes torn and blotched with dark stains. From behind him, gently, I put out a hand to touch him, needing to be reassured. My fingers came away sticky and smeared with red. I held my hand out in front of me, staring at it stupidly, thinking it was not like when the pig was killed: this blood came from a person. I was afraid with a fear worse than in any of my childish nightmares.

"I am a dead man," he said. "The King's army is destroyed and the King fled. They hunt us like rats."

"What are we to do?" My mother wept, and more frightened now than ever, I ran to her and buried my face in her lap.

My nurse alone kept all her wits. She roused John, our boy who turned the spit, from his pallet by the kitchen fire and set him to blow the embers and heat water. She hurried my father upstairs and stripped the clothes off his back and the boots from his feet. She washed him clean and put him into his nightshirt and into bed and drew the bed curtains round him. She came downstairs with the telltale garments in her arms and bade John take the lantern and bury them where the privies were emptied in the garden. "None will care to look there," she said. Then turning to me she took my hand to lead me back upstairs.

"If any come asking for your father, he is sick of an ague and has not left his bed these ten days. Will you remember, Sarah?"

My nurse was the rock on which my infant life was built. It was on her lap that I poured out my sorrows and on her knee that I thumped my fists in rage. Her words were law.

I nodded my head. She tucked me in and kissed me, and blew out the candle, closing the door softly behind her. But my feet were too cold for me to go to sleep. I lay awake listening to the sound of running to and fro in the passage as Nurse and my mother made up the bed in the guest chamber for my mother to lie in, so as to give credence to my father's illness.

Through all this our maids in the attics never woke. Which shows how sound wenches sleep.

When Cromwell's troopers came next morning, thundering at the hall door, the house was quiet and Nurse sitting watching at my father's bedside, contriving a dress for me out of my mother's old petticoat. I was with my mother in the parlour, where the weak September sunlight fell winking on her needle as it pricked in and out of her embroidery. I clung to her skirts and hid my face when she rose to go and meet them.

"We have reason to think there are cavaliers fugitive from Worcester fight hidden in this house," their captain said. "With your leave or without, my men must search the buildings."

"There is no one here," my mother answered. "Go where you please, look where you will, but I beg you to tread softly upstairs. My husband has been sick in bed these ten days and I would not have him disturbed."

When the captain insisted every room be searched she said "Then, sir, I will take you to him myself. Sarah, leave go my skirts. You will stay here like a good child till I return. These men will not harm you."

Nor did they. One of the troopers took me on his knee and played with my curls, and asked me when my Daddy took to his bed, and when he last rode out.

But the Roundhead soldiers in their shining helmets frightened me so I burst out crying, and all they could get from me was "I don't want my Daddy to die." Which was true enough. I thought they were come to cut off his head.

Nurse liked to tell the story how my father shivered so with fright the bedhangings shook, and she curtseyed low and begged the captain not to make a noise because her master lay sick of the ague and could bear no sound.

The soldiers turned the house upside down, searching every nook and cranny from the cellars to the attics. When they were finished here they combed the outbuildings. Though they found nothing I think they were not satisfied. The captain asked my mother at parting "How comes it there is only one riding horse in the stables?"

"Who these days has horses?" she answered. "If one side does not take them they fall to the other."

"Madam," he said stiffly, and I can see him now, a tall dark man, not unhandsome if he had only worn curls and a feathered hat. "My men are not thieves."

All the same, they took away the hams that were smoking in the kitchen chimney and the sacks of flour already ground in the store, so we went short. When they were safely gone my father told us that his horse had been killed in the fighting and

3

he had snatched another man's, loosing it the other side of the Severn above Bewdley, and stealing a boat over under the noses of the Roundheads in pursuit.

For a while after this time I saw Roundheads in every shadow along the terrace walk, so that at every sudden noise I ran to find my nurse and clutch her skirts. But at last my fears died away. No more soldiers came. My father went about his business as usual. The deprivations he suffered and the troubles in the world outside the forest made no mark on my childhood. Till the eve of my eighth birthday my life flowed unruffled.

I was grooming my pony in the yard under the watchful eye of Jacky, our stable boy. The pony had that very day been given to me by my father and was still too new and too precious to be entrusted to any hands but mine. I lifted up his near hindleg to see whether the hoof needed cleaning out.

"You had better let me do that, mistress Sarah, till he knows you better."

"Carlos would never kick me," I answered, and I crawled under his belly to get to his other flank.

Jacky, though only five years my senior, was to me the very fountainhead of wisdom in all the things that most concerned me: horses, dogs, and the signs and portents that foretold the weather. But of this situation I felt the mistress.

From the stables my greyhound bitch whined.

"She'll whelp tonight like as not," Jacky said.

"I wish I could be there."

"Your nurse would never allow it. Don't fret, for this night I'll make my bed on the straw beside her. We'd best put the pony in now, they'll be calling you to your supper."

I sighed and looked up, and where before had been the dark empty way into the forest by the hawthorn tree, stood a pony and rider. The pony might have been twin to my own. The rider was a boy of a beauty such as I had never seen: fair curls tumbled over a fine lace collar; blue eyes gazed straight out of a comely face, smooth skinned and rosy. I thought at first to have seen one of the fairies Nurse told me of in her tales. Then I saw the boy was a child like myself and near to tears.

I handed Carlos to Jacky and went to meet him.

We stared at each other as children do on first encounter.

4

"Who are you?" I asked.

"Oliver. I'm lost. I can't find my way home. I have ridden miles and miles."

"This is Bradstock Manor and I am Sarah. You aren't lost now, my father will know. He knows all the Forest." Then remembering that travellers are always hungry and should be offered food, "Come with me and find Nurse. You can share my supper."

He dismounted, but hesitated to loose his pony's bridle. "She will be quite safe," I added, "Jacky will look after her with mine. What is she called?"

"She's Hetty. Her name is Henrietta, but I call her Hetty."

"Mine's Carlos." We looked at each other in wonder. "Is your father a cavalier too?"

"My father is dead."

In silence, hand in hand, we walked into the house.

We encountered my father in the hall before ever finding Nurse. I was surprised at his greeting Oliver gravely, and asking whence he came as if he were speaking to another man, not a child. In my innocence I never thought that my father would know at once from Oliver's dress that he was gently born. When Oliver said he was from Nuttley my father knew not only, as I had been confident, where that might be, but also who Oliver was.

"So your mother is returned from France. I had not heard, or I would have ridden over."

"It was only two days ago."

"And what news of your father? He is my very good friend."

"My father lies buried at Sluys." Then Oliver told how his mother had made her peace with the Parliament and brought himself and his two sisters home to the Forest. "I am squire now. 'Tis true in barely more than name, but there are still my mother's lands. We live," he said grandly. And then his manhood left him. "Sir, please show me my way. My mother will think me lost for ever. I have been riding all this long afternoon."

But my father insisted that it was too far and growing too dark, and that both Oliver and his pony were too tired to ride

5

home now. "I will send my man Martin so that your mother will rest easy. He shall go at once. He knows the forest and will be with her within the hour. You shall sleep here tonight and Sarah will entertain you to supper."

Oliver's face brightened. " 'Tis true I'm famished," he said. "And weary."

Nurse led us away to wash our hands. But when we were alone, sitting on stools in front of the hall fire over our supper, I could contain my curiosity no longer. How was it, I asked, that Oliver could be lost in the Forest, when it was peopled by foresters and charcoal burners?

"Any," I said, "would have put you on your road." He hung his head. "I was afraid. They looked so wild and so fierce. I thought they might take my pony or even harm me. So I turned away from them."

"The charcoal burners would never harm anyone who belongs in the Forest. They only hate Old Noll and his Parliament men who ride roughshod over everyone, and take their food and their goods, and all in God's name."

"But I have been away. They don't know me."

"I will tell Old Sim. He is my friend."

The charcoal burners were nobody's men. They loved you, or they did not. They loved my father because I was his child and sat by their fires. Old Sim taught me all I know about the forest creatures; when I was scolded at home he dried my tears.

"They do look fierce," I said, seeing Oliver's shame. "I would have been afraid too, had I not known."

We had finished our suppers, our plates were clean. Nurse came with candles to take us up to bed.

That night I was to sleep in the big bed with Nurse, Oliver in my truckle bed at the foot.

"I cannot take off my clothes," he said. "I have no nightshirt."

"You can have one of Sarah's," Nurse said firmly. "You are of a size. Come now, into bed with you."

Little children have no false shame. We undressed together and our pleasure in each other's company was innocence itself. Nurse smiled as she looked from one to the other, twins but that Oliver was fair and I brown. She tucked us up, and as was

6

her custom till I drowsed, she left the candle burning.

There were no hangings on my nursery walls, the plaster-work was painted with strange animals and flowers. In the flickering candlelight they moved and came alive, and nightly in imagination I walked into another world. I wondered how this would be now.

Oliver said sleepily "Our house is grander than yours but I like this one better. It is more magic. See, Sarah, it all changes. If we should get out of bed we should find no walls to hinder us."

When Nurse came to blow out the light I was still awake. I shut my eyes and pretended. I was too excited at finding a companion with whom I could share my secret thoughts. Jacky and Tom the blacksmith's son were all very well, but I could never speak to them of how the painted animals moved.

I woke late the next morning, bewildered to find myself in the big bed next the warm hollow where Nurse had lain. Then Oliver, half in enquiry, called out "Mother?" not remembering where he was and thinking himself still on his travels.

" 'Tis me, Sarah," I said, and we both sat up.

Once the strangeness of our waking passed we could think only of our ponies, and the tedious minutes till Nurse came to dress us dragged like prison hours.

"Hold still," she said as she fastened my shift. "You are not going out naked. And you'll eat your breakfasts first."

We bolted our bread and milk and made for the stables.

In the yard we encountered Martin, just returned with a letter for my father. Oliver's mother would be sending a groom for him later that morning: but the morning stretched before us with no end, as is the way in childhood.

The ponies were glossy with Jacky's grooming. They whinnied softly to us as if they had known us years instead of their being but new treasures. We stroked their velvet noses and learnedly compared their points. Jacky joined us, to ask should he saddle them up? We could try the jumps in the orchard.

Oliver, lordly, opined no. "Hetty will be tired after yester-day's journeyings, and I am to ride her home. We will jump another day."

"As you please, Master Oliver," and Jacky touched his forelock. "May I wish you a happy birthday Mistress Sarah? The bitch whelped last night, six fine pups and no trouble at all. She's a natural born mother."

We went to see.

"This is her first litter," I explained to Oliver. "Think on it. Six!"

She looked up at us from the straw with big proud eyes. The blind pups lay side by side in a row at her belly, their paws scrabbling to get at the milk. They were all heads and mouths, their ears flat shells.

"You can have one if you like, when they're grown," I offered.

"That one," and he pointed. "If you please."

We stared awhile in silence.

"What next?" Oliver asked.

"I will show you all there is to see."

We wandered out of the yard into the garden, down the terraces and out into the meadows beyond, our footsteps tending naturally towards the brook which separated the home farm from the village.

"How old are you?" Oliver asked.

"Eight this day. I had forgot it was my birthday, 'tis because Carlos came yesterday I think."

"I shall be eight on Sunday."

"Then I am the older," I triumphed.

"But I am the man. Boys can do things girls cannot."

"I can ride as well as any boy." Jacky had told me so many times.

"Ay, but do you know how to catch fish with your hands?"

"No," I admitted, dashed somewhat.

I knew the brook was full of trout that lay like shadows in the current, darting away as soon as I came near to see them. To catch them seemed a marvel.

"You must come on them from behind," he explained. "They lie looking upstream watching for what it may bring, but they are a wonderful fish, they seem to have eyes in the backs of their heads, and if you do not go softly they hear you. See, I shall crawl."

He crept on his belly through the yellow ragwort that grew along the bank and then, lying flat prone, rolled up his sleeve and slid his hand gently into the stream, so slowly that it seemed an age till the water closed round his elbow. I held my breath. Then a sudden jerk, a splash, and one of the lovely speckled creatures flew through the air to land jumping at my feet. He caught it, and putting his thumb into its mouth, with a quick movement upwards broke its neck.

"We will take it home. They make good eating," he said. "Now we'll move further up where the fish are still unwary and you shall try. You must slide your hand right under a trout so you can tickle its throat, then whoosh, and out it comes."

My first fish got clean away. But on the second attempt I managed better.

"You learn fast, for a girl," Oliver said, and I swelled with joy.

When Nurse came to find us we were both soaked to the skin and a scattering of speckled trout lay on the bank. She scolded us all the way back to the house. Nonetheless she had gathered them up, stringing them on a stout rush to carry them home.

Oliver's groom was waiting and Hetty saddled ready. But Oliver had to be dried off before he could ride, and then it was time for dinner, and my father said he must eat first; that he would write a letter, and would himself ride over next day to make his peace with Oliver's mother. I cared not. The delay pleased me well. When they left I rode partway with them, escorted by Jacky, so as to try Carlos's paces.

We ate the trout for dinner. It was a birthday to remember.

After this first meeting we became as inseparable as it is possible for children living ten miles apart to be. Formal visits were exchanged by our elders; soon, an invitation came for me to spend a few days at Nuttley.

My mother looked up from the letter and asked would I like to go? I was too full up with happiness to do more than nod my head. She smiled indulgently.

"Then that is settled," she said, and I began to count the hours.

I rode over accompanied by Martin, my emotions a mixture of excitement and apprehension. I had never before ridden out attended by Martin as if I were a young lady. This was the first time I had ever spent a night away from my mother, or under another roof than my own. Nor had I been so far into the forest. The first part of our journey was familiar, blue smoke from the charcoal burners' kilns rose above the trees, we passed Old Sim, busy building a new stack. But soon we were traversing unknown country, riding through coppices where no one was at work. Now I understood Oliver's distress when he had been lost. Suppose I were to find myself here alone? The presence of Martin beside me was some reassurance; he, after all, had been to Nuttley and returned safe.

"Nearly there, Mistress Sarah," he said, and all at once the ride ended and we came into the open.

How big the house seemed; how much grander than ours, indeed. Oliver and his mother and his two little sisters were drawn up formally to welcome me. In memory I see them like a family group in one of Mr Lely's pictures.

Oliver took me by the hand.

"Today, *I* will show *you*." So all was well, and the tremors in my stomach vanished.

I was somewhat taken aback to find that he had his own bedchamber, with his man sleeping in a closet next to him; and that the nursery in which I was to sleep with the two little girls was wainscoted and so had no pictures on the walls. When his mother came to tuck us up and bid us goodnight she took away the candle and I lay awake wishing it was morning. But when the nursegirl came to bed and tossed and sighed under her covers, snoring gently like Nurse, I was comforted.

My shyness towards these new surroundings soon vanished; in time, indeed, Oliver's house was to become like a second home to me. But I was never quite easy with his mother. She was as kind to me as could be, but I sensed that she found me a rough country girl. Oliver could read and write, and speak French. I could do none of these things. I did not even know my notes on the virginals. The manners of his little sisters who were too young to be of interest were better formed than mine. One by one my shortcomings were uncovered.

"You cannot play? Yet I am sure you can sing," she said to me, sitting down at the keyboard and turning over a page of music. "You have a sweet voice, come, try."

I had to blush. And then I wished to cry. "I cannot tell the words."

"Sarah knows all about ponies, and puppies. She's going to give me a greyhound," Oliver said. "We don't want to sing, do we Sarah? Come, you will want to see that Carlos is happy after the night in a new place."

Gratefully I took his hand and he led me away. Gravely, we inspected the stables and the ponies, and I forgot my shame.

That I was unlettered made no odds to my friendship with Oliver. We were deep in the discovery that life held the same magic for us both. Moreover, as I soon observed, anything that he asked for he was given, and this included my companionship. He was king of his mother's heart, that was plain for all to see. After many dangers she had brought the young heir home; now, as he stepped into his father's shoes, growing daily into his natural rights and duties, her eyes followed him with anxious love. The two little girls, Bess and Ann, worshippers too, counted for nothing beside him.

Another boy would have been spoiled by so much indulgence; but such was the sweetness of his nature that Oliver remained unaffected, only that he put a distance, not knowing that he did so, between himself and the servants and the grooms about him. Jacky might call me Mistress Sarah but we went ferreting together after rabbits as equals.

I enjoyed visiting Nuttley, but I much preferred it, and so I think did Oliver, when he came to Bradstock. At Bradstock, with me, Oliver could be wholly a child. We sat together at Nurse's knee, listening to her stories of hobgoblins and fairies, and next morning searched the forest to discover them. But we only found the rings of toadstools where they had danced the night before.

"We should stay awake and come here at night," Oliver said. But though we tried, we never could succeed. Watching the changing pictures on the walls our eyes closed in spite of us.

"If the fairies won't stay for us let's go bird's-nesting," I said.

From a nearby coppice the sound of a forester's axe came over the still air, the regular clunk, clunk, of two men working perfectly together.

11

"They're felling timber, that means Old Sim will be there to take his share. He will know where the best nests are. Come."

But before we could reach the clearing, with a clatter of wings a wood pigeon got up from its nest ahead of us. The untidy platform of twigs had been built at the top of a hawthorn, an easy tree to climb, but its thorns a hazard.

"I'll go," Oliver said. " 'Tis not fit for a girl. Your skirts will tangle with the prickles."

I watched him from below as he inched his way up between the branches.

"Eggs!" he called, drawing one cautiously from the nest.

"Carry it in your mouth and bring it down so," I advised. "It will break otherwise." This, Jacky had taught me.

Oliver's shirt did tangle with the thorns, but he came safely down, the egg unbroken. We examined it as it lay in the palm of his hand, white and almost round.

"What now?" he asked.

"We take it home and blow out the inside, else it will rot and stink."

"How?"

"I'll show you." This, too, I had learned from Jacky.

Oliver's shirt was torn and there was a rent in his breeches, but we reckoned nothing of this. He carried the egg back to the house as if he held all the treasure of the Indies in his hand.

"Nurse! Look!" I said, "a pigeon's egg! Oliver climbed after it and now we need a pin."

"A needle and thread more like," she said, and scolded him for spoiling his clothes as he never would have been at home.

But she found a pin at last, and I blew the egg.

"Like so," I explained. "You make a prick in the big end and one a little bigger in the smaller end, and mind you break the yolk. Then you put your mouth to the little hole and blow, thus."

Slowly, out came what was inside, and I handed Oliver the empty shell.

"Wonderful!" he said, and my content grew with thinking that in some sort our skills were equal.

We wanted to go then and there to find some more nests, but Nurse had the clothes off Oliver's back to mend and it was not till after dinner that we were free to leave the house. Cautioned against thorn trees, we took the ponies and rode out to watch the foresters at work. We reached the edge of the clearing, but there, on a sudden, had to draw rein for safety, lest the ponies take fright and bolt. One of the big trees had begun to sway; the foresters were standing back. Two pieces the shape of giant wedges had been cut on opposite sides of the trunk, leaving a slender stalk. To this a woodman now laid his axe. Very slowly, the oak inclined one way; then with increasing speed and a splitting noise of tearing fibres that sounded like the lightning's crack, fell crashing among the undergrowth.

"It cried out!" Oliver exclaimed. "Did you hear? It takes one by the throat. I do not like to see such a one fall."

"The tree is old," I said, feigning indifference. "The men measure first to be sure. The old ones must come down to make way for others." The leaves whispered and sighed as the branches settled. I did not like to think that the tree might suffer. "There's Old Sim! Now we can safely go," and we rode forward.

I had no notion how old Sim was. Some I think called him "old" from affection, and some because he was the most knowledgeable in his village. To me he was in truth old. His back was bent, his face lined and blackened with the charcoal he worked. His eyes were old too, with the look that comes from understanding and amusement at the follies of mankind. He was a small, lean man with the presence of one much bigger.

I jumped from Carlos's back and he lifted me in the air.

"This is Oliver," I said when I could draw breath. "He is returned home to Nuttley and is become my friend."

Oliver dismounted and courteously they shook hands.

"We knew you was back. It was all over the forest the day you come. 'Tis good to have the squire back at Nuttley."

Oliver accepted his title as a matter of course, and I sensed that my special relation with these people was something it would be of no use to explain.

We told of the pigeon's egg and Old Sim showed us where a missel thrush's nest had come down among the branches. By some miracle the eggs were unharmed and we carried them

13

home, nest and all, for Oliver to try his hand at blowing them.

Later, I took Old Sim to task for letting Oliver ride lost about the forest when all the while he knew he was from Nuttley. The charcoal burners were engaged in removing the covering of turves from a fired stack. Old Sim did not stop for me. His movements were as precise and unhurried as the rise and fall of the woodman's axe.

"He never asked us, did he?" He lifted a turf from the kiln. "We don't interfere with gentry." The turf was laid carefully on the ground to one side for future use. "If we'd have started shouting after him he'd have been more frit still." Another turf was lifted off. "He was heading for Bradstock, he wasn't going to come to no harm." The turf laid beside the first.

I was not satisfied. "You wouldn't do that to me."

"You're one of us, girl." He moved back to the kiln. "As native as one of them conies." One more turf joined its brothers. "Besides, after all I've learned you since you could walk," he was back at the stack, "you'd never get lost." The turf was carefully laid to start a new row. The pile was as neatly built as the stack itself.

"Well, now you must love him for my sake."

Old Sim smiled, not pausing even now. "He's a good boy."

I had made my point. This was no time for idle chatter, I knew. The charcoal burners were busy at a task that demanded their whole attention. The round kilns, like vast bee skeps, called for exact judgement in their building, firing, tending and now at last in their opening up if the wood were not to be spoilt. I lingered awhile to see the brittle black skeletons of the once-green boughs uncovered, then I left them to it.

And so the year slipped by. Our friendship grew. Autumn came, and with the rest of the village we went nutting like squirrels, to lay up winter stores. But when the leaves began to fall meeting became less easy. The ways through the forest grew foul, deep waterlogged ruts in the clay made hard going for the ponies, and as the days shortened our parents refused permission for us to ride out. Each village was cut off for the winter. Only the charcoal burners and the woodmen moved.

I turned fiercely to learning, determined to astonish Oliver's mother in the spring. In this new adventure time passed swiftly

14

so that I scarce missed my companion.

When I approached my father he was contrite.

"You should have had masters," he said. "But the times have been against it. Little one, I fear I shall make a poor fist of it as a teacher, but we will do what we can between us to fashion you into a scholar."

First came the cutting of a pen from a quill taken from one of the geese that were fattening for Christmas; a delicate task, performed by my father while I leant at the table holding my breath. Next I tried my hand at copying the alphabet as he wrote it out for me, the big letters and the small. As the first snows fell, pothooks began to turn into words. This was delight; and then I clamoured for books, and he found me in his chest a copy of *Aesop's Fables*. Aesop and the Bible were my spelling books, and I cried when Adam and Eve were driven from the garden of Eden never to return.

We both enjoyed these lessons and once I was fluent in my own tongue my father led me into the mysteries of Latin grammar, translating for me the tales of Ovid, because he had no other text. Then I clamoured for English poets too.

"Poets!" he said. "They write like angels, but ours support a rotten system. They have to get their bread, but I'll have none of them."

So I fed my fancy on the verses in my mother's song books. Verses led to notes, and these too, with pains, I mastered.

I was a diligent scholar, but the domestic arts I would not learn. When my lessons with my father were over I ran outside to Jacky; Nurse called me in vain, my mother's complaints fell on deaf ears. I found no pleasure in sewing seams or stirring pots. The construction of mince pies held no charm by compare with a Latin sentence.

We celebrated Christmas in the old, forbidden way that the Puritans called pagan; my father would have been punished had it been discovered. But the forest could be an evil place for strangers, and so deep in and in such weather the Parliament agents did not care to venture.

The yule log came and went. The burning bush was carried out and scattered and the fires for the new year twinkled in the fields at night to ensure their fruitfulness. When trees began to bud and March winds dried the forest ruts, then one day Oliver came riding into our stable yard, the greyhound puppy, now grown into a fine dog, at his heels.

"Look, Sarah! How splendid Jason is become!"

"The bitch has pups again," I answered.

We took up where we had left off.

Bird's-nesting led us far afield that spring, and on one warm day we stopped in our straying to rest in the shade of a wild cherry tree. We lay on our backs on the grass, looking up into the white blossom and chewing the gum that comes from under the bark. Townsfolk do not know of this pleasure.

"I wish I could have Bradstock," Oliver said. "I like it better than Nuttley."

"Bradstock is mine," I stated, "to have it you must wed me."

"And will you, Sarah? Wed with me?"

"Yes," I said.

We got up from the ground and solemnly took hands to plight our troth. One or two petals fell like a blessing on our heads.

Now I smile to think how we kept this secret to ourselves. There was no need. It was commonly held through all the forest and in both our households that such a marriage would take place.

CHAPTER TWO

But what of me?

In my fourteenth year on a sudden my contentment vanished.
The midsummer sun shone on a scene that had lost its charm.
My occupations had grown stale. I wanted to know what was
outside in the big world. Feigning that I was taking Carlos to be
shod, I rode off instead by myself to where the Forest came
down to the bank of the Severn. From the shelter of the trees I
watched the traffic moving on its flood; the heavily laden trows
floating unaided down to Bewdley and beyond towards the
sea, but with what effort up river towards Bridgenorth, hauled
by teams of rough men. One such passed along the towpath,
the men straining on the ropes, sweat running down their
faces. The broad boats pushed like the breasts of swans against
the water, throwing up waves on either side. So our timber and
charcoal travelled, but I knew nothing of these towns through
which the river passed. Travellers at the door and a visiting
tailor brought what we could not supply for ourselves. I sat on
my pony wishing I could by magic be transported on the
stream, and half envying the toiling men who knew so much
more of life than I.

"You were an age," my mother said when I returned. "What
kept you?"

I lied again. "I was speaking with the minister. Would my
father do you think let me go to him to learn Greek?"

"You think too much of books, and if not books, of
stables," she answered. " 'Tis time you turned your mind to
household arts."

But even the stables had begun to pall. I wanted fresh
companions. I watched the village girls with envy as they
walked entwined to pick the early blackberries, whispering
secrets in each other's ears. What were they talking of? I picked

17

blackberries with Nurse, and when I carried them into the kitchen, Susan and Mary were throwing apple peels over their shoulders to tell who they would marry. They tittered and blushed, and as I set the bucket on the table I blushed too, because I wished for friends with whom to play such games myself. Oliver's sisters were too young.

Nor was I any longer wholly at my ease with Oliver. He was but a boy, his voice not yet broken. I loved him as much as ever, but in my growing had outstripped him. I wished him to fill a mould he could not, and so he was diminished in my eyes. In body I was already a woman though in mind still a child. I dreamt of cavaliers in feathered hats.

That autumn the Protector died. The news reached us on a still September morning, brought by a travelling pedlar along with his ribbons and pins. In her excitement my mother paid him twice over, and when she discovered the mistake let him keep the money. By midday all the Forest knew. Change was in the air, and through Bradstock expectation ran high, but none could guess what might happen.

"If you eat so fast Sarah you will choke," my mother said. " 'Twould be a pity if Old Noll's dying gave you the stomach ache."

I was in a hurry to ride out. I had fixed to meet Oliver and go nutting. I could hardly wait till our ponies were tethered before I asked "Have you heard? What think you? My father says the King will come back and we shall have our lands again." I saw a whole new prospect open before me.

Oliver shook his head. His face was solemn.

"Who will bring the King back? We want no more wars. Should he come home I doubt if many lands will change their owners."

I stamped my foot. "How can you be so stupid? *Something* must happen. Old Noll is dead!"

"The King has no money. I have seen it," he said, putting nuts into my basket. "Without money no one can move."

"I hate you!" I cried in my disappointment.

" 'Tis not my fault, Sarah."

Then I said I was sorry. But I had felt less dashed had his eyes shone or had he taken my hand.

18

In truth, for the time being nothing did change.

But now my father could not settle to anything and even my lessons with him came to an end. One day he put down his pen and said "My Sarah, you are a child no longer. 'Tis time your mother took on your education."

I felt a great desolation: the first in my young life. I was about to be cast off, abandoned by my father, the one being who gave me daily converse with a wider scene. True, it was a world of books only that he opened to me, and false maybe, but a window nonetheless and now to be shut. In my hurt I ran to Nurse for comfort, and as I had done in infancy, buried my head in her bosom and wept.

She stroked my hair and murmured soothing words till she had drawn from me all my troubles.

"My lamb, you are at a hard age for girls — grown out of one gown and not yet ready to fill the next. Book learning will not satisfy your longings and your father knows it. Have patience. In another year's time you will be old enough for what you need. Oliver likewise needs time. You must not press him. Boys grow slower than girls. Do not cry so. All will be well."

A whole year passed.

"Your father neglects his lands," Oliver said, as we hunted rabbits in fields where the thistles grew and brambles from the forest encroached.

"He is melancholic with disappointment. At every rumour that comes and proves false his spirits rise and fall. Now our lands are in decay perhaps you will like Nuttley best." I turned my head away so as not to see his face.

"I still would have Bradstock," Oliver replied and I felt comforted. "My mother has had news out of France," he went on. "It seems the King is dickering with General Monk and some agreement likely to be reached. We may yet see what we all want, Sarah."

This was in the spring before my fifteenth birthday and once again Oliver proved right.

Imperceptibly, rumour turned into solid fact and by the end of the first week in May we all knew the King was to come back. At Bradstock the common people were so sure of what was to come that they threw off all restraint. May Day was

19

brought in in such a way as had not been seen since the Commonwealth began, and the maypole was raised on the village green. The minister kept to his house and turned a blind eye to what was happening on his doorstep. He began, I think, to be afraid for his future.

My father said he dare not himself countenance such sports till the King were safely home, but nor would he lift a finger against them.

"Bless the lads," and he smiled. "They are discreet. They do not tell me what they intend to do."

On May Day eve, wishing I could go too, I listened as Susan and Mary slipped from the house and passed giggling under my window to join the rest of the village lads and maidens to bring in the green; but I did not hear them return.

Next day the fiddler's music reached us across the fields.

"I go to watch," I said.

Jacky was absent, playing truant with all the rest. I saddled Carlos myself, and crossing the ford drew rein outside the vicarage. I was wondering in longing how I might without loss of dignity join in, when a stranger passing through the forest on his way to Ludlow took my bridle.

"The prettiest wench to be seen cannot stand aside," he said. "Come! Dance to the King! The Parliament sends for him today, I have it from my cousin." He lifted me down and gave me a smacking kiss. Then he tied my pony to the vicarage railings and led me into the dance.

My cheeks were burning, my heart beat like a bird in my chest, but my feet floated over the ground in happiness as I passed in the dance from the stranger to Jacky, to Martin, to Tom, at one with the general merriment. The smell of hawthorn blossom everywhere, on the hedge round the church, decorating the May Queen's bower, proved a heady wine. The arbour was empty except for the May Queen's posy; little Ellen herself, Tom's sister, was already dancing. I was a girl among all the rest, chased like the others and caught with shrieks of laughter by the Jack in the Green. In his leafy headdress he was a wild figure but he offered us no rudeness with his kiss. As dusk fell bonfires were lit. The stranger had long since gone on his way. I slipped home and saw Carlos

20

safely stabled, knowing it would be dark, or daylight more likely, before Jacky returned.

My mother said "Sarah! Where have you been? Your supper waits."

"Watching the dancing," I said. But I think Nurse guessed from my flushed cheeks that I had done more than watch, for she smiled.

That night I could not sleep for thinking of dancing and kisses and that a man found me pretty, and that now I was in truth a child no longer, but a maid.

The rejoicing went on all May and I grew to think it would last forever. Up and down the country bonfires blazed again when the King landed at Dover; the smell and smoke hung in the air, an incense I shall never forget, and the evening sky showed pink with their flames. For four whole days my father in his joy kept open house, and there was dancing in the hall and barrels of ale broached for all who came. In honour of the King's return I was measured for a new gown and petticoat by the tailor, the first I had ever had that was not made at home from garments discarded by my mother. Gown and petticoat came out of their wrappings stiff with newness; smooth to the touch. When Nurse hooked me up and dressed my hair, so transformed was I that I barely knew the girl who I saw in the glass.

"There!" Nurse said. "My pretty one looks as she should at last."

Myself yet not myself! Later I grew vain, but then — 'twas beyond belief.

On the last of those four days Oliver and his whole family came over for the night, that old friends might toast the King together. From the cellar my father brought wine, long saved against such a day. But I had no need of wine to lift my heart. I was already drunk on my new gown, and the coming and going and the rearranging of bedrooms, the clearing of the hall and the fiddlers tuning up, and the horses in the yard, and all the company arriving. Then, of a sudden, there was Oliver, comely, looking at me as if he had never seen me before.

We opened the dance together and as he handed me he whispered "Sarah! How pretty you are! Like — like the wild

21

cherry in the forest." The words came all in a rush.

My happiness was complete. We moved in the dance in a world as enchanted and apart as the private country we had travelled together in childhood, when the candlelight danced on my bedroom walls at night. Our watchful parents, standing side by side, for us were vanished. We had eyes for none but each other; the music of the fiddlers was the only sound we heard. When silence fell and the movement stopped we stared at each other tongue-tied and questioning.

Afterwards, at Nuttley, I stayed as a young lady, with a chamber to myself.

I was wearing my fine clothes, the sleeves of my white chemise falling in a frill below the blue satin, and my hair was tied up with blue ribbons.

"What now?" I asked Oliver, as I sat at the virginals, picking out a tune with one hand. What I meant was — Are we to wed?

"I go to Oxford in the autumn."

"Then what of me? What am I to do?"

"Be patient," he said. He leaned across and kissed me. It was clumsily done. We both reddened.

Then Bess and Ann came running in, demanding that I sing *Greensleeves* for them. So nothing more was said between us.

Perhaps because of the new petticoat he and I were no longer left alone together; wherever we chose to go his mother sent his sisters tagging after. Now that I was grown I had become a danger. I had no dowry and she wished for Oliver to make a better match. She made quite sure I knew of this; I had it from the innocent mouths of Bess and Ann:

"Our mother says that Oliver must marry an heiress if we are to get husbands. Sarah, who do you think she will be?"

But before I could answer Bess's question Ann went prattling on: "We wish it could be you; we cannot think there is anyone half as suitable."

I tried to tell myself Oliver was in all things his mother's master and would do as he pleased. Nevertheless I smarted.

At Bradstock there were no little sisters to intervene. But when he next came and we rode out as of old, there was a new constraint between us. On account of that first kiss I found it hard to meet his eyes. It was not repeated. What passed between us then and in the dance might never have been, and I wondered whether his mother had spoken to him.

But in truth I knew not how to feel. I wished for Oliver to kiss me again if only to end my confusion. When the stranger had lifted me down from my pony he stirred my senses. I was angry that Oliver did not move me so; yet I loved him with all my heart. How cruel a time is youth! When I look back now, it is easy to see my trouble was but the difference between a boy and a man.

Oliver at this time was much occupied with his tutor. When I could not have his company I sat about sighing, deaf to my mother's reproaches, pulling the petals off daisies to tell if he loved me, eating my heart out for I knew not what.

I was picking apples in the orchard for want of anything better to do, when from the yard I heard a shout of "Sarah!" This was Oliver. My heart bounded, but I didn't run. I went softly to meet him, the basket, half full, on my arm. Jacky was holding the bridle of his horse; it was one that I had never seen before.

"Is he not splendid, Sarah?" Oliver said. "He is to carry me to Oxford. I call him the Black Boy."

"He is handsome indeed." But it was the rider I was thinking of. The sun turned his curls to gold, his skin was brown from being so much out of doors yet had a bloom, his eyes were clear and shining with excitement. He had now outstripped me by a full head, and when he dismounted I had to look up at him. I felt myself blushing. "What of Hetty?" I said.

"Hetty is for the girls. I'm too heavy now; she will no longer carry me."

He took my basket from me and together we wandered back into the dappled sunshine under the trees. Every single thing about that moment is memorable to me.

"They are sweet," I said, "try one," and we each chose and ate a rosy fruit, warm from the sun. Neither of us spoke. For the length of our eating an apple we shared the enjoyment of the noise of the hard flesh crunching as we bit, the sweet taste, and the juice running over our teeth and threatening to run down our chins, only we licked it back first. There was the

23

pleasure for me too that Oliver carried my basket as we walked side by side. I was warmed more by his presence close beside me even than by the sun.

The apple finished he said: "Sarah, I have great news. I ride with my tutor tomorrow. I am come to say goodbye." He looked where he flipped the core gaily away into the grass, merry as a boy throwing a ball.

The day fell apart for me.

"So soon?" was all I could say.

"Don't pull such a long face. 'Tis not forever. Spring will come soon enough, then I return. Sarah, look pleased."

"How can I? It is very well for you, you go out into the world; but whom have I here to be with once you are gone? What is my life to be?"

"But Sarah, we part every winter." The last word came out in a squeak. His voice had begun to break; it rose and fell uncomfortably and in embarrassment he turned his head away. "It is no different from last year, it has been the case for all of six — nay seven years, you know it well."

I felt no pity for his discomfiture. Why was he not a man, in spirit at least? For me it *was* different. I had changed. But how could I explain?

"Of course I must go to college, every gentleman does." And now his voice was in his boots. "My father would have wished it. and since the King is back my mother will not fear every moment for my safety. Think, Sarah, what life is like for me at Nuttley. She watches every step I take, my sisters trot after me like puppies. I'm sick of petticoat government. I need my fellows. What man have I to talk to other than my tutor? Tell me, what quality has he?"

I shook my head. With this there was no argument. The tutor was a sad man, a poor scholar, clinging to scraps of Latin and a safe refuge.

"But what is to become of me?" It was my constant cry.

"I shan't forget you, Sarah. Come, wish me well."

"I wish you were not going."

I held out my hand and also my cheek.

It was my hand he took.

I walked with him back through the orchard; I watched him

24

mount and ride away into the forest; it was as if he took life itself with him.

When I could see him no longer and the branches had stopped moving behind him as he brushed past, I picked up the basket of apples, discarded like myself, on the stones of the yard. All unthinking his hand had carried it for me, meaning nothing, and I had thought it was because he loved me. I felt such an ache of sorrow in my chest I wondered it did not split. I was angry with him too because he would not recognise my trouble. At this point in my life one kiss from him would have held me forever.

That night I cried myself to sleep, stifling my sobs in my pillow. My hurt was too deep to tell even to Nurse. When I had moped all next day and she pressed me to confess my trouble that she might comfort me I complained of the lesser evil: that I missed his company, not that he would not talk of love, or that our betrothal had dropped like a stone into a muddy pond.

"Oliver goes to learn," she said, "to learn what he must. And, Sarah, you would do well to do the same. If you were to busy yourself about the house with your mother, who has much to teach you, time would not hang so heavy on your hands. Now is your chance to fit yourself to be a wife."

But for this I had no heart. Oliver had not spoken. I wished myself dead.

Old Sim was no comfort either. I made him pause in building his stack to listen to me, but what he said was unwelcome.

"You would not want a milksop, girl? A mother's boy would be no use to you."

"Oliver is no milksop," I cried, and raised my whip, half ready in my vexation to strike my trusted friend.

"Nay, lass," he said, unmoving. "A lad must grow, like timber. You fret without need."

To counter my distress I rode out on Carlos, morning and afternoon, galloping like a wild thing, till at last Jacky protested.

"You're riding the pony too hard, he cannot stand it. If you go on like this he will be foundered."

I threw him the reins. "Then, Jacky, what am I to do? There's nothing for me here. Nothing, nothing."

"Another year and Mr Oliver will be able to do as he pleases."

"Hold your tongue!" I said and flounced into the house. He had understood me too well. I was sore, envying him for his own happiness. Jacky was courting Susan. I was jealous of their kissing in the loft, and that when Susan grew big they would marry.

It was on one of my wild rides that I found the dead man. I was deep into the forest somewhere on the way that led from Bradstock to Bridgenorth, not caring where I went so long as I was on the move. Again I was riding too hard, in a rage with Oliver that was beyond reason, pitying myself for unnecessary sorrows, calling him false because I wished for love now, not when he could give it me. I saw myself as a lady of romance left forlorn by a heartless lover, and was half enamoured of my pain.

My head was full of this moonshine when Carlos shied, jinking like a snipe; had I not been so practised a horsewoman I would have gone over his head. He was unwilling to go forward, sidling and trying to turn back, so that we scraped among the twigs. It was not till I had got him pulled up and clear of the bushes into which he had plunged that I saw what had frightened him. His senses had been quicker than mine, he must have smelt what was there. Or, with the foreknowledge that animals sometimes possess, had he suddenly become aware that a dead thing lay in our path? In either case, I am persuaded to this day that the pony knew that it was a man, before ever I could tell the same myself from the hat that had fallen by the wayside, and the loose horse grazing beyond.

I felt the strangest thing: not I, but another whom I watched, dismounted and tied Carlos to a tree, walking forward calmly to make sure in all particulars what lay there.

It was like something thrown away. Empty. Of no consequence any more. So that the gash on the scalp and the buzzing flies meant no more than the shreds on a bone on the rubbish heap. I gathered my skirts and passed by it. The horse was of more importance, it was alive and couldn't be left where it was, saddled and bridled and without water. I observed dispassionately that he was a fine bay gelding, such as would

26

belong to a person of some substance.

There was no trouble in catching the animal, he came towards me, whinnying softly. I slackened the girth and slid the stirrup irons up the leathers so that they no longer dangled against his flanks. I had to coax him to pass his dead master. But once safely by, I drew the reins over his head so as to lead him, and mounting Carlos rode soberly back to Bradstock.

Jacky's face clouded when he saw the led horse.

"We have come quietly," I said, "don't scold me. He is in sore need of water. I found him in the forest. His master lies dead, I would think many hours."

Jacky held my bridle and looked searchingly up at me, more troubled than I had ever seen him.

"Mistress Sarah, you bring bad news. I know that horse. He's been shod at our forge. He carries the collector of the King's monies. My master should know of this at once."

"I will go to him, Jacky. See to them both," and I left him standing there, shaking his head.

My father was in the parlour with my mother. I told him all, from first to last, and when I had finished his face was grave.

"This is a heavy business," he said. "I know not when I shall return. Sarah, say nothing of this to anyone," and he left the room.

Not till then, when there was nothing more to be done and I was alone with my mother in our quiet parlour, did I take in fully that the bundle of rubbish I had left behind in the forest had indeed been a human being, and in a rush I was both sad and afraid. I thought: is this what we come to? Then: what will this death mean to the living? I began to shiver and my teeth clacked. I wept for the poor man cut off from life, and for us, who had found him.

My mother called for Nurse, and a cordial, and they sat me down by the hall fire. I had never known such shivers, the fire could have been ice for all the heat I had from it.

My mother said "Sarah, you are a brave girl, a true soldier's daughter. Your father will be proud of you. Do not fret. These shudders will pass."

But her words were meaningless beside my visions of mortality. Nurse was obliged to hold the glass to my mouth my hands were shaking so, and my teeth rattled on the rim. The liquid went down my throat and through my body like fire; and after a time, I was calm again, and trembled no more.

We were at supper when we heard a commotion in the yard. We guessed that it must be my father returning, but he did not then come into the house. We learnt later that he had taken Jacky and Martin with him and gone himself to fetch the dead man back, bringing him out on a hurdle; that they had stopped for a cart on their way to the village; this was why we had heard them.

He was still not home when my mother sent me up to bed. I was glad to go. But in my sleep I had nightmares. The dead man sat up grinning, the blood running from his wound, and I shouted "Murder!" Nurse, hearing me cry out, came in with a candle and slept the rest of the night beside me, holding me in her arms as she had done when I was an infant.

The next morning my father summoned all of us in the household into the hall.

"It is as well that you should know the truth of what happened yesterday," he said. "The dead man, whom my daughter Sarah found when riding in the forest was our Under Sheriff, who these many years has collected the monies due to the Crown. I went with Jacky and Martin to see for myself. From his injuries and from the way he was lying I surmise that he was thrown against a tree. It is possible that his horse stumbled on a root, or maybe smelled deer and bolted. But no one can tell exactly what happened; it is a wild place where he was found, and none working near who might have witnessed the accident. There has been no robbery. The man's clothes had not been disturbed, his rings were still on his fingers, there was money in his pocket, and the taxes he had collected were untouched in his saddlebags. He lies now closed in a coffin in the church, waiting for his family to arrange for burial. I have sent the constable with all the monies and a full report to the Sheriff, and we must all hope that this is the last we shall hear of the matter. I am obliged as a Justice to make investigations in the forest, in case there is a witness maybe afraid to come forward. But there is no reason to suspect foul play."

I was astounded. When the hall had cleared and everyone

28

gone about their business I went to speak with my father in his closet.

"A man did that," I said. "The gash I saw could not have happened otherwise."

He answered "That is a thought you must keep to yourself. Sarah, I know better than you that no tree made that wound, but if I had every man in the forest up in front of me none would testify against the killer. Let us hope we shall be allowed to leave ill alone."

I understood. I had not known, when I found him, who the dead man was. But like everyone else at Bradstock I knew the Sheriff's man to be much hated in the forest. He was a hard man, without pity for the poor, taking the last penny due and lining his own pocket into the bargain. I had had it from Old Sim that a charcoal burner's child had died last winter for lack of food and care when sick and the father had sworn revenge. The charcoal burners would protect their own people; moreover my father was a humane man and a forester first and last; his sympathies would lie with the man who struck the blow.

I said nothing of what I had seen, not even to Jacky or Martin, who knew as much as I, and for love of the forest and loyalty to my father held their peace also. But no one in the village believed my father's story, and the murder of the collector of the King's monies frightened them. They wondered what retribution from outside would fall, and who would come in his place? Hated as he was, he was a known evil, having held his office without a break from the time of the martyred King.

When the coffin was removed from the church and the horse from our stables and no inquest followed, all Bradstock breathed more easily.

Indeed, we heard nothing further on the score of the dead man, and except that I no longer had the heart to ride far abroad, which pleased Jacky, life returned to normal. My father had had no compensation for his losses, as Oliver had foretold; his hopes began to fade. The iron bands of winter were now closing in. There was nothing to relieve the tedium of the days and I fell into a melancholy as heavy as his own.

I was passing the morning playing sad tunes upon the

virginals when there came a knocking on the hall door. It was just such a knocking as the one sounded by the Roundhead soldiers and my heart leapt into my mouth. Then I told myself this was foolish. There were no Roundheads now, and had there been, it would be they not I who would have need to be afraid. But all the same I was still in a flutter when I went to open the door, wondering who this could be?

In spite of his lace collar and the feather curling round his black hat, the man standing there looked too like a Puritan to be pleasing to me; he had "Puritan" written all over him, whether it was that his coat was sober, or something about his lean figure and pale eye, or that his aspect was solemn, I know not. He asked politely for my father, saying he was a certain Gilbert Fearnshawe, and that he was one of the surveyors of His Majesty's woods and forests.

I called for Jacky to take his horse and sat our visitor down by the hall fire while I went to find my father. I think neither man remarked that I stayed to listen, half hidden in a corner, making a show of working the sampler I had been at ever since I was six years old and never getting beyond the first row of stitching. My mind had leapt at once to the murder. I was determined to hear what the stranger's errand was.

I proved to be right. It was indeed the murder that was in question.

"Let us come straight to the point," Mr Fearnshawe said. "In this matter of the death of your Under Sheriff, it appears to me, shall we say strange, that a man who had ridden the forest for thirty years should come to his end in so foolish a manner. His horse smelled deer? If I may say so, and as one who knows the forest himself, it is a tale that itself smells somewhat. Who found the body?"

I trembled.

"Myself," and my father smiled. "Strange it may seem, nevertheless there was nothing to show there had been foul play. The man was not robbed. If, and mark you I say if, there was murder done you might question and hang every man in the forest before one would testify against another."

"I trust you do not compound a felony?"

"I trust not." Then my father changed his ground. "You are

30

not by any chance kin to the Mr Fearnshawe who buys our timber?"

"His brother," and now our visitor appeared to me to shuffle somewhat.

"In that case, it is perhaps of some consequence to you who holds the office in question?" and I saw from his manner that my father in his turn was attacking. "There are some practices to which an Under Sheriff can turn a blind eye; the matter of felling timber, for example."

"Let us say it would suit me if all could go on as before. My brother's furnaces are always hungry, he would no doubt be pleased to take some more timber from yourself. Times, I would hazard, have been hard for the King's supporters." He paused and stroked his nose. "There is no need to count or measure over-carefully."

So Mr Fearnshawe was himself in the habit of cheating the King, and was suggesting that my father do the same. "It is no part of my duties to oversee the King's forests," replied my father.

"I see we understand each other." Mr Fearnshawe uncrossed his long legs and crossed them again. "And no doubt it would be as well if the new man were one who did not lean too heavily on the poor?"

I dropped my wools and as I bent to pick them up the stool I sat on slipped. My father turned his head.

"Sarah! Go at once and tell your mother Mr Fearnshawe stays to dine. She will, I'm sure, be glad of your help."

I curtseyed demurely and left the hall.

I gave the message to my mother, but did not stay. Instead, for the half hour there was till dinner I wandered in the orchard where the last apples still clung to the branches, turning my father's words over in my mind. He was a good man. He had lied without a blush to protect me. I refused to countenance that he should cheat his King. For that same King he had willingly suffered so much, refusing to bow his head; indeed, had he not risked his very life?

But I saw it was so. He had been both threatened and bribed. The threat had left him unmoved; but the bribe he was willing to take. It was as if the very foundations of my life quaked.

During dinner I studied closely this man who had the power to undermine my father. He was neither young nor old, of that lean build that once past first youth does not show the passage of time. His sandy hair was rough textured like a terrier's, and, like his years, neither short nor long. He made himself agreeable to my mother, praising the dinner, saying his housekeeper could not do as well. He spoke of the scenes in London at the King's return, of the rejoicing in the streets, of men toasting him on their knees; he told of the King's graciousness to those he found ready to serve him of whom, we were told, Mr Fearnshawe himself was one. And all the while as he talked he stole glances at myself. I lowered my eyes, but I was woman enough already to know he found me comely, and I was flattered, finding him less unpleasing than I had first thought he was.

When our visitor had left my father took me on one side.

"Sarah," he said, "Mr Fearnshawe is a man of substance and consequence. He is not only concerned with the King's forests, but also holds lands in Gloucestershire and has a place high in the Exchequer. He is in a position to help put Bradstock back on its feet. Whatever his past history, and he makes no secret that he was a Commonwealth man, he serves the King well. We must treat him kindly. And Sarah, do not try to understand those things that are beyond your years."

I was sickened; by my father, not by the man he talked of.

That night Nurse was unusually silent as she helped me to undress. I had expected her to remark on our visitor. Persons of importance calling at the door were a rare occurrence at Bradstock. Moreover, since the murder, we had all been apprehensive.

I turned my back that she might unhook my bodice.

"Nurse, in conversation with my father I heard Mr Fearnshawe say that he knew the forest well. How could this be? I have never heard tell of him before."

She gave a sharp tug as she undid the next hook. "Those Fearnshawes! Their father was steward to the Ryder and master forester of Cleobury Chase, one of the Blounts of Kinlet, the Earl of Leicester's man. The boys ran about these woods barefoot. 'Tis Blounts not Fearnshawes should be

32

visiting this house. Your father plays with fire. There's only one person's advantage any of that breed cares for and that's their own."

"They must be clever, Nurse, to have climbed so high."

"Clever!" and she tugged at another hook. "As clever as a shipload of monkeys. Who wants clever?"

I sighed. I was thinking of the streets of London which I had never seen.

Mr Fearnshawe called again, this time to inform my father of the appointment of the new Under Sheriff, and then yet once more, to discuss, so he said, a new system of drainage that would improve our pastures. On each occasion he stayed to dine, on each occasion I was conscious of the interest he took in my person.

The winter put no stop to these visits. There were matters in these parts, he said, that required his attention; though why this should be so much the case, seeing his estates were in Gloucestershire, I did not understand. But I had had no company since Oliver left for Oxford, and for me his appearance was a diversion.

One day we had a fall of snow, the first of that winter, and even then he came. It was already late afternoon and growing dark, the skies leaden and the snowflakes swirling every which way, thick in the air, lying white on his hat and on the cape of his riding coat. The storm raged into the night and he was obliged to stay; which I think was what he all along had intended. I put on my cloak and went across the yard to the stables to see that all was well and Jacky grumbled, saying the man was a snuffling Puritan and had no business to show his face in a house such as ours. Neither he nor his horse.

"The horse is not to blame," I said.

"Poor creature, to have to carry such a load."

Nurse was not best pleased either, and murmured as Susan and Mary bustled to see the spare room aired and sheets put on the bed.

Mr Fearnshawe did not disclose the purpose of his visit till supper was cleared and we were sitting round the parlour fire. Then he announced that the King had honoured him for his services at the Exchequer by making him a knight.

33

On the instant my interest was roused. This man now sitting by our fire had seen the King face to face, perhaps even touched his hand. Addressing him directly for the first time I blurted out, "What manner of man is our King? How does he look?"

Mr Fearnshawe smiled indulgently at my excitement.

"A tall man, above the common even for such, lean-faced, his hair black with no trace of grey, his eyes penetrating. He walks among the common people and listens. A gracious monarch, only — "

"Only?"

"I fear he is too fond of pleasure. His ministers, nay, all who serve him, would like to see him take a wife."

I fell into a dream, seeing myself at court, curtseying to this paragon among men.

I heard my mother say gently, "Come Sarah, it grows late." Already she had laid down her embroidery.

We collected our candles from the hall and went upstairs to our own chambers, leaving the two men sitting together in silence, waiting, I think, till we were gone before they talked.

The following morning my father called me to him.

"Sarah," he said, "Sir Gilbert Fearnshawe has made me an offer for your hand."

I thought at once: what was their bargain? And who was to be bought and sold? Was it, after all, myself? I stared through the window. The snow lay thick outside, turning the landscape into a prison, the yews along the terrace walk so many white-caped gaolers. I feared our visitor would be obliged to stay, and I wanted him gone.

"I am promised to Oliver these six years past," I said.

"Come now, such childish vows made without a parent's consent count for nothing, as you should know. Oliver is not of an age to bind you to him."

"He is old enough to marry if he chooses."

"Hardly, my child. He is still a student but just gone to Oxford. Nor is he yet full grown. If when he is turned eighteen you both still should feel the same we would have to think again. You must consider, Sarah, Oliver has a mother and two sisters to care for. Nuttley is as badly encumbered as Bradstock. Such a marriage would be a folly; although in other circumstances I would welcome the union."

We were in his closet where we had spent so many happy hours together in time past, his head bent with mine, puzzling out the Latin of Ovid's tales. Now he would not meet my eyes, but looked instead at his desk and played with his pen.

"I would not have you marry against your inclination," he continued. "But think on Sir Gilbert. Do not decide in haste that you cannot like him. He can give you what I cannot: the place in the world that is your right, a handsome establishment, the society of your equals, pretty gowns, the toys that women crave for. Nor does he ask for a dowry. It is a match such as I have not dared to hope for. The prospect else is bleak. Pretty as you are, without a dowry mothers will not welcome you to their houses to tempt their sons. I cannot hawk you round the country to be humiliated."

I was silent. My cheeks burned.

"Well, what am I to tell him?"

"That I cannot give an answer. That I wish to have more time."

"I will make your maidenly excuses," and then at last he laid down his pen and looked up at me.

"I do not wish to meet him," I said. "I am not well. I keep my room till he is gone."

Sir Gilbert left that morning, making his way through deep snow that would have kept other men close.

All the while the snow lay and then turned to slush and mud I was forced to keep to the house, shut up with my thoughts. I longed to speak with Oliver and know his mind, but he would not be coming till spring; and he did not write. If he cared for me he could at least have sent one small word to tell me how he did, and what he did, in his new life. I trembled to think of how comely he was and of the company he was in: the young sparks and loose women, in taverns. And here was I, mewed up like a hawk with doves. I had no company save Nurse and my mother. I wondered how I was to endure two more such long winters. And what supposing Oliver then no longer wanted me? What would be my fate? Wife to some small tradesman glad to do my father a favour?

Then I quaked to think what secrets there might be between

35

Sir Gilbert and my father. That I had to know.

When at last hard frost turned the ground to iron, I put on my cloak and went to seek out Old Sim. The day was brilliant. Every branch in the woods glittered and shone; the leaves on the floor of the ride instead of lying limp and sodden crackled like parchment underfoot. The air was sharp in my lungs and my heart beat fast with the joy of escape to the wilds. Blue smoke rising thin above the trees led me to him. He was watching a kiln, waiting for the exact right moment to close in the top.

I forgot I was now a young lady. I flung myself into his arms and for a moment he held me close.

"My little girl! What brings you here in this cold, to warm my heart?"

"I'm troubled sore. I need your help. I need your wisdom. There is no one else will do. It concerns my father and one Sir Gilbert Fearnshawe."

"*Sir* Gilbert?"

"Yes, Sim, just newly made so. There is something between him and my father that I don't at all understand. Nor do I trust it. They talked sideways of felling timber, and now my father wishes me to wed this man. You know all that happens here in the forest, from where the thrushes nest to what men say. Spell it out to me."

"Spelling books? I know nought of they." He smiled. "But it doesn't need spelling books to figure out that one's game. Since you ask me I'll tell you. My girl, you're no better than an animal taken to market."

"I still don't understand," and I did not. My mind refused to admit his words.

"Then 'tis time that little head did some thinking. Fearnshawe means to buy your father's silence. This new Sheriff's man is in his pocket like the last one. All the forest knows. With your father's mouth stopped Fearnshawe can sell acres of timber to that rogue his brother and no penny go into any pocket but his own. What matter so long as Sheriff and Justice too turn a blind eye?"

"And my father?" I said in a small voice. "Then he is a rogue too."

36

"Your father cuts more timber than he ought. I cannot altogether blame him. After all the troubles there've been. I reckon he takes no more than the King would give if he could. He does no great harm. He cheats no more than other men. The Fearnshawes and their like are a different kettle of fish altogether."

"Sim, if I marry or if I do not, will it not be all the same? Sir Gilbert will do as he wishes. As well as my father's own cheating, there is this matter of the Under Sheriff, the man who was killed."

"No. That doesn't come into it. Girl, I like to think your father would put up with so much and no more, if you don't tie his hands for him. No Bradstock man would care to see sheep graze where now the deer run." He looked at me straight. "Young Oliver would not have it."

Judging the kiln ready, he closed the chimney up. The cold was biting into my bones and I shivered. I liked nothing of what I had heard.

Still no word came from Oliver; nor did Sir Gilbert call. With each day that passed my tedium grew and I thought less of the persons of the two men and more of what they could offer me. As Oliver's wife I should be obliged to be obedient to a woman who did not like me, seeing no fresh scenes, living a life I already knew too well. And then I thought of Sir Gilbert's talk of London, of his familiarity with the court and the King, of his great wealth and his land in Gloucestershire, of carriages, and gowns, and above all of escape: escape from the forest into a wider sphere, the great world itself. I told myself Old Sim had been mistaken. Sir Gilbert was my father's friend; he could not be an evil man. And I was no part of any bargain; Sir Gilbert liked me for myself, had I not noticed as much?

By the time he next came, early in March, I had perfectly weighed it up. I told my father I would do as he wished.

"Then I will send Gilbert to you."

"Gilbert?" I said, struck with discomfort. "You speak as if he were one of the family."

"And is he not to be so?" My father was all smiles.

I waited in the parlour like a dumb image for Sir Gilbert to come, and I gave him my answer looking at his boots not his face.

He kissed my hand, and before I could pull it away, slipped a gold bracelet on to my wrist. He had it ready in his pocket, confident indeed what my reply would be.

I showed my new bauble off to Nurse, turning my hand this way and that, and she called it a slave's bangle.

When I think back on the innocent days of my life at home at Bradstock and try to recall those who nurtured me, I can no longer remember my mother's face. It is grown vague and indistinct. Of my father, I see only his eyes, for those eyes I have inherited; daily they look out at me from my own mirror. It is Nurse's countenance that remains clear in my mind, as it was at that moment: loving and creased, and clouded with grief, which, in my silly satisfaction, I refused to heed.

CHAPTER THREE

I get married

The news of my betrothal was greeted throughout Bradstock with long faces.

Jacky said: "Oh Mistress Sarah! We thought it would be Mister Oliver!"

"He is not yet a man," I answered shortly.

Jacky shook his head. "More man than the other."

At that I coloured and told him that he stepped beyond his station.

I did not care to tell Old Sim of my decision, fearing that he would scold me. When the weather cleared and I could again ride abroad I avoided the coppices where I thought it likely I would find him. It was by accident that I came upon him. He stood in my path so that I was obliged to draw rein.

"What's this I hear, lass? Is it true what they say, that you are to wed Fearnshawe?"

"Yes," I said. It was all I *could* say.

"Well, you've properly cooked your goose now. You should have listened to your old friend."

"But you're wrong, Sim. He likes me, I can tell. He marries me for myself."

"A man like that doesn't marry for the sake of a pretty face. He married for his advantage. Mark my words, girl. If you think you are to have pretty toys and gay cavaliers to play with you're mistaken. What's more it will be goodbye to Bradstock. You'll see no more of your old friends."

"But Sim! He comes here often enough himself."

"What a man does himself is another matter. He won't want his young wife travelling rough miles to sit by my fires. You'll be kept at home to mind the house and rock cradles. Once he's shut your father's mouth, to breed is what he wants you for."

39

But again I did not believe him. I passed by, leaving him standing in the ride, and for once he did look old.

Now lawyers came to draw up the marriage contract, a dingy pair, who remained hours shut up with Sir Gilbert and my father in his closet. I took no notice of them, not even troubling my head as to what it was they bound me to. I was given up entirely to the preparations for my wedding, such a profusion of seamstresses and tailors and chemises and gowns, not to speak of ribbons and garters, as I had never known. I did not ask who was to pay for all this finery. Had I thought, I would have seen it could not be my father, it could only be Sir Gilbert himself. I think my father felt the shame of it, but he did not murmur, and I saw only the pretty things laid before me.

The wedding was to take place in the first week in May when I should be full sixteen years old. As April and my birthday itself drew near, I was unable, in spite of tailors and seamstresses, to put thoughts of Oliver out of my head. With every sign of spring, each primrose, each new green bud, each soft breeze, I wondered: When will he come? What shall I say? How can I tell him?

As so often before, he came without warning, riding into the yard and shouting "Sarah!" and demanding that I ride out with him.

In the six months since last we met he had matured. There was a new look in his eye. I was convinced some wench had taken him to her bed and I was displeased already. But Jacky saddled Carlos and I went meekly, following where Oliver led. He drew rein under that same wild cherry tree where we had plighted our troth in childhood. I swear it was done on purpose. We stared at each other angrily, two children again, but this time at cross purposes. He was unsure and I was obstinate, knowing in my heart of hearts that what I had planned to do was wrong.

He did not dismount.

"Sarah, is it true," he said, "that you are to wed this Gilbert Fearnshawe? I like it not at all."

"What then would you have me do?" I answered stiffly.

"I would offer for you myself if I were *Sir* Oliver, and — "

40

"And what?" From a nearby tree a cuckoo was calling.

He said nothing, but reddened and jerked at his horse's mouth so that it danced and sidled.

"And I had a dowry your mother would accept. Is that not so? And what makes you think I would have you?"

"I'd make you a better husband than a man twice your age and a canting Puritan at that. I — I would wed you in June and crown you with dog roses. Oh Sarah, do not have him!"

My heart turned over inside me; there was not to be this country custom for me. Sir Gilbert had brought a chaplet of pearls.

" 'Tis too late now, and my father wishes it," I said.

I knew that Oliver could sway his mother if he chose, and that had we been steadfast my father would have put away his dreams. I waited for Oliver to speak. If he could go to some whore's bed why could he not snatch me from my pony's back and kiss me? Why could he not tell his love? I wished for rescue, but none came. He was mute as a fish.

I taunted him. "Sir Gilbert is a *man*. I shall have house and servants and a carriage of my own and new gowns, I shall go to court and see the King."

"A husband is not new gowns and carriages. You wed a man, you wed him body and soul. This marriage of yours — 'tis a shameful thing. I will not see it done. No, nor shall my sisters neither," and he laid heels to his horse and galloped away down the ride.

I was left among a sea of bluebells with the wild cherry blossom in white clouds above my head and the new green all about me. The cuckoo was still calling, and then another, mocking, took up the note. I wept, tears of rage; but as well, my heart was sore.

Poor babes! Now I can pity us. Oliver in his situation, his duties to his family heavy upon him, might wish, but was too young to do. And me, I was too young to understand.

Oliver had meant what he said. His sisters declined my mother's invitation to them to be my bridesmaids; instead, I was obliged to make do with the two daughters of our new high Anglican parson, lumpish giggling girls, who came from Ludlow and did not take kindly to our forest life. Our old minister, a true Presbyterian, refused to swear the new oath the King's Parliament brought in, and had lost the living, as he had feared. He was a kind man and preached short sermons; when I stopped to think of it, I was sorry it was to be a stranger, not he, who would hear my vows.

But it was seldom that I thought at all. My wedding was to go forward. That being so, I blocked my mind to all else, walking in a dream of how it would be to be "My Lady". The tailor came for a last fitting of my bride dress. He unfolded the apricot satin — a shade that was new to me — and I tried the gown before the glass in my mother's closet, turning this way and that to see myself the better.

"It becomes you well," my mother said.

"The young lady is indeed beautiful," and first here, then there, the tailor moved a pin.

The colour was kind to my chestnut ringlets and brought out the rosy tint in my cheeks. Pleased with what I saw, I ran to show myself off to Nurse.

She was in a sour mood and shook her head.

"Nurse, do not be churlish. Do I not look pretty?"

"Pretty, indeed."

"Well, then, smile for me."

"I cannot smile for such a thing as this. My nestling is too young to wed."

"Too *young*, Nurse? At sixteen? You said yourself a full twelvemonth and more ago that it was a husband that I needed. Many wed at fourteen."

"But not to such as he. For you he is too old. For him you are too young."

"He is but thirty-four, in his very prime."

She looked at me earnestly. "Tell me, Sarah, what do you feel when you take his hand?"

"Why nothing! What should I?"

"My poor tawny bird!" and Nurse shook her head, "bought and sold and none to lift a finger. What of young Oliver?"

I stamped my foot in anger, forgetting my new dress.

"I am tired of this talk of buying and selling; and of Oliver too. All the world cries Oliver, but *he* says naught. I will not hear his name. I do as my father bids me. It pleases me to do so."

Nurse sniffed. "I had rather you wed our Jacky."

"A *stableboy*, Nurse?"

"Good red blood flows in his veins. *He* never truckled to Old Noll. And if your little head is not too addled to take it in, the day was when his grandfather and *Sir* Gilbert's worked side by side in Dog-hanging Coppice. Jumped up cold-blooded time-server!"

"But Nurse! 'Tis no disgrace to rise in the world," I said hotly. "Besides," and I defended my choice, "he is not so unpersonable a man. He has a flat belly and a fine calf in a silk stocking. He wears his own hair and there is no grey in it. I could wish it were black and curly like the King's and a trifle longer, but that's no great matter. I could wish too that he were a trifle less grave and spoke to me softly, instead of all the time of fields and ditches with my father. But his countenance is not displeasing."

My head was running all on London and courts and dancing, and how it would fare with me. I curtseyed to my image of myself. "My Lady Fearnshawe . . . Is it not a great thing, Nurse, at sixteen?"

She sighed. "Why do you think a man such as he should come to marry a girl without a dowry and outside his own county too? 'Tis because he wishes to be master where his forebears once were servants."

"Nurse, what nonsense you do talk. At Bradstock my father is master."

But Nurse refused to smile and said I was an innocent, and who would be master of my children?

My wedding was fixed for the 6th May, when the May Day junketings would be over. The best bedchamber was opened up and aired to be a bride-chamber, and preparations for feasting went forward as they had done in celebration of the King's return. Bradstock was to be packed out. The stables were made ready, and to make further room for the press of horses, Carlos was put out to grass in the orchard. I was not to take him with me, and I went to say goodbye to him while I was still my own mistress and could do as I pleased and weep a little on his back, unseen by any but Jacky.

"What will become of him, Jacky?" I said. "Take care of him for me."

Jacky's smile was sly.

"What is it? Out with it!" I commanded.

"The master says he is to go to Nuttley, for young Mistress Ann, that the two girls may have one apiece."

I burned with rage. And yet, later, I was glad.

I was with my mother in the hall when the first outrider passed by the window. A commotion of wheels followed and Mary threw open the door.

At the arrival of Sir Gilbert and the ironmaster I turned pale. The coach and six they brought to take me away, to me had the air of a hearse. My mother asked anxiously:

"Sarah my child, you are not ill I trust? Nothing ails you?"

"Nothing, Mother. I am quite well."

" 'Tis natural for a bride to be alarmed," she said. "Marriage is a great step for a girl. I shook when I married your father, yet in the event I need not have feared."

"I am not afraid," I said. Indeed, I was numb, feeling nothing.

The ironmaster was tall like his brother, older than Sir Gilbert and grizzled somewhat at the temples.

"So you are to be my sister," he said, with a smile that seemed to me to mean nothing. "What a pleasure thus to seal my acquaintance with your father."

I curtseyed and murmured polite nothings and he fell into conversation with my mother.

My bridegroom took my hand. "I trust you do well?" he asked, and I answered him "Yes." And there our converse ended.

The ceremony went forward according to custom. We walked to church across the meadows and over the stream where once I fished for trout, and the village children strewed our path with rosemary and spring flowers. I wore my hair loose, as a virgin bride should, crowned with Sir Gilbert's chaplet of pearls. But when he put the ring on my thumb and we were pronounced man and wife I felt nothing; except perhaps that I blushed for his fancy breeches. They were the new sort, called "petticoat" breeches, which describes them aptly enough, for they were wide, like skirts, and edged with lace, made of blue velvet, with lace-edged stockings turned down over the tops of his boots. I could tell, to my shame, that the household thought them foolish.

When we came out of the church the bridesmaids' knots of ribbons were cut into small pieces and thrown among the girls, while the young men jostled to be first to snatch my garter. I had loosed it artfully in the vestry that the winner might not grope too far up my skirts. Tom the blacksmith's boy headed the pack, and as we came out through the lychgate, bent to pull the ribbon from my leg and ran whooping off in triumph among his fellows.

The whole company followed us home. The bridecake was cut, and the feasting went forward till late. But in truth, though the village folk made merry in their own homely way, the rustic jollities clearly did not please Sir Gilbert or the iron-master, and with all Nuttley absent, it was but a lame occasion.

As the drinking went on apace I could see that Nurse grew troubled.

"The child will be worn out," she said to my mother, and I was led upstairs to be put to bed. As the custom is, the bridesmaids undressed me, and — clumsy girls both — left pins behind in my gown. My mother slipped my new cambric nightdress over my head, and she and Nurse were both sniffling, neither of them dry-eyed, as they helped me into bed.

My bridegroom was undressed by his man and brought to me in his nightshirt. I think most women will agree that no man looks his best in such a garment; true, Sir Gilbert's was frilled and embroidered, but none the better for that. Moreover his legs below were hairy, and this I did not care for. Close on his heels the sack posset was brought in by Mary, for us to drink as we sat up in bed, side by side, rendered speechless by our sudden intimacy.

Then the company came in, as many as could crowd into the bedchamber. The young men and maidens, Jacky and Susan among them, were eager to take their turn at throwing the stocking, to discover who would be next at the altar. They sat at the foot of the bed with their backs to us and threw blind

45

over their shoulders: a girl must hit the bridegroom, a man the bride. My stockings were tossed to and fro without mercy till one fell in my new husband's sack posset, and my father seeing the disgust on his face, cleared the room and drew the bed-curtains to.

"Blessings on you both, my children," he said, and left us to it.

Sir Gilbert put his spoiled drink to one side.

" 'Tis a most barbarous custom. I would not have exposed you to such had I had the choice." He took my empty cup from me. "I need no candle to tell me I have a wife to please any man," and so saying, he snuffed the flame.

He lifted my nightdress and felt his new treasure all over. For the first time his mouth met mine. Then without more ado he took me.

No girl raised as I was, virgin though she be, could fail to know what coupling meant; my wedding night came as no shock. But my lord was less than kind. I bit my tongue that I might not cry out — in pain, for there was no pleasure. No words passed between us. When he was done, he turned his back to me and slept at once.

I lay awake, bitterly sad that it had not been Oliver tumbling with me in the bed. He would never have hurt me so. At least any mistakes we made would have been merry ones. My head and body both were in such turmoil I thought I must lie thus till dawn; but the sack posset put me to sleep in spite of myself, which perhaps was its purpose.

He took me again before morning, but this time I bore it better, and tired out, slept again after.

We were woken by Sir Gilbert's man bringing his clothes and water to wash and shave. My husband turned on the pillow and kissed me.

"My dear," he said, "you would like your breakfast in bed, would you not? George shall inform the kitchen."

This kindness to me reflected his keen satisfaction with himself. Drawing back the bed curtains, he shed his nightshirt in front of me and I was forced to allow he was a fine figure of a man.

"May I send your maid to you, my love?" he inquired as he

46

dressed, and I was relieved to see that the blue velvet was put by and today he was to wear his usual snuff-coloured cloth.

"I have no maid, but I would like my nurse to come to me."

These were the first words I addressed to him as a wife. I do not think he found this strange, attributing my reserve to a proper modesty.

He answered me smiling. "So she shall," and stepping forth, mightily pleased, he left me to myself.

While I ate my breakfast Nurse busied herself about the room, putting my clothes ready for me, eyeing me the while, hoping for me to make some comment on the past night. But that I would not do. The gown I had worn the day before came in for particular scrutiny. At each pin she found she exclaimed, murmuring at last to herself:

"Married in May, and crowned with pearls, and pins left in the bride-dress, three ill omens at once!"

"What nonsense you do talk, Nurse." But I was uneasy.

"Nonsense is what it is not, as you well know. Married in May, rue for aye, and one pin left in the bride-dress and nothing will go right. And tell me, what good man would crown his bride with anything so sorrowful as pearls?"

"What's done is done, Nurse, and this is no time to make me fearful," I scolded.

"My little bird, these signs are none of my contriving. For my darling I would spirit them away if I could, no matter what the cost. There now!" and she came to my bedside. "You shall have this!"

She undid the chain from round her neck, whence hung a delicate ebony and silver cross. From early infancy it had been my plaything as I lay in her arms.

"You shall wear it for me!"

That Nurse should part with her cross, this guard against evil without which I never remembered to have seen her, day or night, frightened me the more, and I trembled.

"Come now," she said. "Let me fasten it for you, and stop this shaking. Wear it always and you may indeed suffer unhappiness, but no worse. Unhappiness in this world is the lot of man and woman both. Keep it always by you but not worn on your person and harm may come to you, but not the worst.

47

Lose it," and here her eyes looked into some unimaginable horror, "and there is no knowing what depth of evil you may not fall into."

"Nurse! Nurse!" I cried out. "What are you saying?" and holding out my arms to her, I leant forward for her to fasten the clasp. Then I hugged her close and buried my head in her bosom, loth to be snatched from her loving care. I could not but take heed of what she said, for she had, as I had long known, a kind of blind second sight; I was "frit to death", as the common people have it, terrified in truth, and comforted both at once.

"There, there, child," but she held me tight. "I must get you ready. That man — what am I saying? Your husband waits for you."

When I was dressed and ready we made our last goodbyes upstairs in private, where none could see. I hugged her again and she wiped my eyes dry with her apron.

The coach and six matching greys stood at the hall door. It was an equipage fit for an earl. This new-made knight my husband was showing himself to be a personage indeed. No one in Bradstock had seen such a vehicle, and drawn by six matching horses at that, greys moreover, an uncommon colour. It was a spectacle not to be missed. All the village who were able gathered to see me depart. It was an added spice, as I well understood, that none among them had thought those Fearnshawes would ever come so far up in the world.

My boxes were already stowed under the seats. I made my goodbyes to the household, kissed my parents, and Sir Gilbert handed me in. The ironmaster had vanished; departed early about his business, of which I was glad.

Thus handsomely conveyed, I left my home. But as I soon discovered it was no easy way to travel. The coach was cumbersome and without springs; the jolting in the ruts was painful because of the soreness in my parts from my lord's rough handling. The leather flaps to the windows for keeping out the weather had been put aside, but even so, unless I leant forward, there was no good view to be had of the country through which we passed. I would rather have been on horseback in the open air. Carlos would have carried me more gently.

At Bewdley, a place I had so longed to see, I forgot my discomforts for a while, astonished as I was at the number of houses and the press of people. The bridge by which we crossed the river was to me a miracle, with buildings standing upon it and boats passing below. I exclaimed aloud and Sir Gilbert smiled, and said we were to pass through Worcester which I should find a greater marvel yet.

"Sir," I said, "since we are to be man and wife by what name should I address you?" This question had been much in my mind.

" 'Husband' will do well enough, my dear."

And then again we both fell silent.

The smell of new leather upholstery and the heavy scent of the may from the hedgerows, of horse-dung and piss and dust in the road, mingled with the strange new smell of sweat from the man beside me, made me begin to wonder to what I had yoked my life; I had no more idea than the man in the moon what was passing in his mind, though I fancy that it was dwelling on cradles filled with little replicas of himself. As I have often reflected since, myself, pretty and well-bred, the daughter of an impeccable Royalist, put the last touch to his canvas: a fine new wife, carried in a fine new coach, to grace his fine new house. For he still wore that same self-satisfied expression when he looked on me kindly at last and said:

"Not tired, my dear, I trust? We reach Worcester soon, where we stop to dine and bait the horses. Should you wish to rest I will hire a chamber."

I shook my head. True, I was tired, but what I wished for was to reach my journey's end.

The town of Worcester, brooded over by its vast cathedral, its streets thronged with traffic, was beyond anything I had imagined. I wondered at the skill of our coachman as he wove his way without slackening speed through the press, all else giving way to us, and turned at last smartly under an archway into the courtyard of the inn where we were to stop. Ostlers came running at once, and I saw that in the eyes of the world my husband was the great man he thought himself. He barely acknowledged their salutes, leaving his servants to attend to our equipage, and offering me his arm, led me indoors.

It was my first taste of being "My Lady", and it pleased me. I held my head high and endeavoured to behave as if the attentions I was receiving were only my due; that I had been accustomed all my life to command such respect. Sir Gilbert, I could see, was pleased in his turn, that he had no raw country miss on his hands to shame him in public.

The woman of the house herself showed me upstairs to a room where I was able to wash and make myself comfortable. Afterwards, somewhat refreshed, I was ushered into a private parlour, where I sat down alone with my husband to a good dish of beef and a sallet, with a bottle of wine.

While we dined, he told me of the places we should pass through; but the wine was making me sleepy and I took in little of what he said. I asked had we still a long way to go, and he answered me yes, but that from now onwards I would find the roads easier.

This proved to be the case. I was able to lean my head against the leather cushioning, my eyes closed, and I fell asleep. The movement of the coach, the changes in the horses' paces, wove themselves into my dreams.

Someone was pulling at my arm. "Wake up! Wake up, my dear!" I knew not at first where I was. "Wake up! We are approaching Marley. The people will wish to see you."

I blinked and sat forward. It was late in the afternoon, the sun declining but still bright in the sky. We were coming downhill into a village built all of stone, the cottages thatched, with pretty flower gardens bordering the road. At the clatter as we passed women came to their doors and curtseyed and the children stopped playing to stare. We crossed a narrow bridge over a stream which ran clear in a stony bed, and then we climbed again, a slight rise, to come to a green and the church with its vicarage on our right, and on our left, a pair of wrought iron gates leading to a park.

"Marley Hall, my dear!" my husband said with pride.

The drive wound uphill through smooth green grass, and at the top, looking down, dominating the countryside, stood my new home. The house was raw new, and to me looked perched on its eminence and not yet settled into its surroundings. Like the cottages, it was built all of stone, and it was much bigger than I had expected. My heart sank somewhat. So many windows, like hundreds of eyes looking down on me, and all cold.

"Fine, is it not?" my husband said. "You see here the work of the best architect there is to be had. You will find every convenience, I think."

"It is very grand," I answered. But I thought the house alarming as well as bleak, and was missing the comfortable black and white timbered buildings I was used to, enclosed by the sheltering forest. I was like a dormouse pulled out of its nest.

The coach drew up on a wide gravel expanse in front of the house. A broad flight of shallow steps led up to the main entrance; lining these, the household stood waiting to welcome us. Had I not seen a boy on a pony disappearing round the corner of the house I would have wondered how they could have known of our arrival. Sir Gilbert handed me out, and as we walked up between the two rows of servants he stopped for me to shake hands with his steward Mr Robbins, and then with Mrs Willis, the housekeeper.

"My Lady is tired after her long journey," he said. "We will take supper in her chamber." Then turning to me, "Now my dear, let me show you to your rooms."

CHAPTER FOUR

My eyes are opened

I slept deeply; so deeply that on first opening my eyes I had no recollection of where I was. I thought that I had woken in my own bed at Bradstock; then, when the light filtered red through the curtains, that this must be Nuttley. But the bed was too wide, and no bed curtains at Nuttley were of this colour. I rubbed my eyes, and wide awake now, with a clutching fear at my heart saw I was at Marley Hall, my new home, by myself in my own chamber; my husband, knowing my weariness, leaving me to sleep alone that first night. Never in my life had I felt so alone. Never before had I so questioned the step I had taken. Then my fingers touched the chain round my neck and I was somewhat reassured, feeling that I carried a part of Nurse with me; so much so that I could almost hear her voice; I felt her farewell kisses on my tear wetted cheeks, and at this my alarms returned.

I sat up and drew back the bed curtains the better to examine my surroundings. I had not understood how spacious the room was, but all in red, a colour for which I had no great love since that night when my father returned from the Worcester fight and the blood on his clothes came off on my hand. The walls were done in red damask, with the hangings to the windows and the bed all in red to match. The effect was somewhat relieved by a hunting scene in tapestry set over the door to my closet. I did not perceive the door into my waiting-woman's chamber, so cunningly had it been cut in the damask, till Dorothy, hearing me stir, opened it and came in to draw the window curtains. She curtseyed as she passed the bed. Her first glance was not at myself, but at the undented pillows beside me on the bed. I thought I surprised a look of pleasure on her face, but so fleeting that I wondered after if I had been mistaken.

52

"Will my Lady take ale or buttermilk or chocolate? And what to eat?"

I chose chocolate and an egg soft boiled. Chocolate was a delicacy that had not reached us in the forest. I hoped my ignorance did not show, but I think from the air with which Dorothy lifted her chin that she knew.

I did not know what to make of my new waiting-woman. She was older than I would have chosen for myself, quite thirty, thin, and her hair so pale an ash-brown as almost to have no colour. Had her expression been animated she could have been pretty, but if her countenance had anything writ on it at all it was a deep reserve, that offered nothing and invited no questions. She had undressed me and brushed my hair the night before with a deftness of which I could not complain. Her manner was faultless. Yet I would have preferred someone younger and merrier of whom I could have made a companion and confidant, or even an older woman, comfortable like Nurse, to whom I could turn if need be for help.

No words passed between us as she once more brushed my hair, helped me into my dressing-gown and, plumping the pillows behind me, made me ready for my breakfast. A little maid I had not seen before brought this to me, blushing. And then I was left to my thoughts.

Two long windows, of the new sash sort, faced the bed. Where from outside they had seemed so unfriendly, from my bed I had to allow their beauty. Light, such as I had never known as Bradstock, streamed in, burnishing the gilt tassels on the bed canopy, falling kindly on the pretty woollen embroidered upholstery of the chairs, and the elegant polished table where we had taken supper the night before. Instead of green trees, as if I had been a bird on the wing I saw soft white clouds floating across a pale blue sky.

My breakfast was perfection. I was savouring the chocolate's delicious flavour, my spirits quite restored, when my husband knocked and entered.

"I trust you slept well?" he enquired. "And that all is to your liking?"

"Very well, I thank you, 'tis all very well, and most pretty."

At this he ventured a compliment. "My wife this morning

looks most pretty herself. Your fatigue quite gone, I trust?"

"Oh yes, indeed."

"Then when you are ready, if you would like, I will show you round the house and grounds."

I made to put my breakfast on one side and he smiled.

"Finish your breakfast my dear, and I will send Dorothy to you. You will find me downstairs in the hall."

And there indeed I found him, a solitary figure, commanding the vast empty stretch of black and white tiles, and pluming himself, standing in front of the empty fireplace below his own likeness, newly taken, as he later explained, by Mr Lely.

The painter had done exceedingly well, for while he had portrayed all Sir Gilbert's pride, the legitimate pride in achievement, he had yet caught the vanity of the man, the overweening self-love; for indeed Sir Gilbert loved himself above all else in the world, more so than any man I have ever known. The man who had posed for this portrait was now imitating his own image as created by the painter; but he was, as I came to understand only much later, oblivious to all in it that was mean, and was reflecting, as he thought, only what was noble. It was uncanny to see a man thus play-acting, mimicking his own picture, and so representing his own representation. I underwent the strangest sensations as I advanced over the black and white checkerboard to meet him.

The disquieting reflection of paint in flesh was gone as soon as he stepped forward to offer me his arm.

"Such light!" I said. "So beautiful!" And, indeed, it took my breath away. Here again was light everywhere, pouring in through tall windows, of the same sash sort, to fill the hall, so that even the heavy doors and the wide staircase seemed airy, the black and white stones luminous in the sun. How chill that light was to fall in winter I was not to know. Nor did I wish to take heed, now that I was his wife, of any darkness in the nature of the man.

"We have somewhat of a tour to make before we are done," smiling in satisfaction at my astonishment, "I doubt you will have seen anything in the forest to equal what we have here."

In truth I had not known such houses to exist, my imagination stopping short with Nuttley. Everything I now saw was strange to me, from the convenience of the back stairs for the carriage of slops, to the multitude of rooms where, it seemed, the servants had no place, living entirely apart; something to which we were not used at Bradstock. I could not imagine what some of these rooms were for, or why we should need so many. It was as if I had been given a vast doll's house to play with and did not know how to begin. And indeed this was near the truth, for I had never owned a doll's house, and of household management in general knew nothing. I lifted my head, nodding graciously to the maids we encountered, holding out my hand to Mr Robbins as if all my life I had been accustomed to such deference, and not, as was the case, but playing at Lady Fearnshawe, at heart still Mistress Sarah, more at home sitting in the stables with Jacky, or picking apples with Nurse.

My husband was pleased at my demeanour, though my pretence did not deceive him. He knew full well the measure of my ignorance.

"You are at a loss, no doubt, my dear," he said kindly, as I stared in dismay at the great parlour, where the chairs stood stiffly round the walls, leaving an empty floor fit only for dancing in.

" 'Tis very grand," I said hurriedly, "and the view fine."

"You will receive here when we have company," and he smiled. " 'Tis only fitting, as Lady Fearnshawe. But come, you shall now see the chamber designed to be particularly your own."

The great piece we were in led straight into a charming withdrawing room, and here my exclamations of delight were unfeigned. The room was done all in soft blues and pinks, and between the two long windows, where the light fell most convenient on the keyboard, a virginals, open, a stool placed ready, as if the player had just done.

"I see I have guessed correctly," my husband said smiling. "Come, look closer."

Above the keyboard my initials had been set in marquetry, the letters S and F entwined. That my tastes had been observed, and such thought given to my pleasure touched me. Had our acquaintance been longer I would have turned and kissed him. As it was, I could only look my thanks.

"I hope that perhaps you will sometimes sing for me," he said.

I knew that he could not tell one note from another, for I had seen him yawn behind his hand when I had played to my father; but I was eager to hear the instrument's voice. I sat down, and as my wilful fingers met the keys some demon prompted them into playing *Greensleeves*, in a desire, I think, to prove my friends wrong, to show to all the world that I cared nothing for the past and was indeed fortunate.

But as I sang, I was back at Nuttley and the tears welled in my eyes, at sudden sharp remembrance of Oliver's clumsy kiss.

My husband thought I wept for joy. Gratified, he held out his arm, remarking, "A pretty woman singing is a gracious sight indeed. But we must not linger, we are not done yet. There is more to be seen upstairs than your own bedchamber."

In fresh anger with Oliver, I jumped up, my tears brushed aside. For better or worse I was Lady Fearnshawe and this man's wife; and as we passed again through the hall I was thinking one day to improve it by adding my own likeness, placing it on the wall that faced my husband's picture.

At the top of the stairs he turned to me. "I think, my dear, that you will find few houses so well planned. Here we have the great dining-room."

A dining-room? I asked myself, among the bedrooms? And so far from the kitchens?

"You will observe," and he flung wide the door, standing back in pride to let me enter, "we have space to entertain on a scale proper to our station."

The centrepiece of this vast chamber was a long table, that to my untutored eye would seem to seat forty. I wondered whether we were to dine in this empty splendour when we were alone; but did not care to betray my ignorance by asking. Moreover, the room was furnished all in green, a most evil colour to go with food, and if I were to be mistress of the house in earnest, something that would need to be changed.

" 'Tis very fine," I remarked, and to my relief, with this he appeared satisfied.

Two sets of guest chambers followed, and equipped to a high

degree of elegance and comfort. I peopled them in my mind with the visitors my Lady would command, and here, the words of glib praise came easily.

Now once more we passed the head of the stairs and turned into the passage leading to my own bedchamber.

"This part of the house," my guide explained, "is devoted to our quarters. You are familiar with your own. You are now to see mine."

My husband's bedchamber lay directly across the passage from my own. With a reverence that somewhat took my breath away as being more appropriate to a chapel, he paused outside the door before opening it, then, standing back, bowed me in.

I found this room on the instant unpleasing, the hangings all in purple and orange, a mixture painful to the eye. All was designed for grandeur; the massive chairs, the carving of the bedposts, the chamber pot in silver. This was where he lay when he wished to sleep alone. Only his man George was allowed to come to him in here, and so he then told me: I was never to share this bed; but he could come when he pleased to mine.

These were bleak words for a young wife to hear. Though, indeed, until this moment I had not stopped to consider what Sir Gilbert's view of marriage might be or whether I should find it agreeable, I now began to fear that it might be different from my own. I had no wish to sleep in that ugly bed, but nor did I care to be thus forbidden. My husband laid down rules for me. Marriage was to be a more formal state than I had supposed.

And yet he was not unfriendly. While I was still lost in these thoughts he laid his hand on mine and pressed it gently.

"I daresay my dear you find so much that is new to you overwhelming. You did not expect such wealth, perhaps."

"No Sir," I murmured.

"But 'tis not all," he continued. "I have now something particular to show you."

The tone of his voice, the glance he bent on me, promised marvels greater than any that had gone before, and I was at a loss to think what these could be. We mounted another flight of stairs, my curiosity rising with every step.

We came out on to a broad landing, handsomely wainscoted. He waved a hand in dismissal to his left.

"The maidservants lie there."

Then, turning to his right, he opened door after door. He was showing me his nurseries, and I understood, to my astonishment, that in all this great house these were the rooms he cherished most. My head spun as I saw that here was provision made for ten children as least, perhaps more. While I was still engaged in counting up the number we arrived at the nurse's room itself, the resting place of the new born. And here indeed my husband might have been in church, for he did not speak. He did not look at me.

My eyes flew straight to the cradle. Lined with silk, equipped in every particular, it waited ready for its inmate. Round it had been disposed all the little things a mother might provide for her baby.

Who in this had been Sir Gilbert's tutoress?

In the same way as did our cat at Bradstock I knew that the furnishing of nests was a mother's business, and what was a cradle but a nest? I had been robbed of my proper pleasure. My place had been usurped by my husband.

Now, too, the purpose of my marriage came home to me, and it was a bucket of cold water thrown over my head. I saw myself perpetually with child, toiling so that all these nurseries might be provided with young. I imagined every place at the great dining-room table filled by our offspring, and at the thought of all those infant faces I wished to scream: only to smile in relief at my folly. No woman could bear forty children: if in this matter of nurseries my husband was over zealous, no more was expected of me than was demanded of all wives. Every girl knew as much. Nonetheless, the longer I stared at the cradle the less stomach I had for my task. I did not wish to think of my flat belly swelling, and that this might be not once, but many times over.

My husband's eyes demanded some comment.

" 'Tis all very charming. You have thought of everything," I said. I was red as a beetroot, and I saw this pleased him. He had taken my disgust for modesty. I hurried on, wishing to change the tenor of his mind. "And what of the kitchens?" I cared not

58

at all for kitchens, but had the wit to see that in my new role it would be well to give at least the appearance of interest.

This too gave my husband pleasure. He patted my hand.

"Of course my dear, a very proper enquiry. We have just time to visit them before we dine."

We dined in the little parlour, where in fact all the meals we ever partook of were served: I never knew the great dining-room used.

Then, after, came the tour of the grounds.

We traversed gardens laid out with gravel walks and orange trees, all new, and leading from the terrace a vista, an avenue of trees planned through the park that would look very fine once they were full grown.

Sir Gilbert turned to me as I admired this view.

"We will walk a little and so look back at the house," he remarked. "When the trees are a trifle further advanced I intend a painting should be done. You may have noticed the hall is somewhat bare as yet. Such a painting would grace the walls, do you not agree?"

I murmured, "Yes indeed." But I was piqued. I told myself that the next picture on those walls should be of me; though by now, even as the thought entered my head, I was quick to see that no picture of me would hang there till the artist could portray the fruits of my husband's loins. There would need to be at least one child standing at my knee and, for preference, two, and one in arms.

From here we passed through the kitchen gardens and came at last to the stables; a handsome set of buildings, built round a yard that was entered under a clock tower.

"The manservants have their quarters here," my husband said. "They are well housed, and less temptation to the maid-servants."

I said nothing. I knew well enough that if men and maids wish to get together they will do it, no matter where they lie at night.

But now from his demeanour I sensed there was to be another surprise, though I never could have guessed what was to come. We inspected the six greys that had brought us here, and the riding-horses for the servants, and Sir Gilbert's own two, and the stable boys pulled their forelocks; and then the head groom, Harrison, who accompanied us, cocked an eyebrow at my husband, who nodded and smiled, and then — oh then! he said:

"This my dear is Kitty. She is for you."

She was a rich bright bay with black points and a sweet intelligent eye. I fell in love with her at once. Harrison led her out into the yard for me to see, and the understanding between the mare and myself was instant, as had happened with Carlos. She breathed out slowly through her nostrils, stretching her neck towards me, and gave a low, soft whinny. I took her velvet muzzle between my hands and kissed her. Never in my life had I dreamt that such a lovely creature could be mine. My heart beat as though it would burst my chest. I looked imploringly from one man to the other.

"I would try her paces, if I may. Please, now."

My husband indulged me. I flew back to the house and made myself ready.

I returned to find Kitty waiting for me, saddled and bridled. Harrison helped me to mount, and I walked slowly under the arch and at last, out into the park.

I made her walk the first hundred yards, both to test her manners and to see whether she moved well at that gait, for a horse that walks well is like to move well in its other paces. Such was indeed the case; she had an elastic tread, and when I asked her to trot we seemed to float on air; when we cantered, my hair flying, it was very heaven. What perfection! She answered to the lightest touch. She and I were as one. This mare could read my mind. Both to please myself and to show off to the men watching me, I wove my way at score between the new young trees, and when we returned and I drew rein, I could see the admiration on their faces.

Harrison said to my husband, "Sir, if I may be so bold, my Lady rides to perfection. She sits a horse marvellous well, and the mare is just right for her. If I may say so, Sir, you chose well." He was a frightened man in constant trepidation for his post. He fawned as he spoke.

It was my husband who handed me down, and now, flinging my arms round his neck, forgetting that I was a lady, forgetting

60

all those standing by, I did kiss him.

"Come, come, my dear," he said, and put me gently from him. Such improper behaviour in front of the grooms embarrassed him. But he was pleased, too, as I saw from his bearing when I turned from him to stroke Kitty's neck. Then he offered me his arm.

"How can I thank you enough?" I said, and this came from my heart.

"Your pleasure is mine," he answered. But I think it was himself that he applauded, for he made no motion of tenderness towards me.

My husband lay with me all night, as I had been expecting, and so enamoured of Kitty was I, and so grateful to him for his gift, that I looked on him more kindly and endeavoured to be fond. I even tried to forget his hairy legs, but could not; then attempted to find them pleasing. But this too I could not.

Nonetheless, there was a certain novelty in having a companion in my bed. Besides, to see a man yawning in the morning and walking to and fro showing off his parts is an education for a woman.

So, though I loved him not, in those first weeks I tried my best to like him. I told myself he had a noble forehead; but this was spoilt by his hair: it was not quite long enough; as well, it was stiff and wiry, and it was sandy coloured which I could not abide. I told myself he had a fine blue eye; but his gaze was in truth pale and cold, his expression calculating. I told myself he was kind; but it was the kindness a man extends to a new acquisition such as a piece of precious procelain. Moreover, I could not help but be aware that he was not always kind to those who worked for him, and had no mercy on their shortcomings.

As I could not then know, he was most at fault in that he was never at pains to please me. He took his own pleasure of me and cared nothing for mine, so that I, a natural lusty wench, was left unsatisfied, ignorant of my body's powers.

I have reflected since that husbands would do well to learn that this is a common cause of restlessness in females. It is all too often the case that a man will busy himself to please his whore, but do no more with his wife than will get her with child.

In truth, as Nurse had seen, we were an ill-assorted pair. Had Sir Gilbert married a meek domestic creature, he might have made her happy; he could indeed have loved her, her subservience all the time pandering to his picture of himself. My misfortune lay in being too wild and headstrong, and thus I encouraged all that was most offensive in his nature.

Yet for a fortnight he was pleased with his bargain and I did not quarrel with mine. I was indeed a Lady, and as I had hoped, mistress of a great house; the servants curtseyed to me, and at every turn I was asked what I desired. Above all there was Kitty. The weather continued fine and I was taken riding daily over new country, carried by this lovely creature beside whom the husband accompanying me paled.

It was at the end of a fortnight that my terms came upon me for the first time in my wedded state. I called for Dorothy, not knowing whether to be glad or sorry, and while so wondering, I noticed once more that strange fleeting look of pleasure on her face. I put it from my mind, too occupied in thanking providence there was to be no baby yet in the cradle upstairs; then fearing that my husband would be put out.

This proved to be the case, and now for the first time I felt his displeasure. That I was not at once with child was a fault in me, and reflected on himself in the matter of his choice.

" 'Tis quite usual, Sir, I believe, that a wife does not conceive at once," I said. "And, Sir, the first time a bitch is put to a dog it doesn't always take."

But this only compounded my crime. He found the comparison offensive and my remark unladylike; though it was no more than the truth and what any child brought up in the country would know.

"Such language does not become you," he said stiffly, and left me to myself.

From this time he withdrew somewhat of his favour. Instead of riding out with me he spent longer in his cabinet and with his steward, addressing to me no more than the most necessary formalities. I saw that now he meant to punish me, and I was angry that a man so careless of a woman in bed should yet be such a prig.

At last he announced: "Well my dear, tomorrow I must to London."

"So we are to go to London! What joy!" Though somewhat uncertain of his response, I clapped my hands like a child.

"*I* am to go to London is what I said. My wife stays at home."

"But I have so longed to go to London, after all you have told of it. Please take me with you," I begged. "A wife surely should be at her husband's side."

At this his face grew cold. "A wife's place is in her home. I go on business, not pleasure. You would find no entertainment. I would have you know I keep no London establishment, nor do I intend one. Lodgings suit my purpose well enough. I shall be gone a week."

I was near to tears with disappointment. I pouted.

"No, my dear, for the time being you have done travelling enough. I would wish you to settle down and learn the ways of Marley. And I would have you exercise more moderation when you ride."

I think it was then that my efforts to like him came to an end.

CHAPTER FIVE

Discontents

My husband trod me that night as a cock treads a hen, and left the next morning before I was dressed. He gave me his orders as I sat in the parlour, drinking my morning chocolate.

"If there is anything you lack, Robbins will see to the matter." And then, with a look that pierced my belly, "And you will please to take care how you ride. Harrison will accompany you." He turned on his heel.

So angry was I that if I had believed that by galloping Kitty I could have shaken his seed from my womb, I would have done so.

While I was still in turmoil, trembling with fury that my person should have been so insulted by my husband, and now yet further degraded by being left in the charge of Harrison in his absence, Mrs Willis came to me.

She asked what I fancied for my dinner, adding "Now that my Lady is at leisure, perhaps she would care to inspect the linen and go through the stores."

She cannot have failed to observe my flushed face and sullen looks, the unfinished cup of chocolate in front of me, and there was kindness in her eyes, even concern. But this I chose to ignore. I had not even the wit to ask her to sit down, caring only to be rid of her presence.

"Oh Mrs Willis," I said hastily, "in truth I know nothing of stores or of linen. I am sure you will care for them much better than I."

Her manner remained polite, but a frost fell.

I blundered on. "I would not wish to interfere with the housekeeping, it is done to perfection and pleases Sir Gilbert. I'm sure anything you choose for dinner will be delightful."

This only made matters worse.

"Very good, my Lady," she replied, her face set, and she did indeed leave me.

I saw nothing of the generosity in her offer. Had I not been in such a rage I might have perceived that she was giving me, an ignorant chit, my place as mistress of the house, and that in so doing she surrendered part of her own authority. In a calmer frame of mind it might have entered my head that indeed she pitied my youth, and guessing that I might find myself lonely, was doing what lay in her power to make me feel at home. Had I but been polite, had I but confessed my ignorance and asked her to help she would, I fancy, have taken me under her wing and mothered me. But I, seeing only the boredom of household duties, behaved as a petulant child, treating her goodwill as naught.

So I threw away the friendship of one who in my struggles with my husband might have been my ally. Rebuffed, she withdrew into herself, marking me down as a featherbrain and not worth her trouble.

Nor could I hope now to succeed with the other servants. They took their tone from her, and the gulf already set between us by the curtsies I had so enjoyed was not to be crossed. Even little blushing Rose, a wench my own age, who had brought my breakfast to me on the morning after my arrival, would not raise her eyes to mine. As for Dorothy, she had disliked me from the start.

It has struck me since that before launching their daughters into marriage, mothers would do well to instil into them the importance of servants: how essential to happiness it is to gain their confidence and respect; moreover, how simple, if the rules of friendship are but observed. It is not to be forgotten that servants will know at once of any disharmony between husband and wife and will take sides. In this I lost to my husband before I began.

All this while the light had been failing. Now, as Dorothy was dressing me, the clouds opened. I sat watching a very waterfall running down the windows and wondered how I was to pass my time.

"How deadly is this rain!" I exclaimed. "I had meant to ride, but the day is spoiled."

65

" 'Tis pity my Lady has no embroidery with which to occupy herself."

"It got forgot," I said. That dismal piece of work! And yet now I could wish to have it by me. " 'Tis well thought of. I would have needles and canvas and wools procured for me."

"And what would your Ladyship require as to colours?"

"Oh Dorothy, I know not. I would make flowers. What pleases you. I would have you see to it for me, I'm sure you will choose well."

I did not care for her smile, reflected in the glass as she dressed my hair. I felt she understood my lack of interest and was pleased that I should suffer. Indeed, what a pass had I come to that I should send for coloured wools to play with?

She waited behind my chair.

"Is there anything further my Lady requires?"

"No Dorothy. Oh no, thank you, you can go."

I sat on staring at the window where there was nothing to be seen but the rain, still with no idea how I was to pass the morning and altogether sorry for myself.

Since I could not count sheets my household occupations were gone; as my Lady, I could not chatter with the maids as they polished spoons or gossip with the turnspit in the kitchen. Nor would I put on my cloak and go out to the stables for the pleasure of stroking Kitty's nose, for in the present state of my feelings I could not bear to speak with that crawling creature Harrison; altogether his master's man, his company was hateful to me.

I was thinking how different it would be if only Jacky were in Harrison's place when someone knocked.

"Who is it?" I said, startled out of my dream.

"Rose, my Lady. If my Lady so pleases I am sent to tidy the bedchamber."

"Come in, Rose." I was glad to change my thoughts. "How it rains!"

"It will go on all day I think, my Lady. So Mr Robbins says." Her gaze fell on the brushes and combs before me on the table.

"Pick them up if you wish. I am about to go."

She examined first one then another and sighed.

"What is it?" I asked, in curiosity turning to look at her. "What troubles you? In truth I'm troubled myself — by this rain," I added hastily.

"I ought not to say, my Lady. Mrs Willis says we are not to gossip. She says — "

"Please to go on, Rose. I am asking you. I am not to be governed by Mrs Willis."

"She says it's best not to carry tales. But oh my Lady, I had thought to be your waiting-woman and Mrs Willis was agreeable to it, only there was Dorothy. Dorothy didn't want the place, but Sir Gilbert wouldn't let her remain in the household else."

"Oh Rose! What misfortune! What pleasure might we not have had!"

In the glass, I saw behind me the door to Dorothy's chamber begin to open and I rose from my chair.

"You may carry on with your work, Rose," I said in an altered tone. "I am finished here." And I went downstairs, my anger stoked again. What was behind my husband's action? Had Dorothy, like Harrison, been set to spy on me? From his portrait in the hall Sir Gilbert looked down on me. His cold eyes in some unknown way accused me, even in his absence, of not performing my duties.

The day dragged interminably. I tried to occupy myself by practising at my virginals, but this soon palled. Playing to oneself in a bad humour with the rain falling calls forth wrong notes. Moreover my stock was small; I knew few pieces by rote and there were no songbooks here for me to learn from: indeed, no books of any kind. As I had early discovered, all the grand lacquered cabinets were empty; bare as when they had come from the maker. The whole of this vast house was a most barren place, a hollow sham, fit only for yawning in.

I thought to write a letter asking for my music to be sent, but the little writing cabinet in my closet, like all the rest, lacked furnishings. Before I could begin I must apply to Mr Robbins for pens, ink, paper, sand and a penknife.

By the time I had found him and these had been procured my dinner was ready. And so the morning passed.

Jess begged at table as she would never have dared had my

husband been present, and knowing it would have angered him, I fed her tit-bits.

By the steely light falling through the long windows, I wrote that afternoon. But then, after this brief happy converse with my absent father, dullness came again upon me.

Most women in my position and alone would have sent for their waiting-woman for company, to sing duets with them, or played at cards with the housekeeper; but even had songbooks and cards not been lacking, after my rudeness to Mrs Willis, and in my knowledge of Dorothy's dislike, I dared not venture.

After an evening spent in such boredom as I had never known, watching Jess biting her fleas, I went early to my chamber and kept Dorothy long before me, inventing little needs, requiring my feet washed, trying to engage her in gossip, asking who were our neighbours? I might as soon have tried to get water from a stone. She answered me in monosyllables, as much only as duty required.

The night carried my discontents away. On a clear summer's day when the air is warm and one is but young, it is difficult to be low-spirited for long. Still in my dressing-gown, I walked out on to the terrace. The housemartins were flying high in the sky, carrying my heart with them; the scent from the box borders was sharp in the air, freshened by the rain. From the poultry yard a cock crowed, opening up the morning. His proclamation of hope was music in my ears. Fancy took my feet along the gravel path between the espaliered apple trees and through the gate into the vegetable garden, where I had not as yet explored.

Here in front of me lay strawberry beds where fruit already ripened. The earth like all else was offering me her bounty. At my feet the leaves were still damp from yesterday's wetting; in childish joy I parted them to find and pick the glistening berries, careless of my trailing gown, eating till the juice ran over my fingers.

A rough voice from behind reproached me: "If my Lady said she wanted strawberries I would have had them sent up to the house."

I jumped up hastily. I was as flushed as the strawberries themselves. I had forgotten the gardener, and what was worse, in the whole of the past weeks I had never troubled to find out his name. He was a large raw-boned man and his feelings showed as raw as his face. In his eyes, as is the case with all gardeners, the gardens were his, not mine.

"There is no fault," I said. "I didn't know I wanted strawberries until I saw them." I added in hopes of placating his resentment, "The gardens are very well."

But his looks made it plain that he did not forgive me for my trespassing, and as if I had been a thief, he watched me out all the way till the gate shut behind me.

So I was found guilty in my own garden.

I hurried back to the house and up to my chamber, and now Dorothy's pained face showed me that I was at fault here also, for keeping her waiting to dress me.

I was hardly downstairs when Mrs Willis came to me.

"Had I known my Lady wished for strawberries I would have sent for them to be picked." And though her manner was all it should be, her voice too was a reproach.

"I didn't know they were ready, Mrs Willis. I do not yet know all the gardens hold."

But I could see that in her eyes I ought to have made it my business to know. So I could not mend my offence.

The word strawberry was now quite hateful to me. But when the fruit appeared with thick cream for my dinner I ate with pleasure. I could not guess the storm to which this little matter would lead.

Nor on such a day could I sustain my disgust with Harrison: the poor man could not help his servitude to my husband, and he had the virtue of admiring Kitty. Moreover, I was eager to ride.

That afternoon we penetrated to the far confines of the estate where it bordered on a wild common; in winter, no doubt, a windswept desolate place, but today, with the peewits crying, it was an invitation to freedom. I longed to gallop as I had done in the forest, and disappear into the far distance, leaving all Marley behind: then picturing Harrison flayed by my husband's wrath, turned the mare's head. It was as well, for on the way back Kitty cast a shoe, and we were obliged to stop at the forge.

Harrison dismounted swiftly, all deference.

"Do you take my mount, my Lady, and I will stay and see the mare shod. Let me change the saddles over."

But I would have none of this.

"I prefer to stay myself and oversee the smith this time."

Harrison shook his head, but he left me.

In the smithy I was once more in my element. The smells of hot iron and burning horn, the hissing steam, the smith with his leather apron and his mouth full of nails, the group of village children standing by, were as familiar to me as the very air I breathed. Such sights and sounds were as wine to me in my present exile.

The smith lifted Kitty's foot and the children stood back, all but one, and his attention was fixed on Kitty, not on me.

My heart missed a beat. For a moment I thought I had seen Oliver, and that time had indeed run backwards: then at once recognised my mistake. In the child in front of me were re-created the same golden curls and fair complexion, but this boy was younger than Oliver had been when he first appeared to me out of the forest; his face was not so round, his eyes more grey than blue, his features subtly different. Yet the resemblance was startling enough, even as to his being better dressed than the other children. He had sprung as suddenly into my sight as had his counterpart. I was strangely drawn to him.

I engaged him in conversation.

"Is it the mare you like or is it watching the sparks fly?"

" 'Tis the mare."

"Can you then ride?"

He heaved a vast sigh. "No."

"You have no pony I daresay."

He shook his head. "My grandad is on the farm," he said, as if this explained all.

"I see. But you would like to learn to ride perhaps?"

This time he nodded, speechless.

I pitied the child, having felt that passion myself at his own age, moreover I was intrigued. The longing in his eyes went straight to my heart.

Kitty was shod, and as I had observed, well shod too. The smith waited, stroking her neck.

70

"What is your name?" I asked the boy.

"Richard."

"Well, Richard, if you would like you shall try the mare out and see how you go."

I made to take off the saddle, for it was of no use to a boy, but before I could undo the girth the smith took all from me.

"My Lady!" he said in horror. "Allow me! 'Tis not fit for such as you."

I laughed. "I have unsaddled a horse often enough," I said. "But do you lift this child up for me."

I led Kitty out of the yard and a little way along the road. The child sat the mare with natural ease, taking the reins exactly as I told him, but wordless, till as we were returning he said:

"I didn't know a lady could do such things."

"What things?"

"Take off saddles and such like. Ladies are for waiting on."

"Ladies are as other folk. I'm only Sarah, as you are Richard. I am but a country girl, used to climbing trees for bird's eggs. If I could not saddle and unsaddle my own mount, I would be truly ashamed. Can you catch a trout with your hands?"

"Yes I can."

"Well, so can I."

He stared at me, round eyed in astonishment.

We stood side by side while the smith resaddled Kitty. "I think, Richard, we must meet again," I said, "but now I must go home."

I thanked the smith. "I have not my purse with me," I added. "I will direct Mr Robbins to see to your fee."

Kitty had behaved, as she always did, like an angel. He patted her neck and smiled.

" 'Tis no matter my Lady, Sir Gilbert settles the reckoning monthly."

He pulled his forelock, and I rode out of the yard up the hill to Marley. My thoughts were full of the child. Who and what was he? But now I trusted none of those about me. Some happy instinct moved me to keep my curiosity to myself.

It was late at night when my husband at last returned from London, and I had long since gone to bed. Though I felt no love for him, when I heard the door of his bedchamber opening and shutting I found myself pleased, if only because now there would be someone besides Jess for me to look at over my meals.

To my surprise, it was not till I had done breakfast and was about to go upstairs to dress that he came to me. His whole expression was unbending and I saw at once that I was in disgrace.

"Madam, I fear you need a governess! Gathering strawberries from the gardens! A child would know better. Should you wish for fruit the proper course is for you to ask Mrs Willis, and you will please do so in future. This improper behaviour on your part has caused Hawkins and Mrs Willis, too, to feel at fault, when the fault, as I must point out to you, was your own."

Then before I could open my mouth, "And you should know better than to loiter at the smithy seeing to the shoeing of horses. It is no fit place, no nor occupation either, for my wife. Servants should be used and left to do the work they are paid for. It is for us to keep our distance."

Here he paused for breath, and I smiled, which was foolish. But he had laid his weakness bare to me, and now that I could speak I was too angry to mind what I said.

"Sir, I would remind you that I am familiar with the manners that are proper to our station, and have been so from infancy. In my experience the servants here are wrongly treated. There should be no such distance. As to the picking of strawberries, a lady born knows when to put her dignity aside and take a common pleasure. Nor is it any disgrace in her to attend to her animal's welfare. It was only proper for me to satisfy myself that Kitty's foot had taken no harm. Indeed, the smith knows his trade. I am happy now to see anyone from the stables take her down to be shod."

I was right as to the distance between servants and their masters but I had been wrong in my behaviour to them as people. Even as I taunted my husband with his birth, I knew the truth in my heart. The grain of justice in his reproof made me sorer still.

A red spot painted his either cheekbone. I knew, and I knew that he knew, that his own gentry was newly come by. At that

72

moment I felt that he hated me. My victory was a dangerous one.

I could see him casting round for some other cause for censure. He took a turn up and down the parlour.

"And am I to understand that you sent Dorothy shopping for you? And that you have been writing letters to your father? Pray, madam, can you find no occupation in my house? In what is it so lacking?"

His spies were everywhere: poor cringing Harrison, trying to protect himself in advance at my expense, Dorothy set at work in my bedchamber, and for all I knew every man, woman and child in Marley. Nothing that I did was to escape his notice; someone else would always run to him with my news before I could do so myself. If an angel had come down from heaven and sat with me to dine, Mrs Willis would have told my husband of the menu before I could speak to him of my joy in this visitation. I wondered that none of his creatures had informed him of my encounter with Richard. I had thought to talk with him about the boy, but not knowing what misery I might bring down on my head or the child's, resolved to hold my tongue.

I had no wish to inflame my husband further. While I choked with fury inside I answered meekly, the false innocent:

"Sir, I understood from you that I was to ask Mr Robbins for anything I might need. I hardly thought you would grudge me the wherewithal for the writing of letters, or embroidery with which to occupy my hands. My father will be pleased to hear from me that I am well, and I would have him send me my music, to learn tunes that I may play for you. And, if you please, I would have books to read when you are away from home."

At this he unbent somewhat. "And what would you like to have?"

"Oh Sir!" I said. "The plays of Shakespeare if you please, and the fables of Aesop, in English for I know no Greek, and the Latin tales of Ovid that I used to read with my father, and I would dearly like the Martyr King's writings and the verses written for our present King's return."

I asked only for what I knew of, and I fancy that my eyes

73

shone; for indeed, when I thought of my father and his closet at Bradstock and our reading together, my heart was moved with love. But seeing this joy my husband took offence, choosing to imagine a slight upon himself. Once more a coolness fell.

"You are not in your father's house now, Madam, but in mine. You will please to accept my governance in the matter of what you read as in all else. Plays are a vanity and Latin a lewd tongue not suitable for females."

At this my temper flew altogether out of control.

"Then perhaps, Sir, the ladies of the great ones with whom you consort in London will advise you of something. They will surely know what is fitting for a well-bred wife to read." I burned at the insult to my upbringing and my voice rose. "If I may not go with you to London I do not care to be kept an idle prisoner. I may not pick strawberries, I am not to ride as I please, I am not to converse with servants, you do not wish me to write to my own father. Am I then to sit, and sit, playing the same tune over and over again?"

"I will see that you have employment." The red spots were back. "And why do you not call on our neighbours? Then you would not want for company."

"It is for them to call first on a newcomer. So my mother taught me. And I am such. It would be ill-mannered in me to presume. Our neighbours do not come; it seems they do not choose to know your wife."

To this he had no answer. If a look could have killed, I would have been dead at his feet. He stalked from the parlour and I heard his voice raised, calling for Robbins.

In his stiff state he looked so like a doll I toyed with the fancy that if I were to prick his skin not blood, but sawdust, would run. Nevertheless, I was half triumphant and yet also half afraid at having crossed such a man.

I sat long at the table before I went upstairs to dress, for I did indeed quake at my own boldness, and in my present state had no wish to meet Dorothy's prying eyes. While she was behind me fastening my bodice, so that I could not see her face nor she mine, I was reflecting that last night my husband had hardly entered the house but I was again in the wrong, and he showing his displeasure in the same odious manner. How was life with

74

such a man to be endured?

That morning we rode separately, taking opposite directions, to poor Harrison's bewilderment. Accompanying me, he knew not where to look or what to say. I let the man be, giving myself up, while I might, to the pleasure I had in Kitty, as she moved so sweetly beneath me.

Between myself and my husband anger built up all day. I refused to let go of mine: he fed his, thereby mending his self-esteem. Each time we met, and always on the most formal terms, it seemed that the gunpowder must ignite. Nonetheless the hours passed without explosion and we sat down together at supper in the most normal way.

I maintained towards him the politeness good breeding demanded of me, determined to show myself in no whit to blame; but the greater my dignity, the colder his countenance became. Had I wept, or begged forgiveness, or said that I was sorry — though for what I could not tell — he would have read me some small lecture, and then in due course patted my hand. But this I would not do.

That evening he told me no little tales of where he had been or what he had done, he made no request that I should sing for him. When the servants were gone he sat in silence, making sure that I should understand the menace of retribution to come.

"Goodnight, Sir," I said at last.

He did not answer, and I went upstairs, and all the while Dorothy was undressing me I wondered whether he would come to my bed.

Even as she left me I heard the door of his bedchamber open. He marched in without knocking.

I have only ever known one man to look handsome in a nightshirt and Sir Gilbert in his cut as poor a figure as ever. But tonight his aspect was alarming. To my agitated mind the hairs on his legs appeared each one to be standing up in rage.

I knew at once that he was ready for what he was about to do, and that it was to be for my punishment, not for his pleasure. It was indeed rape; he took me forthwith, without a word, without a kiss, to prove he was my master.

Afterwards, I cried into my pillow, and that pleased him.

"Tears of contrition become you. I am glad to see you contrite." With which he turned on his side and fell at once asleep.

My tears were of anger only. There was no sorrow in them, no, nor even of bodily hurt, as I could swear that he had hoped. For next morning he rose smiling, mighty pleased, his vanity restored, in the mistaken belief that he had broke my spirit.

He walked up and down at the foot of the bed that I might admire him, stretching in the sunshine that poured in through the windows. Little scarlet lights winked in his sandy hair.

"Well my dear," he remarked, as if nothing but the agreeable had passed between us, "in two days I go again to London. You will find that to be the pattern of our life. I shall be obliged to be away for a week or two and then back at Marley for as long as business permits. I shall hope to bring you back some gew-gaws to amuse you. The French write pretty romances, I am told."

"Thank you, Sir," I murmured, my breath quite taken away, my anger now outrun by astonishment at his affrontery, and astonishment chased out by disgust at his ideas of what was proper to the wedded state. I was to be disciplined as he would his dogs: a whip in one hand, a bone in the other. Even as a child I had never been so treated.

He had done showing off his body, to how ill an effect he was not to know. "I will leave you to dress," he said. "We will take breakfast together downstairs. This morning I have matters to attend to with Robbins. But the weather is delightful, we will ride out this afternoon and see how the hay cutting goes on."

I could feel my face red. It was still so when I sat down at my mirror. Dorothy again wore that hateful smile and I made no attempt to disguise my ill-humour, finding fault where none was as she brushed my hair.

At breakfast my husband was all affability, explaining where the meadows lay that we were to visit later.

"Pleasant though it is to sit talking thus, I must to my cabinet," he said, rising at last from his chair. "And how will my wife spend her morning?"

76

"I think to take a walk," I said. "On such a day 'tis a sin to remain indoors."

Indeed, I found myself in sober mood, needing to order my thoughts in peace, away from this house where I never felt unobserved.

Finding the wind on the terrace blow cool, going back therefore to fetch my cloak and turning into the passage when all supposed me elsewhere, I surprised Dorothy in close converse with my husband in the doorway of his bedchamber. At my approach she glided away towards the backstairs, and my husband stepped inside his door and closed it in my face.

Not until I was out in the Park and well distanced from the house was I able to think about what I had seen, so disturbed was I.

To see Dorothy in collusion with my husband set my heart thudding. I had taken them in conspiracy; this was hateful to me. How well placed my distrust of her had been! My most unguarded, most private acts, were open to my husband: the sighs a woman gives when she undresses, the half spoken word, the indiscretion let slip in the languors induced by hairbrushing, were all to be recorded. I could be in no doubt now how alone I was. Moreover, it crept into my head to wonder whether there was more between Dorothy and my husband than the spying? Was it her hand behind the cradle upstairs? Hers, and not someone else's? Was she perhaps his mistress? Was this indeed why she so much disliked me?

For a moment my heart sank utterly as I came face to face with the prospect that there was to be no happiness for me in my present life. I drew my cloak closer about me. I was walking between the avenue of trees, in and out of which I had galloped so gaily when I was first presented with Kitty so short a time ago. How different my spirits now! My position was in truth not one to be envied.

My husband did not love me: of that I was convinced. I doubted that he even found me pleasing, except as a means to breed him children and then only if I were subservient altogether to his will. I had married him to get out into the world of men, but the world of men had no place in it for women. At Bradstock my captivity had sat lightly, and whereas I had been

77

my father's, I had imagined myself to be the Forest's prisoner. Here all was made plain. I had exchanged one master for another: a good for a bad. A woman had no rights in her own person, be she daughter or wife she was but a chattel to be passed from one man's hand to another as they pleased.

I was learning the first lesson that all females must learn, that in the world of men, it is men through whom she must live.

My reasoning before deciding on this marriage had been but the imaginings of an ignorant child. Why had I not had the wit to heed the voices of those who saw more clearly? And yet, does not every caged bird long to spread its wings and fly?

I had now come to the confines of the park where labourers were putting up tall palings that deer might be added to the other ornaments of the place. The rhythmical knocking of beetle on wood had accompanied my thoughts. It was the knocking of nails into the coffin of my hopes.

But what foolish hopes they had been! It had taken me but a fortnight to become disabused of my husband. I had now discovered there was to be no wider life.

"Morning, my Lady, morning my Lady," came in a chorus as the men paused to touch their forelocks.

What a hollow joy I had gained in being addressed thus!

I was tempted to take Kitty and ride home to the Forest. Then I considered what harm this might do to my father. Moreover, Sir Gilbert would surely fetch me back, and what cause would my father have to keep me from him?

I resolved to see my blunder through. I must learn to manage my husband.

I wondered if I were to bear a child would it ease my path? I imagined breeding one up who would be a companion to myself. But any child of mine would be even more my husband's, and one year was too long to wait.

Then I thought of Richard. Here was a boy, presented to me as if by fate, to whom I had been instantly drawn. My need now was to see him at once.

Not far below the rise where I was standing the brook ran alongside the Park. With a picture of my own childhood self in mind, I walked upstream to the bridge at the foot of the village, hoping that I might find him fishing but did not encounter a

78

soul. It was but natural, no child would dare to fish in the grounds of Marley Hall.

My steps turned towards the smithy, but before I could get so far I saw the very one I was seeking, playing in a cottage garden beside the road ahead of me. I could not be mistaken in those bright curls; I was about to call to him when the door opened and to my astonishment Dorothy appeared, calling "Richard?"

What had Dorothy to do here? And such a different Dorothy: her face, her whole person altered, softened and flooded with life, a comely woman any man might desire.

With the child she was loving and laughing. In a passion of envy I watched them together as I drank in the heavy scent about me, feeling concealed though I was not. But they had eyes only for each other. He leapt now into her arms and she covered him with kisses, and it was as if a knife had been driven into my vitals.

At last in play she chased the child indoors, he squealing with laughter, and I hurried past the cottage and on up the hill.

What was I to do? Without Richard I could not endure my present situation. But how to come by his company? I tried to persuade myself that he and Dorothy were but kin, that he was a late-born brother, or a sister's child. But the more I thought on it the plainer it became that he must be her own. Those had been a mother's kisses that I saw. What a perverse turn of fortune that the boy I so longed to befriend should belong to one who was my enemy! I determined nonetheless that I would do so, no matter what this might entail.

I had reached the top of the hill, and in front of me, across the grass, the church beckoned, offering me sanctuary in my distress. Instead of going back to the Hall I turned and entered.

In the fighting at Marley during the late wars, Cromwell's Roundhead troopers had broken the stained glass windows and torn out the carved box pews, so that there was neither the soft light nor the privacy I had been used to at Bradstock. A white beam shone full on the Squire's seat. I knelt in all humility at the back of the church and prayed for help in my difficulties, and my tears trickled a little at what I had lost.

A hand fell on my shoulder.

"My child, what troubles you?"

This kind voice reminded me of my father, and though it was but the vicar, at the words "My child", my tears redoubled.

Now he saw who I was. "Lady Fearnshawe! And in distress! I cannot see you like this. Let me take you to my wife. Come, dry your eyes and calm yourself."

I followed meekly through the vestry door and to the parsonage, observed by none, and he led me into a small parlour where his wife was sitting at her mending.

"My dear," he said, "I have brought Lady Fearnshawe to see you. I think that, like many another, she may need your help."

She lifted her head and a pair of friendly eyes met mine. Her face was homely and full of goodness. Something in her hands, working on the mending in her lap, reminded me of Nurse. She smiled.

"I do not feel like a lady," I said, and then in a burst I poured out my heart, telling all my loneliness but, with some instinct of caution, speaking no ill of my husband himself. "I don't understand," I concluded, "why no one wishes to know me here. I cannot believe there are no neighbours near enough. Even in the Forest, which is a wild place, we were never alone."

The vicar cleared his throat. "Sir Gilbert is much respected in the village. He is a good landlord, and a just employer to those who do their duty by him. But this is Royalist country, and I fear he is not forgiven in having succeeded where the Brandons were the squires before. Marley Manor was half destroyed in the late unfortunate wars, and Robert Brandon fled to France and died there in poverty. When his estates were sequestered they were acquired by your husband; in pulling down the old house and rebuilding he alienated his neighbours further."

"But I am as good a Royalist as any!" I said hotly. "My father fought for the King at Worcester and he too suffered much for his loyalty."

"My dear Lady Fearnshawe," the vicar's wife said, and she laid her hand on my knee. "They judge you by your husband. I beg you to be patient, for as I expect you know yourself, in country places curiosity can be relied upon, sooner or later, to move women in particular to forego their prejudices. You are but young. 'Tis hard to be so far from home. Of course you miss your parents, and all who were about you. It cannot be easy to be mistress of Marley with no mother standing by to guide you. But take heart, learn to do your duty by your household and you will find you have friends."

She went on to say I was welcome to come and sit with her when I would, that this would be entirely proper in my situation. "Moreover," she added, "it might interest you to come with me when I visit my sick. Help from the Lady of the Manor never comes amiss."

My tearfulness now quite gone, I seized on this opening to ask about Richard and enquired who the pretty boy I had seen might be. "Well dressed," I added, "for one in such a situation."

"That will be Richard Blackett, indeed a lovely child. His grandparents care for him, they are good folk and do their duty. 'Tis the usual sad story. They had but the one daughter — "

Here the vicar shook his head and his wife left her sentence unfinished, seeming at once altogether occupied with the next stitch she had to make.

I had learnt what I needed to know. Richard had to be Dorothy's own child; it could not be otherwise.

I rose to take my leave. "Thank you for your kindness," I said. "I will come again if I may."

The morning was far advanced. I hurried across the green and through the park, fearful of being late for dinner. My head was still full of what I had seen and heard, even as I sat down at table with my husband.

He took my silence for submission, for he smiled at me kindly. "Well, my dear? And where did you walk?" he asked.

"I paid a visit to the Vicar's wife," I answered. But I was busy puzzling out what lay behind the Vicar's shaking his head? Why had his wife stopped in her story? The getting of a green gown is common enough in country places and not all young men keep their promises. Had this been the whole of Dorothy's misfortune there could be no harm in telling me, I had been an unnatural prude else.

"She is an estimable woman," my husband said, "and knows

81

where her duty lies. I am pleased that you should make her acquaintance."

I barely heard his words. How blind had I been! There could be but one reason for her sudden silence. If the squire were the father of Dorothy's child, to tell the tale to his new young wife was indeed not fitting. Richard was my husband's son! Here was his hold on Dorothy herself!

I trembled at his hypocrisy, and bent my head that he might not see the blood rising in my cheeks.

"She asked me would I care to go with her when she visits the sick in the village," I said, speaking I knew not how, the words sticking to my tongue. "Do I have your permission? I believe 'tis the custom. But I would not go against your wishes," I added, playing the hypocrite myself. I was learning to deceive, astonished to find myself so apt a pupil.

This too pleased his vanity. "A very proper activity," he remarked.

All that afternoon as we rode, with the sun shining above and the smell of the new mown hay on the breeze, all the while we watched the women in their sun-bonnets moving rhythmically along the rows as they turned the drying grass with their long wooden rakes, their chatter and laughter mingling with the shouts of the children at play round the edges of the field, my mind was elsewhere. I answered their greetings, I replied to my husband's remarks, as if I had been a puppet in a show.

Was it a man or a monster riding so polite beside me? Was he not worse, even, than I had imagined? To set his mistress to be my maid was indeed an insult to myself. But baser still, revealing a deeper turpitude than I had thought his nature to possess, what cruelty to Dorothy! She must watch me take her place, and from day to day live in anguish, waiting to see my lawful issue supplant her own son.

We passed a field where the cutting had but just begun.

"A good crop," my husband remarked, "if the weather holds. And a pretty scene do you not think my dear?"

"Yes, indeed."

As the men moved forward and the scythes flashed in the sunlight I was thinking how fortunate that I did not love this

82

man; for indeed, this being so, it mattered nothing to me how many Dorothys or what number of bastards he might have. But Richard had won my heart before I knew of his parentage, and knowing it, I was all the more determined to befriend him, not only for my own pleasure, but that I would not, if I could prevent it, see such a child suffer. It offended my deepest sense of justice that Richard should be unlawful and without rights as my husband's child; and I was in indignation for his mother. She had conceived him in love. That he had been begotten in lust was nothing to the matter, except as a stain upon his father's character.

My hands were freed and my mind clear to use my secret knowledge of my husband as I would. I sensed I had a power over him, though what it was I could not tell as yet.

I felt his eyes upon me. "The Forest, you will agree, is beautiful," I said. "But the prospect here — these rolling hills and fertile fields quite take my breath away. Never have I seen the like."

He swelled visibly, and touching his horse with his heels, he capered a little, showing off his horsemanship by executing a half passage as we approached the gate to the field.

He was still in a good humour with me that evening, for after we had taken supper he asked me to sing.

I knew that this was done to signal his approval and that he would only yawn behind his hand. I answered:

"I had thought to sit and further my embroidery but if it would please you for me to sing, I will put it by."

"No, no, my dear, I like to see your hands busy. And what is it you are making?"

"A cover for a tabouret to rest my feet on in front of the fire." Before I opened my mouth no such idea had entered my head. My needle had but devised a shapeless primrose in the middle of the empty stuff, knowing not at all to what end.

My husband crossed and uncrossed his legs, and smiling patted Jess's head. "The jade!" he said fondly. "She is in pup." And such was the pride in his voice, one might have fancied he believed he had sired the puppies himself. I marvelled to see a man so lost in his own conceit. "I intend she shall found a line of Marley spaniels. Perhaps, my dear, you would care to have one of them for your own? Or would you prefer one of these little lapdogs ladies appear to fancy?"

"I am used to greyhounds, but a spaniel will do very well I daresay." I lowered my head that he might not see how I despised him. I wondered would he look on me with that same doting gaze when I should be with child? Despite all his cruelty he could love, for he loved the bitch, and surely all the more would love his own children. I fancied he would breed little tyrants, treating them with total indulgence, watching and smiling, standing by while they trampled on their mother and the servants about them. It flew into my mind that in all likelihood he loved his bastard, not indeed as he would a lawful heir, but as he might one of Jess's pups.

In the corner of the parlour the grandfather clock was ticking the seconds exactly towards the hour. With a like exactness I was picking my words.

"A truly pretty boy, the Blackett grandson," I remarked. "One would think him nobly born, his quality above what one would expect to find in a cottage."

"When did you see him?" My husband was disturbed.

"He was at the forge watching when I had Kitty shod. The child looked with such longing at the mare that I put him up and walked him round. He took so naturally to the business I could not but think his father to have been a horseman of more than usual merit."

I bent my head over that hateful embroidery, and out of the corner of my eye watched him expanding under my flattery. He was suddenly rubicund. I had never seen him thus.

"I would not encourage the child to think above his station. But 'tis pity that one so gifted should not have the opportunity to learn."

I dared not look up; I felt my remarks go home.

"What had you in mind, my dear?" he said at last, a little stiffly.

"I wondered, could Harrison spare the time to instruct him? The stableboy's pony would be of a size and temper for a child."

"Well, well." He cast about him, uncertain what to say. "I see no reason why not. I like it that you should consider the welfare of our village folk. Yes, very well, my dear, I will explain your wishes to Harrison."

"And who is to tell the boy of his good fortune? I would like to have the pleasure of it myself; but perhaps it would be better for Harrison to carry the message."

Again my husband's face was tinged with pink. I watched him struggle with the dilemma. If Harrison were to go, the village would talk. But if I went they would laugh, thinking me a blind fool.

In the end he preferred to let it be seen as a piece of feminine folly: "I find no reason why you should not go, if it would give you pleasure. Personal kindness from the lady of the Manor never comes amiss. I see, my dear, that you begin to learn."

Now at last I could look up. I gave him my thanks, tumbling out the words, my face flushed. He smiled indulgently, thinking me overwhelmed by his praise. But my joy and my excitement were all at the success I had achieved. Moreover I had discovered how this was to be done again: I had only to keep my temper and apply flattery. I had learnt my lesson indeed, but not the one intended.

When he departed for London we took our leave on the best of terms; he fancying he left a docile wife behind, I, all impatience to see him gone.

I could discern from his bearing, from his very swagger as he mounted his horse, that he fancied this time to have got me with child, and by his kindness to me in bed to have made his point that now I behaved as he wished.

In truth, I dissembled, pecking his cheek in duty, all the while thinking how I might contrive to call on Richard while Dorothy should be safely occupied elsewhere. I looked forward, in my lord's absence, to supervising the child's riding lessons myself.

As I came into the hall from the terrace, Rose passed me with her arms full of soiled shirts, blushing that she used the front stairs, which were out of bounds for such purposes. I remembered that this was the household's monthly wash-day and every female servant would be busy in the laundry. I went upstairs to make sure that Dorothy, also, would be thus employed.

I came on her in my bedchamber, changing the linen on the bed. She thought herself unobserved, and held the sheet against her cheek, kissing it where my husband had lain, the tears running from her eyes. She was rocking to and fro as if she cradled his child itself in her arms. I had not thought that any woman could so love a man, and such a man as he. But, in truth, I saw she did.

She had neither seen nor heard me. In pity, not wanting to add to her distress, I backed softly away.

I made a clatter in the passage before I approached again to enter the room. The clean sheets lay on the table waiting to be put on the bed. Dorothy had gone. But her misery hung so strong in the air I felt that I intruded.

How earnestly I wished it in my power to help her! What pleasure to me could I but take her place, and she mine! I pictured the joy of giving her everything: my husband, my house, my position as my Lady that had once seemed so delightful. A servant's life appeared full of charms.

I forgot my dislike of household tasks; seating myself in all idleness at the table with the folded sheets in front of me, I fancied what happiness it would be to live as did our Susan, free to lie in the woods with Jacky and marry only when she must.

But here I was at Marley and no help for it.

Poor Dorothy! At last I understood. Hers was in truth the hand that had arranged those nurseries upstairs. And had she been led to hope that she was herself to be their mistress? Such a refinement of cruelty was in keeping with all I had come to learn of my husband.

Yet as I rose to hasten to the village I had no smallest thought for what she must feel at seeing Richard happy in my company. I needed his love too much.

Of my intentions towards him I said nothing to her for it never entered my head to do so. Looking back as I write, I fear that she must have been in an agony lest I meant to steal her child, only to cast him out later in favour of my own.

So in my ignorance I fed her hatred.

CHAPTER SIX

An obedient wife

Meanwhile, with my husband gone and my plan going forward it was as if a thundercloud had left the sky. The days passed in innocent pleasure, the one melting into another as in my childhood. The mornings were but dreams, preludes to afternoons spent with Harrison and the child in the Park. Once or twice I was aware of Dorothy at the window, throwing up the sash and pausing to watch from a distance on pretence of airing my bedchamber. But this spoiled my enjoyment no more than did the gnats that rose and fell in the shade under the trees.

Richard was making fast progress. That I might the better observe how he did, I held Kitty back and let him go ahead of me with Harrison.

We drew rein, the three of us together. And now I said: "Harrison, your pupil comes on, don't you think he could be let go without the leading rein?"

Richard was pink with pleasure, his eyes big and starry.

"Please! — Mistress — Lady — "

"Mistress Sarah will do."

Harrison looked down his nose in disapproval of this liberty, yet daring to say nothing.

"He is but a child, Harrison, it pleases me to be thus informal."

Richard was pleading, "I can do it, I shall not fall!"

Harrison let him go, and side by side we watched him canter into the distance. The pony was broad for Richard's short legs, but he was altogether its master.

"Your schooling is to perfection," I said, and saw how he forgot my lapse in dignity. "The child does you credit."

" 'Tis easy, my Lady, the boy does as he is told and no argument."

I forgot the passage of time. I forgot even that I was a wife. It took me quite by surprise when I once more heard my husband's regular tread in the passage and the door to his bed-chamber close behind him. As on his last return from London it was late and I already in bed. I waited, but he did not come to me and at last I fell asleep, resolving as my eyes closed that since I was a wife I would appear an obedient one; moreover, while he should be at Marley, to refrain from showing too great an interest in Richard's lessons. For I had no wish to lose my new joy. I well understood how it would please my husband to use such deprivation as a punishment.

The sight of him in his snuff-coloured suit, rising from the breakfast table to bow to me as I entered, put an instant damper on my spirits. In his absence I had in some sort made Marley my own. This was all fancy, and as it fled I was reminded of the difficulties of my condition as a wife. The very manner of his sitting in his chair showed that he was master and I an under-dog, different only in degree from the rest. I looked at him in some apprehension that I might once more be in disgrace. But he spoke to me kindly:

"And how has my wife been occupying her time? Worthily, I trust."

I knew full well that he would have already found out my every movement from his spies. But I swallowed my anger, and rejoicing in finding myself able to dissemble I answered meekly:

"Quietly enough. I have walked, and ridden, and endeavoured to learn from Mrs Willis something of household affairs."

In truth, to occupy an evening I had summoned up courage and commanded Mrs Willis to sit with me, and of what else could she speak? For hours on end, with my mind elsewhere, I had listened to talk of conserves and sheets. I was never to mend my position with her, but this overture led to a show of friendship between us, and news of it I fancy, lay behind Sir Gilbert's smiles.

I remembered that a wife should ask after her husband's affairs. "And I trust you found all as you desired in London?"

I had spoken as he wished. "Well enough, my dear. And

88

now I have some trifles to show you in the withdrawing-room."

On the table under the looking glass two packages waited to be undone.

"I trust I have met your wishes," he said. "Go carefully! What you are handling is fragile."

He stood over me, breathing hard, as I undid string and paper and fine shavings, to discover altogether six small porcelain bowls decorated in the Chinese manner, with six saucers to match. So fine were they that when held up to the light the sun shone through as if through water.

"They are pretty indeed," I said amazed, wondering for what purpose they were intended. Puzzle as I might, I could see none they would serve, for they had no handles and indeed would hold but a mouthful of drink.

"In these is drunk the new beverage, tay, that is come from the East," my husband informed me. "I have not sampled it myself, but I am told it is to be all the thing with ladies. Now, my dear, you have somewhat few women can boast of."

"They will look very well in my cabinet." I saw no object in filling shelves with useless trifles; for what is a piece of china that is only for show? But nonetheless I was pleased that the piece should no longer stand empty, and I arranged the precious objects carefully inside, before addressing myself to the second package.

Here I found a novel in four volumes and two new song-books.

"I trust these will occupy your leisure hours, my dear. My acquaintances tell me that Mademoiselle de Scudéry should be to your taste."

I thanked him as prettily as I knew how, but as I laid the song-books on my virginals my attention strayed, and my mind was all on Richard's having taken his first leap and had not fallen. And how would he go this afternoon when I dared not be there?

And now my husband's eyes too were drawn to the window by the distant sound of the workmen's hammering, and his face stiffened.

"What is that obstruction I see in the Park?"

89

" 'Tis a little brushwood jump for the child. He rides like an angel. Your trouble for him has not been misplaced."

Sir Gilbert coughed, and we heard no more of it.

I fancy his vanity blinded him to the fact that I well knew Richard to be his child. He must otherwise have guessed, for he was no fool.

For the whole week that my husband was this time at home there was peace between us. I forebore from taking any part in what was going forward with Richard; I made no enquiries of Harrison. Every afternoon I rode out with Sir Gilbert, and was in all ways dutifully attendant to his wishes, impatient only for him to be gone and once more to have Marley to myself.

Such that summer was the pattern of my life. Harrison was in a curious way my ally. We came, I know not how, to have an unspoken accord, based on our mutual love of Kitty, by which certain things would not be mentioned to my husband. If I chose to loiter at the Smithy, or if I went out riding with him when he was instructing the child, nothing would be said; no one would be the wiser save Dorothy, and whether she knew or not was of no consequence, for she would not wish to spoil Richard's pleasure. At last I became so sure of Harrison that on occasion I ventured to ride out with the boy alone. But there was a comradeship between the three of us, based on admiration of each other's skills, which meant an easy enjoyment of each other's company, and Harrison's presence was indeed a part of it.

I had this advantage in the management of Harrison that I was in the stables daily, and he came to depend on my words of praise as he did on his morning draught of ale. Nor were they undeserved, for he was a gifted horsemaster. Moreover, I made a point never to be displeased, and always to show interest in the smallest detail of the creatures' welfare, and so earned the man's respect. I could speak with knowledge, and for this I came to bless Jacky and his teachings in animal lore.

In my husband's absence I watched over Jess with Harrison. I stood beside him when her time came and chose my puppy from the litter almost before she had finished licking them clean.

"I wish for that one, Harrison. 'Tis a dog and will be a fine

90

one. I shall call him Caesar."

My husband on his return objected to what he was pleased to call a heathen name for such an English creature. But I said what was Gilbert but good Latin; and at that he gave way.

Contentment revived my interest in what was going on around me, and I wondered again who, if any, were our neighbours? This I was soon to discover. One by one, during the summer months, the County called to look me up and down and stare and walk round the house, and offering no friendship, go away again. It was curiosity, no more no less. My father was not known outside his own county, and no matter that I was a lady, I was in their view too small a catch to wipe out Sir Gilbert's sins.

My eyes were opened to the general purpose by a Lady Cobleigh, to whom and her two daughters I took an instant dislike. She was a large, heavy woman, pulled tight into a purple silk gown which contrasted evilly with her high complexion and her black hair, which was already turning to pepper and salt. The girls were both older than myself and I rejoiced to find them plain: tall and raw-boned, one in yellow and one in green, neither colour kind.

They arrived in the morning and in all politeness I offered them dinner, knowing that Mrs Willis could be relied upon for this and that the gardens were stocked with the season's delicacies. But my offer was brushed to one side as if Marley Hall had been a cheap hostelry and nothing we could provide fit for their fine bellies.

Announcing "We have but time to look round, Lady Fearn-shawe," my visitor proceeded slowly through the house as if it were her own and she inspecting the work of a negligent housekeeper. She poked her nose into every room and every closet, going ahead of me up the stairs and into the dining-room, at last laying her hand on my husband's bedchamber door.

"Sir Gilbert does not care to have his bedchamber visited," I said, unguardedly.

"A Bluebeard, is he? And what has he to hide?"

At this, I was of course obliged to usher her in. "Your ladyship may observe for herself."

"Hmm," she said, and we passed on.

At last every inch of the house, except for the attics and the kitchens, which were fortunately beneath her interest, had been gone over, every cabinet opened, and standing in the middle of the great parlour and looking all round her she observed:

"We were all so very sorry when poor Sir Robert was turned out by Sir Gilbert and Marley Manor pulled down to build this house."

At this I protested. "But am I not right in believing that Sir Robert died before ever my husband bought these lands? And was not the manor burnt down in the fighting?"

"In part, child, in part. I doubt Sir Gilbert will have told you all. We do not love him hereabouts."

"Then why do you come?" I said hotly.

At this she reddened, and calling to her daughters, made to depart.

The two girls had sauntered into the withdrawing room.

"This virginals was bought for you I daresay, Bess," the one remarked, "when he offered for you."

"Indeed," I said, with some coldness. " 'Tis news to me that Elizabeth begins with an S." At which she had the grace to blush.

As they drove away I thought in triumph of our coach, drawn by my husband's six splendid greys. For theirs was dragged by but four horses, indifferent as to quality and not matched as to colour, the whole as ill-found as the ladies within.

I went straight to Mrs Willis's room to tell her that if these women called again she was to say I was ill and turn them from the door.

My husband came in late that morning from riding out on business. She reported to him before even he sat down to dinner. He came to me frowning.

"Madam, what do you mean by forbidding Lady Cobleigh my house? I particularly value the acquaintance. There is much for you to gain from it."

"Sir, I hardly think you would have me do otherwise. She does not forgive you for having been the Protector's man, no matter what you are now. As your wife, I, too, incur her scorn. I do not choose to be insulted in this house, nay, nor to see my husband insulted neither." And I told him all that had passed, omitting only that I had learned that he had offered for Elizabeth and been refused.

When I had done, I again observed the pink spots of rage upon his cheekbones, though this time his wrath was not directed against me.

"I am sorry you should have been exposed to such treatment," he said. Then, after a pause, "I do not imagine Lady Cobleigh will call again, but should she do so, I do not think it necessary you should receive her." Finally, as if to make amends, "I have matters to deal with concerning the Forest this autumn, and as well must visit my brother. Perhaps, my dear, it would please you to spend a week at Bradstock?"

I was speechless with joy; my tongue faltered as if it had forgot its use. He smiled indulgently.

"I see, my dear, that you would like to go. Very well then, that shall be arranged. Come now, let us dine; I have been busy all morning on account of a new roof required by a tenant for his barn, and am famished."

Till this visit was proposed it hadn't occurred to me that such an event was possible. I felt that I had left home for ever and would never see the Forest or my family again. I had received no answer to my letter to my father and counted myself cast off and forgotten. Now my head and heart were full of Bradstock, and I could hardly bring myself to wait for the day of our departure. In spite of my married station the thought kept springing to mind: what of Oliver?

Two weeks later a letter at last arrived from home. My father wrote: "Dearest child, I hear from your husband that we are soon to have the pleasure of seeing you. This being the case, I am not sending your music as you will more conveniently carry it away with you yourself. I am glad to hear you are well. The Forest goes on its usual course. Jacky is to wed our Susan and we are to have a new girl in the kitchen, and I am led to believe this is to be her sister, Jenny. Your Mother and Nurse send you their love. Your affectionate Father."

So all was as I had left it! I was not forgotten. I saw I had been too hasty. I should have remembered that my mother was never known to put pen to paper; that Nurse could not; and that my father was dilatory beyond words.

Summer turned to autumn. The blackberries ripened on the hedgerows, and when we rode abroad Richard begged for us to stop that he might cram his pockets with nuts. When the first frost brushed the grass and dew picked out the spiders' webs like lace among the brambles, my husband said: "My dear, today you will make yourself ready. Tomorrow we leave for Bradstock. I have ordered Dorothy to pack what you will both need."

"But I don't require Dorothy with me, surely, to go to Bradstock! There is Nurse!"

"My wife does not travel without a waiting-woman to ride with her in the coach."

"The coach! But I had thought we would ride! I had so looked forward to taking Kitty."

"For what are a fine coach and horses if they are not to be used? Come, my dear. It is the proper way for one in your station to travel. I must ride, for I shall be leaving you at Bradstock and travelling where no coach will go, therefore you will need Dorothy."

"But we should go safer on horseback. At this season, should it rain, the forest roads will be quags no coach can pass. Could not Dorothy ride pillion behind George?"

"You forget yourself, my dear. I know the Forest as well as you do. Nay, better, for I have ridden it in all weathers, and from my youth. If the roads are bad, we will leave the coach at Bewdley and take horse from there."

The next day as I stood waiting while Rose packed our baggage under the seats, I had to admire our equipage, and my heart swelled. My eye told me that the horses were fat from idleness, but nonetheless, splendid indeed. Yet, as I stepped inside with Dorothy following behind to settle beside me I felt my foot dragged a ball and chain.

The leaders took the strain, and then the wheelers, managed to perfection by our coachman, began to pull and we were moving forward, till in style, we swung out of the Park gates into the high road. I glanced at Dorothy. Respectful but silent, she was like a leech fastened upon me, that I could not shake off, nor could I ignore her. I could have wished her a thousand miles away.

All the village turned out to see us pass, lining the road at their garden gates, the children sitting on the wall to wave. To my chagrin, I was on the wrong side of the coach and could not wave back to Richard; it was Dorothy who suddenly coming to life leant from the window and blew kisses. When she sat back in her seat there was triumph on her face. She had unbent wholly in front of me and I could not fault her. Moreover, she had made her farewells to Richard without my coming between them. Now it was I who had been shut out and put in my place.

While Dorothy continued to look about her from the window, I sulked in my corner till we came to Worcester where, as before, we were to dine; and here I woke up and enjoyed playing the lady. For what sixteen-year-old could resist the attention our party called forth?

From here onwards it was I who hung from the window, and Dorothy who slept, till we came at last to Bewdley and the bridge across the Severn, where, in my excitement, I shook her awake.

"Dorothy! Dorothy! Look out!" I cried. "The Severn! 'Tis a great river and you will never have seen its like!"

She rubbed her eyes and stared and shivered as we crossed the water.

Now at last we entered the Forest, and the coach shook in the ruts.

" 'Tis a wild savage place, a very desert," and she shrank into her corner as if to escape out of the coach altogether.

But I sniffed the familiar scent of rotting leaves and of woodsmoke rising on the air and my heart sang.

"Not at all," I said. " 'Tis only that it is strange to you," and I began to wonder where, tomorrow, I would find Old Sim.

My husband and George had ridden on ahead and when we arrived at Bradstock all the household waited on the terrace to greet me. I flung myself out of the carriage before it even stopped moving and into my mother's arms.

"Have a care, child!" she said.

When I had hugged my father and then Nurse, I remembered Dorothy, who stood waiting, the luggage at her feet, and that remote expression on her face which I knew well to mean that she disapproved of all she saw. I presented her as politeness demanded.

All at once I found myself in the parlour, alone with my mother. My father had carried Sir Gilbert off to his closet. Dorothy and Nurse had disappeared upstairs. We stared at each other. How strange it was to be here again! And how small and how dark my old home now seemed!

I pushed the thought from me.

My mother had eyes only for my belly.

"Not yet with child?" she asked.

"No, Mother. Is it any great matter?"

She sighed. "I had hoped for a grandchild. But 'tis early days."

"Well, Mother, tell me. What news? My father said nothing in his letter. Where is Old Sim working? And what of Oliver? And are Jacky and Susan wedded?"

My mother sighed again. "I'm afraid, my love, you will not find Sim. He is dead, not long since. They found him in his hut, as if gone to sleep watching the kiln. No one can tell how old he must have been."

I sat down, feeling that with Old Sim gone the world had come to an end.

"Oliver is at Oxford still. He sees out another year and then he is to wed: an heiress from Worcestershire. They say she is the sweetest girl and he is much enamoured of her."

Less than six months and all forgotten! It was another blow to my heart.

"Jacky and Susan!" and now she smiled. "They have been wed these six weeks and Susan swelling already. The babe is due in March. Your father found them a cottage in the village and Susan is quite the proud housewife. Jenny does very well in her place. And now, my child, you must wish to wash and make yourself comfortable."

"I can find my way!" I said. From habit, I went straight to my old bedchamber, only to find Dorothy unpacking her clothes.

96

"Did you require me, my Lady?" she said.

"No Dorothy, no. I wished to see that you were comfortable and had all you required," I said hastily.

She lifted her head and looked at the painted walls in some disdain. "As comfortable as could be expected," she said flatly.

Of course, I was now a married woman! I was to sleep in the best spare bedchamber where I had spent my wedding night.

None of this visit passed as I had hoped. Jacky was too busy with the extra horses and our coachman to gossip with me; moreover, he was inclined to treat me with distance, as a grand lady. There was no riding out into the Forest to talk to Old Sim. My father was sunk in his usual melancholy. The woods by the cherry tree had been cut down.

Nor did I have one minute alone with Nurse till the night before we left, for Dorothy interposed herself between us; waiting on me morning and evening, and at all other times everywhere at Nurse's elbow, assuming this to be her rightful place as an equal servant.

Nurse came to me as I was getting read for bed, and dismissed Dorothy from the room.

"I wish to have a word alone with my nurseling," she said. "Dorothy, you can go to your chamber."

Dorothy left without a murmur, such was Nurse's authority, nor did she loiter to eavesdrop at the door. I heard her footsteps patter down the passage.

"Oh Nurse!" I said. "What am I to do? I do not conceive, and though I care not at all, my husband grows impatient. All he wishes of me is an heir."

"And a good thing too that you are not with child. There is time enough for that. I advise you, Sarah, watch Dorothy. She wishes you nothing but ill. And since you are married to that man, mind your Ps and Qs and do not anger him."

"Nurse, I know it all," I said sadly. "There is nothing you can tell me about my husband or Dorothy or what has been between them," and I poured out all I had discovered.

But Nurse only shook her head.

"See, I wear your cross," I said, and I touched it where it hung at my neck. "Smile, Nurse, and kiss me, for tomorrow Sir Gilbert will be here and we shall not be private at all."

Hug me and kiss me she did, but she could not smile, and her eyes were full of tears.

Sir Gilbert arrived betimes on horseback, and ordered the coach round to the door almost before we had done breakfast.

I was nearly in tears as I kissed my parents goodbye. I could not speak. I dared not look at Nurse. I stepped in silence into the coach. As we departed, and Dorothy settled herself beside me for the long journey, my heart cried dumbly to the trees for help — to stop the coach — to alter my fate. But no comfort came. I had in my pride forsaken the Forest to marry a stranger, so now it turned its back on me. As we went forward, I could fancy the way behind us vanished and the trees closed over it.

Whether the coach shook in the ruts or its wheels rolled smoothly, the message was the same: outcast, outcast.

And yet what use had I now for Bradstock? A cold hand touched my heart as I saw plain that the answer was "None". For I myself was changed, a child no longer; there was no salvation in laying my head on Nurse's bosom or hiding in the Forest.

In my musing, I didn't notice when we left the Forest to enter Bewdley, nor that we crossed the Severn.

Indeed, I belonged nowhere, and at this I shivered.

Then I thought of Richard. I saw him standing in his stirrups to reach the nuts on the bushes, and fancied the way to re-capture innocence lay here; not in going back. I must go forward. If Marley gave me this, my marriage bed was no worse a place to lie in than my maiden's chamber.

I was unaware that we had come into Worcester and the horses had pulled up. Dorothy shuffled and stretched and my husband opened the coach door.

"My dear," he said, "wake up! We are at Worcester and will dine."

As on going, so coming back I was on the wrong side of the coach to wave to Richard as we came into the village. Again it was Dorothy who leaned out of the window as if she, not I, were the lady. I cared nothing for it. I was tired, and soon would have the child to myself.

To my surprise it was a comfort to return to Marley; to see in

98

the dusk here and there light shining from a window, to find a warm fire in my bedchamber and the candles already lit, and Rose, blushing at being discovered still setting the table for our supper by its blaze.

Indeed, since at Marley even in bad weather it was possible to ride out, that winter I was less confined than ever in my life before; and in the company of Richard and Kitty and Harrison, with Caesar growing up and needing training, with tales of romance to lose myself in over the fire in the evening, and the Vicar's wife to talk with, I forgot to be unhappy. I even enjoyed the country Christmas activities and the great gathering given for the tenants in the hall, where the Yule log burnt day and night in the grand hearth below my husband's picture.

But spring came to my undoing and I began to sigh.

I was sitting at my virginals singing one of Dowland's sad airs and pitying myself, because the leaves on the trees outside were already pale green and today was my birthday and no one had remembered, when my husband came prancing in; or as near to prancing as so sober a man could get. He had a pair of the new petticoat breeches but just come from the tailor; now he was parading this finery, expecting my applause.

"They are very fine," I said.

The flowered apricot satin of which they were made was pretty indeed. But in these breeches, which to my eyes were no better than full skirts cut off short, with his drawers tied above his knees to fall in a frill to his calves and what was left of his legs below dwarfed to toothpicks — though indeed they were good legs, apart from the hairs — the effect was so ridiculous I was hard pressed not to laugh.

"And what are these for?" I enquired.

"Why, for the occasion of the King's marriage. The Portuguese princess is expected from week to week and I am required to do her honour. I shall need to hold my head up with the best of them," and he paused to smirk at his image in the mirror.

My heart began to beat in hope and fear at once.

"Am I then to have a new gown?" I asked.

"You do not require one I think. You have gowns enough." And I saw in the glass that he frowned.

"But I must hold my head up too!"

He coughed, his words were for me but his eyes were still for himself. "You will not be coming. You will stay here."

At the insult of being addressed thus in total insensibility as to my feelings, I leapt from my seat, all my good resolutions flown from my head. I paced up and down like one of the wild women in the Forest who stare from the charcoal burners' huts.

"Not go to London for the King's wedding! How can you be so cruel!"

"The King, I think, will be married at Portsmouth," he said drily.

" 'Tis all one. Portsmouth or London, why should I not go with you? Am I not young enough and pretty enough to stand beside you?"

Now indeed he turned from admiring his appearance to look me over, and his eyes were grey stones.

"Madam, it is not for a wife to question her husband's decisions. Put this folly out of your head. If you think I would expose one who knows so little how to conduct herself, to a court that is nothing but a nest of whores and lechers, you are much mistaken."

"Folly, Sir? Is it folly to wish to be with you to see the King wed or to welcome the Queen? Am I then never to go to London, never to meet the grand company you talk of, but to remain at Marley till I die for lack of distraction — and yet be content? Are you perhaps ashamed of your marriage? Do you in truth fancy that your grand acquaintance will despise you for your wife? That they will know my father cuts no great figure in the world and smile at you for a fool? Had you not been refused by Lady Cobleigh for her daughter you would have taken that hoyden with you, you would not have dared do otherwise."

I had never seen him so taken aback.

"How did you know of this?"

"From the creature herself."

"And pray, why did you not tell me?"

"I did not choose to. You would be obliged to take her, plain and stupid though she is, for fear of her mother's tongue and

100

her mother's eye, and her mother's position in the County. Then, indeed, the company in London would have laughed behind their hands to see you yoked to one so ill-dressed and provincial. I am right, am I not, that what I did in forbidding that harridan the house you would have done yourself, but that you did not dare?"

His colour was changing from red to white and back again. In his shame he could say nothing. He was left floored; like a woman in his drooping petticoats.

I pressed home my advantage. I was beside myself with rage. I did not care how much I hurt him or if I wrecked my marriage. I cast round for anything that would pierce his composure.

"I am deceived in you," I said, gazing on him in his fine clothes as if they were but a wrinkled skin and he a toad in my path. "I see it plain. You do not wish me to find you out. You keep no grand company, for you are nothing but a clerk, feathering your nest at the King's expense and cheating your way to fortune. And 'tis, I think, your whore that you lie with in London, who walks with you at court among the rest. I am to stay here that I may not see you in your sins, but all virtue, as you wish me to be."

I saw that he trembled, and at this I exulted. The red patches were back on his cheekbones, but he spoke with cold restraint.

"You are mistaken, madam. I am no petty government clerk. On the contrary, I am high in the counsels of the Exchequer, as you would learn if I chose to take you to London. No. I do not keep a mistress, though," with a glance at my flat belly, "for all the satisfaction I get here none would condemn me if I did."

"I have endured my duty as a wife," I said hotly, "nor cried out at your unkindness. If all you say is true, nonetheless you still lie to me." And now I knew the blackness of his heart. "It is out of meanness that you do not take me with you! Because I am not with child and deprive you of what you most desire, I am to be deprived also. You punish me for what is no fault of mine."

"The fault's not mine, that I do know," and he appraised my person as if I had been a bitch that had failed his expectations.

101

"If you know that, you are no better than the lechers you affect to condemn. And do not — I beg of you — offer me the common cry of men, that what a youth does in his salad days is neither here nor there."

To this too he could find no answer.

That I was privy to his secret I kept to myself, not wanting to endanger Richard. I racked my brains for something to taunt him with elsehow.

I loved this withdrawing room in which we stood; indeed, the house as a whole had beauty. Nevertheless I lied, to wound him:

" 'Tis a hard fate you condemn me to, Sir, entombed in this garish mausoleum till I should happen to breed."

The look he gave me was so venomous I knew he would have put me away if he could, for a less barren stock. For one long moment he considered me, not only with venom, but in cold calculation, so that my rage was frozen and I trembled for what he might do. Then in silence he left the room, closing the door softly behind him.

My legs crumpled under me and I sat down on the stool in front of my virginals, listening to my heart beating, the blood burning in my cheeks. I was frightened now, for I saw that I had worsted him at every turn, and this he would never forgive.

Thus all the good that had been done by my obedience, was undone, and we were back at the beginning again.

I cannot now wholly blame my husband. In his eyes I must have seemed a bad bargain: I neither bore him a child, nor cared for his house, nor furthered his standing with his neighbours. Nay, I, a useless chit, had the temerity to set myself up against him, and to cast in his teeth all that he had laid at my feet: his establishment and his house, the pride of his heart, the monument he had raised to his achievement.

Indeed, at this stage in my life I could have been a good wife only to a husband I loved. For I was not ready to make the smallest concession, or willing to see any point of view but my own.

I had been ill-advised to forget Nurse's words and speak as I did. And yet, what weapon has a woman, save her body and

102

her tongue? They are all she has in her armoury. And my body my husband did not love.

In truth, the villain of the piece was the custom of the times which, even now, treats women as chattels, and even their right to say yea or nay as to the disposal of their persons allowed them, if at all, only by courtesy.

While I still sat staring at nothing Rose entered the room.

"My Lady, dinner is ready," she announced. Her eyes were downcast and her voice unsteady. I fancy that already the household knew that peace had fled.

I know not how I sat through dinner, nor why it did not choke me.

In the days that followed I waited for retribution but none came. My husband withdrew himself altogether from my bed, for which I was not sorry. Indeed, in perfect politeness, he practised a studied withholding of himself at all times, as if I were not there; neither asking me what I did nor telling me what he did himself.

Although this new form of cruelty did not touch me, I was yet left strangely uneasy; for I could not believe this was the whole of his intention. The servants performed their duties as if I had been a condemned felon, or infected by the plague. Only riding out with Richard at my side could I forget my circumstances.

I was waiting happily on Kitty, watching in affection the child's excitement as he reached into a blackbird's nest to steal the eggs, when it came to me that I had missed my terms. A wave of horror ran through my body.

"Four eggs, Mistress Sarah, four!" Richard cried.

"Leave one for the poor bird."

He set about making a nest of moss in the pocket of his coat to carry them safely, and all the while I was thinking how it would be an even worse fate to bear my husband's child than to exist in my present barren captivity. I fancied him hard put to it not to rejoice for himself, yet harder still to forgive me; I saw myself living in a perpetual limbo, tolerated for my body's sake.

As we rode home Richard's chatter floated unheeded below me.

Now I noticed that Dorothy watched me with apprehension in her eyes, lest there be a child on the way to supplant Richard, and had I not been in turmoil I would have pitied her.

Then, twelve days late, my terms came upon me, and I lay in bed, relief flooding through me as the blood flowed.

"I do not feel well, Dorothy," I said. "Tell Mistress Willis today I keep my bed and will take my meals here."

In truth, I did not feel the least inconvenience, but I did not wish to face my husband. I fancied watching neither his frowns nor his concern nor even the blank sheet his countenance had been this last fortnight.

I was enjoying my chocolate, listening to the sparrows as they quarrelled in their nests above the window, watching idly a feather drift down, first this way then that on the still air, and thinking what clumsy birds they were and yet how they managed to survive at all, when my husband burst in upon me. He stood at the foot of my bed, his face cold with anger, and for a whole minute stared at me in silence.

At last he spoke. "So you miscarry! Had you controlled your tongue this loss would not have occurred. Had you not given way to wanton rage I might yet have had an heir. Your wilful conduct has killed my child." Before I could open my mouth he turned on his heel and left the room.

For I know not how long I was too stunned to think. Such a knot tied in my stomach that I feared I might vomit.

Why did he not let me speak? Now he was gone all those things I might have said in my defence flooded into my mind.

If I were indeed miscarrying, what else but his unkindness had brought it to pass? And how cruel was his conduct now! Was I not, like him, a human being? Might not I too be suffering? Would a child not be mine also? Did he then accuse me of murdering my young?

But in truth my inconvenience was so little I doubted I miscarried. Every woman knows that her terms can be delayed by a shock to her feelings, and had he not most deliberately insulted me? In this too it was he who was at fault. He alone was to blame. Had he not upset me he could have saved himself both his false hopes and his grief. Had he not kept a spy in my bedchamber, by which means he was made privy to the workings of my body, he would have been none the wiser as to my delay; for had I thought myself with child, at so early a time I would have told him nothing of it.

My breakfast tray was still on my knees, my chocolate cold and forgotten. I touched Nurse's cross and prayed that I might never give him the heir he craved.

I kept my bed the next day also, not indisposed, but too sick at heart to move. From now on I hated him. I carried my hatred where his seed should have lain; and every time I looked on him it grew stronger.

CHAPTER SEVEN

I ride wild

The morning on which I decided to rise and go downstairs it was Rose who came to draw the curtains and let in the pearly light.

I had been awake some little while already, occupied in wondering why my husband delayed so at Marley, with the new Queen expected from Portugal. I had never known him absent himself from London for so long at one time, and I could only think that his purpose was to torment me.

I yawned, blinking at the sunshine.

"Oh my Lady!" Rose said breathlessly, "I'm sorry you should be called late, but Dorothy has fallen and hurt her ankle. Mrs Willis thinks 'tis a sprain and says she is to rest it. So I am to come instead. If my Lady is agreeable."

"Perfectly, Rose. But poor Dorothy!"

"And I have brought you your breakfast, my Lady. Mrs Willis didn't know what you wished, and everything being so behindhand she thought it best to send it up."

" 'Tis very well, Rose. And when I have done you can dress me, for I am recovered, and it is too splendid a day to waste in bed."

Caesar had escaped to creep upstairs with Rose; I heard him whining outside the door. Now, on her return, he slipped round her skirts and into the room, eager to satisfy himself that all was well with me. While I sat at my table for her to brush my hair, he was playing, contented, at chasing a fly, growling, pretending it was hidden under my slipper.

We were laughing together over his antics when Dorothy opened the door. She paused to draw breath as she closed it; then hobbled, limping, to the nearest chair, and supported herself with both hands on its back.

With no by your leave to me, she addressed Rose. "Mrs Willis requires you downstairs. I will see to my Lady. And take the dog with you. Sir Gilbert doesn't allow them in the bed-chambers."

Her commanding Caesar brought the blood to my cheeks. Rose looked from her to me and back again.

"Help Dorothy to sit down, Rose, for I think she should not stand."

Dorothy looked daggers, but was obliged by her very pain to submit.

"Now, Rose, fasten my gown, and then you may go. And, Rose, since I think Caesar might trip Dorothy in her present lameness, you may take him with you. I will send for you later."

Rose left the room, chasing Caesar in front of her. Dorothy and I confronted each other, openly at last, fighting for supremacy.

"What does this mean?" I said. "I understand Mrs Willis ordered you to rest."

"It is my place to wait on you. I can manage quite well."

"I think otherwise. Moreover it is not your place to disobey her."

She looked at me insolently from where she sat, as if I were a child and a mere cypher.

"Sir Gilbert wishes it," and there was sly triumph in her voice.

"Dorothy, I do not intend to have Mrs Willis's orders countermanded, even by my husband. I do not choose to be waited on by someone who is in pain. You will go to your room."

She kept a mulish silence, but her eyes changed. I have seen that look in a rabbit before the blow falls that breaks its neck. I knew what she feared.

"I am not going to dismiss you from my service, nor will I complain of you to my husband, for I do not wish to harm your child. That Richard is your child I have always known. And I would indeed be a fool if I could not guess the father. Let us have this clear between us. I pity you from my heart."

All the stuffing went out of her; I did not care to watch, she was like one who has been whipped. She could control her pain no longer, her face drawn, her limbs shaking. I went to help her as she raised herself from the chair, but she shook off my hand as if it had stung her. Then she pushed me rudely aside and limped into her chamber, shutting the door in my face.

I sailed downstairs on air. Her venom was drawn, she could no longer hurt me. What did it matter if she were my enemy? With every step I trod her underfoot. The sun shining in broad bars across the black and white tiles caressed my face as I passed through the hall to find my husband.

He was in his office, deep in discussion with Robbins. I felt at once on entering that something of moment was afoot. Both men fell silent, waiting for me to go away.

"Mr Robbins," I said, "would you please be kind enough to leave me alone with my husband? There is something I would say to Sir Gilbert in private."

My husband did not lift his hand from the paper.

"Will it not wait? You can see that Robbins is engaged with me in business."

"I would be obliged if Mr Robbins could see his way to do as I ask."

The steward bowed and left the room.

"Sir," I said, before Sir Gilbert could speak. "I will not have Dorothy sent to wait on me when she cannot put her foot to the ground. Do you wish me to go unfastened? My hair improperly dressed? Am I to suffer her groans all day? It was cruelly done, to Dorothy and myself alike. If I am to be mistress of your household, Sir, I do not care to have its governance interfered with." He opened his mouth helplessly, like a fish pulled out of water. "Your countermanding of Mrs Willis's orders is not to my liking; I intend to inform her that you change your mind. And should you seek to punish me by night for exercising my due rights by day I will lock my door against you. I hardly think you will so lower yourself as to send for a locksmith, or come upon me through my waiting-woman's bedchamber."

Sir Gilbert remained speechless in astonishment, his hand motionless upon the table, as if made of wax. I curtsied deeply. "And if you lay a finger on me in chastisement I will leave the

108

house and tell all the world why I do so."

All the signs of rage I had learned to expect appeared in his face. Then, on a sudden, he put up the shutters, his countenance lost all its expression; I could no longer read his mind.

He spoke with perfect calmness. "I am glad to see you assume your proper duties, Madam. Now send Robbins to me, if you please."

For a moment I stood nonplussed. But recovering my poise, I swept from the room and sought out Mrs Willis. Assuring myself that I was in truth mistress of my household at last and could indeed act the part, I ordered that cold compresses should be put to Dorothy's ankle and that she was to be cared for in her bedchamber till she should be fit to work again.

"Rose will suit very well meanwhile," I concluded. "And Mrs Willis, do not fear, I have made all right with Sir Gilbert."

I left her, dumbfounded among the clean linen she was counting.

That night my husband softly crossed the passage to my bedchamber, tried the door, and finding it unlocked, went away again. I slept like a baby.

The sun shone as bright as ever next morning and Rose chattered like the sparrows outside as she dressed my hair; but my spirits were heavy as lead. For I saw that for all my triumph I was now at war with both my husband and my waiting-woman and must live in consequent discomfort, and no future anywhere to be seen. Moreover I mistrusted Sir Gilbert. I could not believe he would forego revenge, nor could I any longer imagine what form it might take.

To throw off my melancholy I began to ride wild again, as I had done once before in the Forest. In tacit agreement with Harrison, I went my own way, to gallop alone and free over the common. Here, where there was no sign of human cultivation, with the wide skies overhead, I left my despair behind, coming home exhausted in mind and body, too spent to think. Unlike Carlos, Kitty enjoyed herself; and Harrison, seeing that she came to no harm, held his tongue, occupying himself in taking Richard over country suitable to his years, till I should be ready to rejoin them.

On the first of these wild rides I found the spring. The clear water bubbled up from the ground below a little hanger on the very edge of the common, where it bordered Marley estates. The grassy bottom was hidden from the Marley side by a dip in the ground and a half circle of thorn trees, so that I came upon it by chance when our galloping was done and we were making our way home. The hawthorn was just coming into bloom. Clusters of tight white buds speckled the green. In the hanger a woodpigeon was calling, the most peaceful sound, I fancy, in the whole world. High above us a kestrel hovered; while Kitty drank, I watched the bird drop like a stone from the sky.

On the second day we stopped again at the spring, though so much had the place taken my heart I was half afraid it had been a dream and I would find it gone. On the third day Kitty quickened her stride as we drew near, and curious to see whether her feelings matched mine, I let the reins lie loose on her neck that she might go as she pleased. She made for the spring as a horse will turn for home.

On the fourth day I scarce recognised where I was. The dell was thronged with life: carts and tents and horses, women cooking over fires, lounging men and everywhere dogs and children. I knew at once these must be gipsies, though I had never seen any before, for none came to the Forest. Their sacking tents reminded me of the charcoal burners. My heart warmed to these wild people. The red cloaks of the women and the brown children running barefoot were a pretty sight, and I envied the freedom of their lives, so different from my own.

I wished to speak with them, and rode Kitty into the half circle of tents with no thought that we might be unwelcome.

At once all activity stopped. The women went inside their tents, the men, as one, turned to stare, their faces hostile. Even the dogs gave up their scratching. I sat like one in a dream. The may blossom had come out overnight and its heavy scent numbed my senses.

But Kitty snorted in surprise and fear, flaring her nostrils, sidling and trying to break away. Along with the may blossom, the smell of fear was in the air, and catching it, I was afraid myself. In a flash I saw myself hemmed in, unable ever to escape, Kitty stolen and myself dead, foolish though I knew this to be. While I hesitated, unwilling to give way to the mare

110

or to myself, thinking to urge her forward that she might not be cheated of her drink, a brown baby ran across our path. Kitty stopped dead, so the baby was in no danger. But the frantic mother, her belly already big with her next child, ran screaming out of one of the tents, her cloak flying, and snatched up the innocent from under Kitty's nose. Startled by the billowing cloak the mare shied and whipped round so that I was almost wrenched from the saddle. While I fought to control her, the men fell back and a crone darted out, waving her fists and shouting in a language strange to me. Her grey hair fell to her waist, her black eyes were pools of jet; evil was round her like a cloud. Her malison was directed not only towards me but at the mare; and the mare, understanding what I could not, bolted.

Behind us pandemonium broke out: men shouting, women screaming, the dogs let loose barking furiously at our heels.

No horse had ever run away with me before. It was a full half mile before Kitty was winded and I regained the mastery, by which time we were well on the way home and all hope lost of meeting with Harrison that we might return together.

By ill chance Kitty and I, unattended, reached the stables at the very moment Sir Gilbert was dismounting and handing his reins to one of the grooms. Kitty was in a lather, moreover cut on her off fore leg by who knows what bush or stone in our wild career; there was a trickle of blood on her fetlock.

My husband looked me up and down.

"Madam, what is the meaning of this? How comes it the mare is injured? And where is Harrison?"

"She was frightened by gipsies and bolted." I was trembling myself, now that my own fright was past.

"Gipsies? Where?"

"On the common. In the dell below the hanger, by the spring." I began to fear now not for myself but for the gipsies. I tried to cover my mistake. "It was not their fault Kitty bolted. It was just that she was surprised at finding them when she went to drink."

"I told them I would not have them there." He was white with rage. "They shall go, I'll have them turned off."

"Sir, they were doing no harm. Leave them be, I beg of you.

111

There is a woman among them who is very close to her time."

"Vermin! Pig stealers! Chicken thieves! They drop their young like cattle. Encouraging gipsies indeed! You have done enough harm today already by damaging the mare. Have a care, Madam! If in future I find that you cannot be trusted to ride soberly, and with Harrison, you shall not ride at all. Meanwhile do not seek to govern my estates."

He strode towards the house, shouting for Robbins.

The men didn't know which way to look. That Sir Gilbert should speak to me so in front of them was an insult such as no gentleman should offer to his wife. Moreover everyone could see, Sir Gilbert himself indeed, that Kitty's injury was of no consequence. It was plain to every man Jack of them that he was but seeking a pretext to find fault with me.

And had the mare been injured, what of myself? But for my comfort he cared nothing.

As for the gipsies, I pitied them, but his callousness towards them was all one could expect from such a man.

I was in a towering passion as I waited to see Kitty attended to and her scratch dressed. The stable boy's face was crimson.

"These gipsies," I said, with what control I could muster. "Where do they come from?"

"Ooh, I don't know, my Lady. They did always come there — in the old squire's day. He didn't mind them. Sir Gilbert thinks otherwise."

"I see," I said. And I did see. They must have been in fear of me, that I would inform on them and bring misfortune; and indeed I had told, not dreaming what would come of doing so.

That afternoon I shut myself up in my closet, unable to bear to have any part in what I knew Sir Gilbert was about. He had summoned the constable from the village to the Hall and, taking every man from the household, intended himself to see the gipsy camp destroyed. I watched them go; riding, as they did, from the stables past my window and down the front drive. His face wore an ugly flush of triumph on his return, but I asked him no questions, unwilling to add one mite to his satisfaction. In the evening, preferring Jess's company to mine, he occupied himself in his cabinet with his papers, and I retired to write to my father; thinking with a sore heart that *he* had rather have lost twenty chickens than that one woman near childbirth should be disturbed.

Dusk fell so that I could hardly see the words as I wrote. My pen moved slowly over the paper. I was just thinking it was time someone brought me candles when the front door bell pealed. I heard Robbins leave his office to see who could be there at this time of day.

Feeling secure with him close at hand, I ventured into the hall, for I was curious; keeping in the background away from the light he carried, standing in the shadow beneath my husband's portrait. Robbins was arguing with a woman: in some uneasiness I felt that somewhere I had heard that voice before. She would not go away, and he shut the door in her face.

The candle flame sank to nothing and then shot up again in the draught.

"Who is it, Robbins?" I said.

I think he neither saw nor heard me, for he left the room without answering; and almost at once my husband, the dogs following at his heels, came striding forth, carrying his heavy riding whip and saying over his shoulder:

"Leave her to me, Robbins, you had better go. I may prefer to have no witness." He threw open the door.

A gipsy woman stepped inside, her cloak like bat's wings folded about her. Her long grey hair was filthy, indeed she stank, the smell reaching even to where I stood. It was the same evil hag who had so frightened Kitty. She had been before me all the while I was writing to my father; now it was as if my own thoughts had brought her here. In the candlelight her black eyes shone with malice.

She saw me at once, and as if it were of no importance and meant nothing to her, flung at me almost in passing:

"Barren you are and barren you will ever be." Then she fell to cursing my husband, up hill and down dale so that the hair on my head stood on end.

To my astonishment he never raised his whip. He was as if paralysed, overcome it would seem as I was indeed myself, by fear of the supernatural powers she was invoking. It was not till she had done, and ran off down the steps to vanish in the darkness, that he came to life.

"Out! Get out!" he shouted. "And if I find you still in the parish by morning I'll have you whipped through the village."

I doubt she heard him.

And now there was no danger, the dogs, taking heart, rushed to the doorstep, from a safe distance barking furiously into the night. He called them to him, and went straight back to his cabinet, without a word to me or so much as looking in my direction, taking the light with him as if I had no substance. Left alone in the dark, I feared I would fall to the ground in terror.

There was no moon to shine through the windows and light the stairs. I crept up, a step at a time, thinking my legs would hardly carry me.

I was never so glad of anything before in my life as when I opened my bedchamber door to find the candles lit and Rose quietly turning down the bedcover.

"Oh Rose I am cold all through," I said. "I think I must be unwell. I wish to go to bed. I would have Mrs Willis send me up a hot posset." And indeed my teeth were chattering as Rose unfastened my gown.

I must have looked strange, for Mrs Willis brought me up the posset herself. She stood by while I drank it; then drew the curtains to and made sure I was comfortable before going downstairs. But my sleep brought little refreshment, for the gipsy's face and the evil she had let loose made me turn over and over again and cry out.

The next morning I woke to hear that Sir Gilbert had left for London.

CHAPTER EIGHT

A visitor

It was Dorothy once more who drew the bedcurtains. The sight of her against the red hangings added to my heaviness.

"I am tired this morning," I said, "please ask Mrs Willis to send breakfast up to me. And will she be so good as to tell Sir Gilbert I keep my chamber."

"Sir Gilbert is gone. Did my Lady not know?"

So my husband had not even had the courtesy to inform me of his movements! My gaoler knew first. A flame of anger brought me wide awake.

Dorothy was not her usual self. She neither made to brush my hair nor helped me into my dressing-gown, nor did she leave to send for my chocolate, but hovered at the bedside. She was fixing me with her eyes as if there was something they would draw from me.

"All the household know of who came last night," she said at length. "The maids go in fear."

I wondered who had been listening and how much they had heard. The gipsy had not raised her voice; but of course, Robbins knew of her presence and that she could only have come on a bad errand. All must have heard Sir Gilbert shouting.

I shivered myself as I thought of her. But to Dorothy I spoke with unconcern. "It is better for the household to go to church and pray, than to start like frightened rabbits. Such fears are all moonshine and wicked superstition."

"They fear for Sir Gilbert." She had turned her face away.

"Sir Gilbert has no need of their pity."

I looked at her where she stood, unable to leave my bedside, pleating the bedcurtain with her fingers, seeking for comfort, begging for it from me whom she hated. "And Dorothy, the gipsy said nothing of Richard."

She flushed crimson and then turned white again, more lily-coloured than the sheets on the bed. I knew then that she feared for her child; but that she feared still more for my husband, and I despised her for her pain, that she should be thus distressed for a man so little deserving of it.

I cared not at all what became of him. And as for myself, at present, silly as I was, I could imagine no worse fate than I endured in being his wife. I did not wish to bear his child. What matter if I should prove barren?

"Dorothy," I said, "you forget your duties."

At last her hand loosed the bedcurtain and she left the room.

But indeed, had I wished to comfort her I could not have done so, for there was no comfort for her in the gipsy's words. Had I had the humanity to take her in my arms and share the night's events her misery would have been somewhat easier to bear. But for this I was too young, the war between us too great. All I did was lie back against the pillows, listening to the sparrows chattering, drinking my chocolate and foolishly rejoicing at my victory.

I did not know what love was, and in my callow state could not comprehend what Dorothy suffered. Alas! 'tis as easy for a woman to break her heart for a villain as for a saint.

I was beginning to wonder what had become of Dorothy and whether I was to remain all morning unattended, when Rose came in. She made a little bob, which she always did when she was upset and in need of reassurance.

"Mrs Willis's compliments and she says to tell you she has taken the liberty of giving Dorothy leave to go at once to pray, because she was in such a taking and good for nothing till she had got back her pluck. She said Dorothy must say 'Lord strengthen now the feeble knee', and Dorothy could hardly put on her cloak her hand was trembling so. And oh, my Lady! What is to become of us all?"

"Mrs Willis did very well. But Rose, there is no call for this alarm. 'Tis all moonshine. Now I wish to dress. Bring water for me to wash, and today I wear my blue." For in that gown I knew I felt and looked my best, setting off as it did my hazel

116

eyes and the red lights in my chestnut hair, and I wished for all the confidence I could muster.

While Rose washed my feet and helped me to dress I chattered of simple things, till at last she was laughing and herself again.

It was plain that all was in disarray, and with Sir Gilbert gone, none but myself to put it to rights. I went downstairs determined to set my household in order. Nonetheless, as I passed through the hall an echo of last night's terror came to visit me. It was as if brimstone lingered in the air. My hand flew to the cross at my neck; but as one fear was dispelled another, more troubling, took its place. Nurse's forebodings on my wedding eve came back into my mind, and it needed all my strength and courage to put them aside and go forward.

I found Mrs Willis in the stillroom, counting preserves. Her eyes travelled twice along the same shelf and I knew her mind to be elsewhere.

"Mrs Willis," I said, and she turned with a start, "I understand that Dorothy is all to pieces and the other girls no doubt not much better. We must show them this is folly."

"Indeed my Lady, they jump at shadows," and her face cleared. Poor woman, I fancy she had been in some dread that not only would she have the maids in terror, but a hysterical mistress on her hands as well.

"You shall take me to inspect them at their tasks, for if they idle to chatter of spells they will only make themselves more fearful. But first I would speak with Mr Robbins."

I knew that Robbins knew that I had been a witness last night; the look he gave me was full of questions.

"Mr Robbins," I said. "I presume that as usual Sir Gilbert has left you with his instructions, and all you need to carry on in his absence." He inclined his head. "As to last night's disturbance, I see no reason to believe any gipsy will come back; they have shot their bolt and we shall hear no more of them. But since the maids are upset it might be as well for their peace of mind to take extra care at night."

"I intend to go round after dark myself to see all doors and windows safely fastened. But would my Lady like me to arrange for some of the men to sleep in the house?"

I smiled. "Thank you, Mr Robbins, but I hardly think it necessary. I don't think an old woman's words will hurt us. Protection by yourself is quite sufficient in these peaceful times."

I surprised a new look of respect on his face as he bowed to me. I saw he would have kissed my hand had he dared, and I was pleased.

I went round the house attended by Mrs Willis as a general reviews his troops. There was something in my new manner which surprised her, but she had no choice but to comply. In every corner the girls were talking and not at work; they jumped apart like frightened does at our approach. I spoke to each one in kindness, giving praise where praise was due and calming their nerves — in truth I knew not quite how; surprising myself.

The morning was now half gone and Dorothy still nowhere to be seen. Mrs Willis began to wonder and make apologies. I cut her short.

"Don't be too cross with her when she returns. I know she is being over long, but no doubt the poor girl needs to take comfort with her child as well as with her God."

It gave me a secret pleasure thus to patronise Dorothy in her absence, and it gave me pleasure too to see Mrs Willis start and stare as she recognised that I was no green fool.

When we were done I sent Rose for my pattens and went out to the stables. The men were no better than the maids, standing about in idle groups, their heads wagging. And with them I found myself angry. I called Harrison to me.

"Harrison, what is the meaning of this? Does Sir Gilbert but have to turn his back for the men to stop work?" I passed my hand over the quarters of the first animal I came to and looked at my palm in disgust. "That horse is filthy." I moved on. "And this one has no water. Why is my mare not groomed and ready?" I berated each man myself till their cheeks burned. "And Harrison," I ended, "if the men are all in such fear on account of one old woman I look to you to arrange they do sentry duty at night for the week to come. After that, I doubt there will be need, for you will all have recovered your spirits."

The groups melted away, each man to his task. Harrison

touched his forelock, too shamed to speak. I picked up my skirts as if the yard would sully them, and left.

But as the day drew to its close I no longer felt so brave, and when Mrs Willis came to me in the parlour to ask would I care for company that evening, I said "Indeed Mrs Willis I would like nothing better."

"And shall Mr Robbins join us?"

"By all means."

And so he did when the candles were lit and his rounds were done. "All is secure, my Lady," he said, then from out of his coat pocket brought a pack of cards, looking at me in question the while. I smiled and he placed them on the table.

"Well now," Mrs Willis remarked with satisfaction, "tonight we have three players. Let us draw up our chairs and be comfortable."

Very merrily we played at gleek, a three-handed game that was new to me.

"My Lady has a natural born head for cards," Robbins said. "Look to it, Mrs Willis, she will end by defeating us both."

That Sir Gilbert had he known how we were passing the time would most heartily have disapproved, I fancy we were all aware; and indeed this added to our pleasure.

Never had an evening flown so fast or so agreeably since I came to Marley, and when at last Mrs Willis put down her cards, I saw with surprise that it was late and time to retire to bed. Robbins lit my way, a kindness for which I was grateful. In truth, now it was dark I did not care to cross the hall or mount the stairs alone. I gave him my hand and thanked him as I bade him goodnight at my chamber door.

To my delight my enemy was absent; it was Rose who was waiting for me.

"Dorothy is still good for nothing and Mrs Willis sent her to her chamber long ago," she said all in one breath, adding, "I reckon nothing of gipsies, my Lady."

"You have a stout heart, Rose, and show great sense. Now please to make haste."

All the time she was undressing me I yawned. I was asleep before she left the room.

When I woke next morning, not even Dorothy's long face

could damp my spirits. How easy it had been to take command! And when I did so, what kindness I had found! It was as though fresh air blew through Marley.

Little by little fear lifted from the household.

My daily rides on Kitty began again, and one afternoon I found Richard waiting eagerly for me. He told me with pride that Harrison said he could manage his pony himself and was fit to ride unattended.

"Well done," I said. "Then today you shall come with me alone."

"And Mistress Sarah, you haven't seen how I can gallop! We could ride to the spring now. The gipsies haven't come back."

"How do you know?"

"Me and my friend went to look. I found a horseshoe nail. My granny says it's lucky."

He touched his pony's flanks with his heels, and I perforce must follow.

"I will show you," he said, when we pulled up on the edge of the common as if the place were his own discovery and new to me.

The spring was hidden as it had been before by the hawthorn trees, heavy with white blossoms, their perfume thick in the air. But inside their circle the grassy bottom was empty. Nothing of the gipsies remained save the charred marks of their fires. Of her own accord Kitty moved forward to drink her fill; and while I waited for her to finish the last of my misgivings vanished.

"It's a good place, isn't it Mistress Sarah? There are nests in these trees, come and look."

Now began halcyon days. The merry evenings at cards continued, and indeed this companionship served to strengthen my position. It became quite natural for me to confer with Mrs Willis every morning, and then, as had Sir Gilbert, to visit Robbins in his office. Thus the whole of life at Marley lay each day before me.

When news came that the Queen had landed at Portsmouth Robbins and I planned together what should be done in celebration.

"Every village will have a bonfire," he said.

120

"And I would have music and dancing on the green. No doubt you know of musicians. And Sir Gilbert would approve the expense in such a cause. But 'tis a matter for all Marley, we should consult the Vicar and the rest of the village as to what they wish!"

"I can lay my hand on musicians, my Lady, but it would be best to move fast. At the King's coronation they played for Lady Cobleigh."

"Do so, Mr Robbins," I said. We both smiled.

It was common knowledge one week after, that Lady Cobleigh had been in person to command the musicians and had been refused. I glowed to feel the slight she had put upon me quite wiped out, and I thanked Robbins for his foresight.

As I did so, it came to me in my new freedom of spirit that if Sir Gilbert could have a suit of flowered petticoat breeches to honour the Queen, why should I deny myself a new gown? Since he had refused it me, he might rage when he found out, but for that what did I care? He would never refuse to pay the tailor.

"And Mr Robbins," I said, "I would have a gown proper to the occasion. Will you be so good as to arrange for the greys to be ready tomorrow morning, and instruct the coachman accordingly?"

For in truth, I knew not where the tailor was to be found; which I fancy Robbins guessed.

I set out as a lady should, with my waiting-woman in attendance; the greys too fat from lack of exercise, but their coats and every inch of harness shining. Dorothy looked all the way as sour as a quince; but indeed, it is no pleasure to any woman to accompany another in the buying of gowns if she is not to have one herself.

The tailor, hearing the horses pull up, came out of his shop to meet us, bowing and scraping and handing me to a seat as if I had been the Queen herself. Then he sent his assistant for one bale of silk after another, holding them up himself for me to make my choice. Blue and apricot I had already, and cream was dull, and brown and crimson for dowagers, while pink did not suit my hair.

At last he unwound before me a roll of yellow silk and laid

121

against it ribbons and trimmings of green. It was like the yellow flags that grew by the stream, and though Dorothy would say nothing, I knew it would be pretty and could see from the tailor's eyes that the colours became me.

"I will have this," I said, and I stood up for him to measure me.

There is not a woman who does not know the pleasure of a new gown, that makes the heart beat faster as she understands just how, dressed in it, she will look her best. As I felt thus, looking upon the shining yellow silk, all enmity left me, and I thought: poor Dorothy! How was she ever to have a new gown? And what liberty had she in her choice? There was none but I to help her to this joy.

"Now Dorothy," I said, "you are to be new dressed too. To honour the Queen I mean to be properly attended."

She chose grey, like any puritan; but this I would not have.

"Rose pink would be more to the purpose. You have a pretty face and should not hide it."

At this she blushed, something I had never thought to witness, but with pleasure or chagrin I knew not.

The morning of the King's birthday dawned fair for our celebrations; but I was in a fever, for the new gowns had not yet come. They arrived but just in time, as I was finishing my breakfast chocolate. The rustle as a new dress lifts from the tailor's wrappings, and the feel of stiff silk, still move me.

As soon as Dorothy had dressed me, I gave her leave for the day. She carried her gown to her bedchamber as if it had been a newborn baby. She liked me no whit the more for my generosity, but in the giving I found myself absolved; what she felt or did not feel was no longer of concern to me. Who, at seventeen, can understand how bitter an enemy's gifts can be?

When I stepped forth on to the green accompanied by Robbins, I no longer grudged Dorothy her child. Somewhere in these festivities Richard was busy in his childish sports, but my mind was on other pleasures. I was aware that every man I passed, every man with whom I danced, gentle or simple, admired me as a woman, and such homage went to my head.

Robbins forgot himself and kissed my hand in public.

That evening while the sparks from the bonfire flew into the sky, I sat down with Mrs Willis to a cold supper. The screams and laughter still mingled with the music drifting through the park.

"The girls will be late," she said, in some concern.

I smiled. "For once, Mrs Willis, you must turn a blind eye. Mr Robbins will wait up and see all is secure."

I think even Dorothy had been kissed, for she was flushed pink as her dress when she unfastened my gown.

The weeks passed. It was hot thick July weather. I had become in truth mistress of Marley: Mrs Willis deferred to me, the grooms in the stables would have licked my boots had I so asked, Robbins followed me everywhere with his eyes. Even Dorothy minded her P's and Q's. Had it not been for the portrait in the hall, I would have forgotten that I had a husband.

One evening when we were not yet at cards, I was remarking to Robbins that there would be thunder, when, without warning, George arrived; he bore a message from Sir Gilbert that he would be returning the following morning, bringing with him a visitor, and that he required the best spare bedchamber made ready. A silence fell between us. It was as if a pall descended over Marley.

"Mr Robbins," I said, "you will please inform Mrs Willis. And tell her from me that I would take my supper in my bedchamber this evening."

I spoke thus in a wild and useless hope that if I so kept Dorothy with me she would be prevented from telling tales to George. Then I reflected that neither Robbins nor Mrs Willis would have anything but good to speak of me. So, one gown apart, what could Sir Gilbert scold me for? And I had reason to believe that our defeat of Lady Cobleigh in the matter of musicians would make up for more than a tailor's bill too many.

For me, what a heavy awakening next day! How blood-red were the crimson hangings closing me in!

This morning I saw reserve again in every face about me; indeed, it must have clouded my own. It was as if the halcyon days had never been. Only Dorothy looked smooth. She was like a cat walking towards a bowl of cream. The secret smile behind her eyes roused all my buried enmity.

With my thoughts fixed on the ironmaster, the only man with whom I had ever seen Sir Gilbert on intimate terms, I could imagine no interest to be had from any visitor he might bring. Nonetheless I decided to wear my new gown. By this means my husband might get used to my disobedience before he had room to find fault; for he would scarce do so in front of a guest.

The sound of horses trotting up the drive announced the end of my freedom. I felt Dorothy's hand pull as she put the finishing touches to my hair.

My own hand trembles as I write what followed. I can feel the bannister rail sliding under my fingers as I descended the stairs. I saw only the man standing beside my husband, and I was comforted that I was wearing my new yellow gown; for I knew before ever he looked up and I saw the admiration spring into his eyes, that I had met my fate.

I heard my husband saying "My love, let me present Mr Kit Selby. His father is my particular friend."

He kissed my fingers and called me Madam in the most formal way, but as he took my hand in his I was aware beyond all shadow of doubt that his feelings matched mine, and my heart jumped like a wild thing inside my breast.

I knew not how to compose myself. I dared not meet his eyes. My own rested on the feathered hat he was holding, and the soft leather boots with the bright spurs.

When I was able to raise my head, as politeness forced me to do that I might bid him welcome, I found myself as dumb as any callow maid.

I surprised a smile on my husband's face, which I took to be directed at my lack of polish, whereat I drew myself up with what dignity I could muster and said, "I trust, Sir, you will find all to your liking. Mrs Willis will show you to your chamber."

Beside our guest, how dusty a figure my husband made in his snuff-coloured suit!

For the rest of the day our visitor behaved with perfect decorum. His attention was devoted to my husband and he noticed me only so far as courtesy demanded. Even his regard, when he chanced to meet my own across the table, was veiled.

In their occupations the two men ignored me and, while they were engaged in inspecting the stables or riding out together, I moved, restless, from one room to another, picking up this and that only to put it down again, listening for their footsteps and, hearing nothing, walking out to take a turn along the terrace, wishing that the cloudless sky might open to send down rain that they might be forced back to the house.

At last evening came. The men returned to find me sitting idly at my virginals, my heart swollen to bursting with wounded vanity and disappointed hope.

"My dear," Sir Gilbert said, "do not rise. I'm sure it would delight our guest if you were to give us a song. It will occupy the time before supper." He turned to Mr Selby. "I think you will find my wife sings well."

The song I chose was *Greensleeves*, for this I knew well enough to sing even when disturbed. Moreover, I found myself wishing to prove that my childhood love was truly exorcised. What I had felt for Oliver was indeed mere brother and sister love compared with the emotion that consumed me now. I forgot till I saw the smile twitching at Mr Selby's lips that I was dressed in green ribbons and the song, therefore, an invitation. At which I found myself blushing in shame, for was I not already a wife and my present sensations wicked?

"Her ladyship has an exquisite voice and a true sense of the music. You are fortunate," he said, "in such a wife."

Sir Gilbert visibly preened himself, as if it had been Jess or any other of his possessions that had been admired.

"You win high praise, my dear. Mr Selby is somewhat of a musician himself. You have brought your lute I trust, Sir? We shall look forward to hearing a duet."

"Indeed it would be a pleasure." He answered Sir Gilbert but spoke with his eyes to me. It was flame put to tinder.

My happiness returned. But what, I wondered, had come over my husband? Were my crimes all forgotten? Did he fancy himself now altogether my master? And so fancying, did he think to move me as a puppet on a string for some secret end? There was that in his looks I did not understand.

When Dorothy was done that night and I was at last alone, I lay awake between the sheets, my thoughts dwelling on the visitor, my body stirring again as I conjured up the look in his eye as it met mine and the strange delight I had experienced as my hand lay in his.

The door to my bedchamber opened and Sir Gilbert came in. I started, for I had quite forgot his existence; indeed, he was so far from my thoughts that for a moment he appeared to me as a stranger.

Instead of coming to my bed he began to pace to and fro in front of the window. It would seem he had forgotten he was in his nightclothes and I was to be treated to a lecture. I found myself thinking, that though it is their custom to do so, a nightshirt is no garment in which a man should hold serious discourse.

His manner was uncommonly gracious, as if nothing unpleasant had ever, in the whole of our acquaintance, passed between us:

"I must advise you, my dear, that our visitor is something of a scamp."

So for once it was not I who was at fault.

"It is a sorry story of careless behaviour. Few young men start with such advantages." He turned and favoured me with a glance; I fancied it was to see whether I was attending, and had pen, paper and sand all ready. For he was behaving as though I were a junior clerk in his department and he delivering a minute at dictation.

"Favoured by the Queen Mother as a youth in exile! On the King's return made welcome at Court! Enrolled an officer in the new regiment of Life Guards! What an opportunity for a noble pauper!" He paused turning meanwhile in his stride that I might have his words correct.

"But all this he has thrown away. He has abused His Majesty's kindness and made the town too hot to hold him. An upbringing in France has I fear been the undoing of too many young men."

I waited for the next paragraph to follow. But here, having found himself abreast of my glass, he stopped to examine his reflection. Did he salute his own superior prudence, I wondered? Or was he but ordering his flow of words?

"Not only has Mr Selby drifted out of his duties, he has

126

further disgraced himself by killing a fellow officer in a duel, and that in a mere quarrel over a debt at cards."

Here Sir Gilbert coughed and looked at his toes.

"His father is close to the King, and these follies might have been forgiven him. But the young fool has had the temerity to get one of the King's mistresses with child."

At this my pen, had I had one, would have made blots. By little and little my sympathy had been aroused, and it was now fully engaged.

Impatient though I now was to hear more, I was obliged to wait while my husband took a full turn about the room in silence, that I might the better understand the whole measure of his disapproval. But in truth, I was watching his shanks below his nightshirt as he walked, and comparing them unfavourably to what I fancied to be inside that other's soft boots. And then what hypocrisy! I felt the blood rise to my cheeks. Had he forgot his own sin? Dorothy or court lady, the offence was the same.

When he chose to resume his address his manner indicated that he was coming to a close.

"Lord Selby lost all his possessions in the late wars and has no seat in the country where the young man can be rusticated till it please the King to overlook his crimes. I am beholden to his lordship; and since for this rascal it is the country or the Tower, I have offered him a refuge."

He directed his scrutiny full upon me.

"You will, I trust, be on your guard, my dear."

I murmured I know not what; and now, having delivered himself of this warning, my husband climbed in beside me and took his pleasure in his usual manner. I yawned, waiting for him to be done.

Dorothy was strangely flustered when she came next morning to pull the curtains. Her cheeks were pink and she turned her head away from the spectacle of myself and Sir Gilbert once more lying side by side. I wondered had she perhaps hoped that he had left my bed forever?

"My dear," my husband said, putting his foot to the floor, "today I have affairs to see to; I ride out this morning with Robbins. I leave you to look after our guest." And at this all thought of Dorothy, and indeed of everyone but one person else, flew from my head.

The gentlemen were to breakfast early. I had no mind to be seen in my dressing-gown and chose to take my morning chocolate in my chamber. While I was still trying to decide which gown to wear and at last inclining towards my blue, Mrs Willis came to me. And I was, with some difficulty, bringing my attention to bear on the relative merits of raspberries and apricots, when I became aware that she, too, was absent.

"What troubles you, Mrs Willis?" I asked. "It is not I think a matter of fruit that is on your mind."

"My Lady, I fear for the peace of the household. Mr Selby's man Thomas has a bold eye and is like to cause havoc among the maids."

I had seen him but once; a lean man with hard grey eyes and sandy hair, too like Sir Gilbert in colouring and build for me to conceive that he could please any woman.

"It will be but a nine days' wonder," I said. "They will blush and bridle and that will be an end of it. The girls have sweethearts already, all but Dorothy, and she, I fancy, knows what she is about."

Mrs Willis shook her head and I could see she disagreed with me; but my thoughts were already dwelling on where I should find Thomas's master and how, this morning, he would look on me.

"Should Thomas prove troublesome I will speak to Sir Gilbert," and there the matter rested.

That morning I chid Dorothy till every curl was in place.

How long the passage seemed! What an adventure the stairs! My steps were led to the withdrawing room by the sound of a lute, eloquently played, the notes following one after another in such a way as to melt a stone. The player did not look up as I stood in the doorway to listen, but something in his manner told me he knew I was there. He began to sing:

"There is a lady sweet and kind,
Was never face so pleased my mind;
I did but see her passing by,
And yet I love her till I die . . ."

128

His voice, neither high nor low, neither mellow nor yet harsh, stirred me as no man before had ever done. Then the thought that he had killed a man, added to such sweetness, made him as magnetic to my eyes as a ferret is to its prey. I ventured in to sit quietly while he sang.

> "... *Cupid is winged and does range,*
> *Her country so my love doth change:*
> *But change she earth, or change she sky,*
> *Yet will I love her till I die."*

He finished, and when I spoke it was without the polite formalities good breeding demands. While listening I had jumped them and left them behind.

"They say you killed in a duel."

He put his lute aside. "He cheated me at cards. A man cannot let that pass," and his eyes were telling me quite another story.

"Sir, is it true you fathered a child on the King's mistress?"

"Who is to say who fathered the brat? She was a handsome wench. It was only after, that I learned she had obliged many. It was convenient to pick on me." And now he came to sit beside me. "But who would complain of such sweet exile, my Lady? Yet I would have it less formal. Can it not be Kit and Sarah?"

I murmured that it could be so. But what was to happen to him after? How was he to live?

He took my hand and drew a line down my palm from the middle to the wrist. "My father thinks that in a week or so I should return to my regiment. But I think otherwise."

And now he drew another line across the first, from the root of my thumb to the root of my little finger.

"I am tired of bugles and parades," and as he elaborated he made little circles and patterns with his finger on my hand. "I have my own idea how I may live comfortably and do nothing men call work."

"What is it?" I whispered. I was so heavy with desire I could scarce lift my eyes to meet his.

"First this," and he stopped my mouth with a kiss, pushing me gently backward against the cushions. When he lifted my skirts I could not resist: and then I felt such bliss as I had not known possible.

There was no thought in my head that we might be discovered until the sound of hooves on gravel announced Sir Gilbert's return. I started from Kit's arms and fled up the backstairs to my bedchamber. I wished to change my chemise, fearing it would betray me, but could not unfasten myself without help and I dared not submit my disarray to Dorothy's sharp eye. I did what I could to put myself in order. Had I been more practised I would have known a chemise was no great traitor, and that I had but to smooth the creases in my gown and rearrange my hair.

When at last I went downstairs again to the withdrawing-room, I was astonished to find Kit unconcerned, joking with my husband, his lute lying across his knee.

"I understand, my love, that you have been making music," Sir Gilbert said, "and are in good voice. This evening you must let me hear these famous duets."

I knew not which way to look.

CHAPTER NINE

Cupid is blind

To my dismay, Sir Gilbert invited Robbins and Mrs Willis to the withdrawing room that evening to listen to our music. Candles were lit, though the evening light had not yet left the long windows; chairs were arranged in a semicircle to face the players. Mrs Willis and Robbins both appeared ill at ease, and I could not imagine why my husband had on a sudden unbent in this way.

To my further dismay the song that Kit chose to play was one that spoke my feelings only too clearly.

"Fain would I change that note," I sang, *"To which fond love hath charmed me."*

I wondered would I reach the end without faltering; but at the second verse he took up the tune himself and as our voices married I took courage.

". . .I serve thee with my heart And fall before thee." We ended and looked at each other, as is common with lovers, conscious only of ourselves.

Kit put aside his lute. " 'Tis for Lady Fearnshawe to play for me now."

I sat down at my virginals and as he leant over me to turn the pages of my book of airs, his arm brushed my shoulder.

"Fine Knacks for Ladies; let us try this."

The piece is all jollity and little sentiment, and to my stumbling accompaniment, he sang merrily but without feeling to stir me; so I regained my composure.

We made music till late into the night, and though Mrs Willis and Robbins asked for more, Sir Gilbert was yawning behind his hand. I closed my songbook and turned in some trepidation to the company, for we had sung of nothing but love: though indeed, apart from hymns, I knew no airs that told of anything else. The curtains had not been drawn and the rising moon shone in to pale the candle flames and cast an unearthly light on every countenance. Sir Gilbert's I could not read; it wore the mask of polite boredom that was usual to him when obliged to hear music; Robbins's thoughts were far away, perhaps with the young person I knew him to be courting in Gloucester, while Mrs Willis had been so moved that tears stood in her eyes, though for what sorrows I could not guess.

"Most pretty," Sir Gilbert said. "We have had a veritable feast of song."

Mrs Willis and Robbins rose from their chairs and took their leave. I dared not meet Kit's eyes as my husband led the way up the front stairs and we parted to go our several ways.

I was hardly in bed when Sir Gilbert came to me. He had no reproof to administer and, to my relief, no desire for pleasure, but was asleep as his head touched the pillow. I wondered briefly why he was there beside me then fell asleep myself to dream of another.

It was a shock, when I woke, to find myself as usual inside the red bedcurtains. My husband, his head in its rightful place, was still sleeping, his mouth half open. Outside the sparrows were quarrelling and shuffling in their nest, occupied with their second brood. Nothing had changed. My head spun. I was in an agony to know whether I had imagined everything that had happened to me.

But I was obliged to wait all morning for a sight of our visitor to discover whether Mr Selby was indeed Kit to me, and I, for him, Sarah. Sir Gilbert, no doubt to satisfy his inflated self-esteem and to bring home to one less fortunate the benefits of prudence, had taken his guest to view the bounds and beauties of Marley, even before I was dressed. Nor was I on their return to have satisfaction; for though I knew as Kit stepped into the parlour that my own feelings were irrevocably engaged, I had no opportunity to be with him alone. Covertly, as we sat at dinner, I searched his face for some sign, and when I could comfort myself with none, told myself he must dissemble before Sir Gilbert; when at last I caught a glance that seemed to me particular, I could not tell whether I fancied it or not. I needed at least to feel his hand on mine.

"I must ride into the town this afternoon," Sir Gilbert said, when the last apricot had been consumed. "I am taking Mr Selby with me, as he tells me he finds himself in need of one or two trifles. No doubt you have duties with which to pass your time."

No flicker of emotion crossed Kit's face: or had he winked? I could have struck them, both the one and the other.

When they were gone I remembered suddenly that I had not seen Kitty for two whole days, nor indeed thought of her. And how was Richard faring? I found him in the stable yard, as restless as myself, and bade him saddle the pony and we would ride together. His face lit up, and in his company, for a little, I was able to take pleasure in the wheat turning golden in the fields and the green hazel nuts thick on the bushes at the side of the track. Though in truth my mind soon wandered, and the child's idle chatter passed over my head.

"Lady Sarah! Lady Sarah! I was watching Mr Selby." And now I heard every word.

"He's a better horseman than Mr Harrison. Or Sir Gilbert. You should have seen him go! I wish I could ride like that. And Mr Harrison says his horse is finer than any in our stables except for Kitty. He carries a pistol when he rides. Mr Harrison says it is because of footpads and highwaymen. And to have such boots! He gave me a penny and let me hold his bridle."

I could see that Richard had found himself a hero and my heart glowed. To give a child a whole penny! What generosity! And how unlike my husband.

On our way back we amused ourselves by racing in and out of the trees that were to grow to make a vista, and we were taken quite by surprise by the two gentlemen, who were returning to the stables from the opposite direction and had drawn rein to watch. Kit was dressed all in black; the velvet now deep and impenetrable, now shining like the bloom on a plum as the nap caught the light. The effect was brilliant; black coat with winking silver buttons, fine white lace at collar and cuffs. Sir Gilbert in his new flowered petticoat breeches was made to seem tawdry. But even in leather jerkin and fustian Kit would be a man to turn a woman's head.

I read unbridled admiration in both faces: Sir Gilbert's was all for his son, but Kit saw only myself. My fears had been for nothing. I could be happy now, even were he to shun me all day.

"Lady Fearnshawe is a monstrous fine horsewoman," I heard him remark to my husband. "And the mare a fitting mount."

He cast a knowledgeable eye at Kitty. But was not part of his scrutiny for the rider?

"I chose the mare myself," Sir Gilbert replied with unction. Indeed, had he not chosen both?

"My dear," he said, as we pulled up, "I trust you have not been riding too hard."

"With the child?" I answered him, raising my eyebrows, and what pleasure it gave me to do so! "I think not."

I knew full well what was in his mind, that scratch on Kitty's leg. But indeed his habit of scolding betrayed him into folly, for he must have known that in the company of a child on a pony such galloping was out of the question.

The boy was off his pony in a flash that he might once more hold Kit's bridle, his father's eye following his every move.

Next day the skies opened. How well I remember the rain; falling, falling, from first light till night closed in, imprisoning me with Kit in my closet next the withdrawing room, while Sir Gilbert shut himself up with Robbins and his accounts — absent, but yet too present to allow of pleasure between us except through our eyes and the touch of hand on hand.

"Let me teach you to play cards, Sarah," Kit said. "We cannot sing all day, even to please my host."

"I have no cards," I said.

"But I am never without." He began to clear my books from the table. "Romances!" I blushed and defended myself.

"I would rather read Latin, but Sir Gilbert disapproves."

"Women need life not books. Now see — we will begin with piquet," and we drew up our chairs.

At piquet I fancied myself, for I had played with my father. But against Kit, whether I held good cards or bad, I could do nothing.

" 'Tis not fair you should always win!" I cried at last.

134

"My sweet Sarah, you cannot win, for I am cheating you."

"And that is not right! *Why* do you do so?"

"For the pleasure, my Sarah, of seeing you blush. Come I will show you how. Then when you play against rogues you can beat them at their own game."

"But to cheat!" I exclaimed.

"All the world does it," he said lightly.

"And for this you killed a man?"

"Ah! It is not the cheating, but to be found out, and the manner of it; *there* is the insult can't be pardoned."

His shoulder pressed mine as he showed me his hand of cards and how he slipped one among the others, and my whole body melted.

"Now you shall try," he said.

He showed me one by one his skills, and how he knew by marks which card was which. By the end of the morning he swore that I could deceive him.

"What a sharper you would make, my Lady Sarah!" he said.

I laughed in triumph at his praise, for that I should please him was all the world to me.

And so my downward path began.

All day we played; when we came to join Sir Gilbert at supper in the parlour I was flushed with the heat of play and our complicity.

Sir Gilbert was fondling Jess. "Tomorrow I must return to London," he said. "I trust, sir, you will forgive my absence. Sarah my dear, I look to you to entertain Mr Selby."

I thanked heaven it was at Jess he was looking and not at me.

All next day the rain continued to fall, lightly indeed now, but enough to keep us indoors. We behaved with the utmost decorum, not wishing to discover ourselves to the servants, and certain, without word said, of what was to come when darkness and sleep at last possessed the house.

How sweet it is to nurse a secret love when fulfilment is assured!

Leaving Kit sitting by the empty parlour fire, picking softly at his lute, I went early to bed. I grudged every minute Dorothy spent in undressing me; I was impatient for her to be done and away and asleep herself.

Oh the difference in the sound of a bedchamber door opening to admit a lover not a husband! Kit closed it softly behind him and set his candle on the table by the bedside before he looked towards me. In modesty I drew the covers to my chin. In his dressing-gown he was enough to melt my heart, but when he took it off and laid it on a chair how magnificent he appeared in his nightshirt, lace ruffles at his wrists and his legs a poem, his calves in truth all I had dreamed. Unlike Sir Gilbert, he shed his nightshirt too, and I saw his person in its full beauty before he came to me.

"My lovely Sarah I need to see you," and he pulled the bedclothes back. "Love requires no covering." And now he removed my nightdress and I powerless to protest.

His hand encountered the cross at my neck. "What have I found? Do I then have a saint to reckon with?" and he was laughing as he lifted the chain on his finger.

"Take care! I would guard it with my life!"

"Your treasure shall have all the care in the world. I find it piquant. Pious ladies are always the greatest sinners for they know they will be forgiven."

I did not tell him that it was not piety, but Nurse's words, that made my cross sacred. Even to Kit I could not explain this. But indeed, having cried out my warning, all I could think of was his hand at my breast and the adoration I read in his eyes.

For the first time I knew what it was to fall asleep in a man's arms, and the sweet agony of waking to a kiss when he left my bed at dawn. I watched while he put on his nightshirt and dressing-gown, and taking the burnt-out candle with him left the room; then slept again at once, worn out with pleasure.

When Dorothy asked me where I would take breakfast, I answered at once "In the parlour", for I wished Kit to see me in my dressing-gown. "And make haste to brush my hair." I was all impatience, and Dorothy this morning moved like one asleep, her eyes straying, her hand pausing aloft as if it had forgot its purpose.

Running downstairs at last and across the black and white tiles to the parlour, I was both excited and shy, as if I had only lost my virginity the night before and a man was new to me. But indeed, this was in part so, since Sir Gilbert had never woken me to the delights of being a woman. I felt the blood in my cheeks, and halted to steady myself before opening the door.

Kit was already at table, and Rose standing at his elbow. "Good morning, my Lady," he said. "I trust you slept well. I have taken the liberty to ask Rose for two eggs with my chocolate. I have a monstrous fine appetite this morning." His eyes were laughing at me.

"Indeed sir, I seldom sleep ill. Are you sure two eggs will be enough? Marley is well stocked, is it not, Rose?"

She blushed and fled the room.

"I thought gentlemen drank ale," I said, drawing up my chair.

"Not always. Not in town. I thought ale a country lady's drink."

"Not at Marley it would seem."

Why had I troubled to be shy? What novelty and what comfort to be thus at breakfast with a man in such sympathy.

At my feet Caesar gave a great sigh, complaining as dogs do when they are bored. I remembered that I must soon speak as usual with Mrs Willis, and with Robbins too, since my husband was away.

A misgiving bored its way into my happiness.

"Kit!" I said, "suppose that Dorothy —!"

Kit was feeding a crust to Jess who, altogether forgetting her master's training, sat pressed against him, her head on his knee. He looked up and smiled.

"My sweet love, Dorothy, I fancy has her hands full enough elsewhere." He finished his feeding of Jess and dusted the crumbs from his hands. "Even had you rung for her I doubt she would have heard you. Thomas confides in me, and he tells me he has discovered a beauty, and a kind one at that. I heard them at their billing and cooing two nights ago and had it from him next morning."

"Dorothy?" I said blushing. "Not Rose?" But then, how absent Dorothy had been that morning. And Thomas, to my eyes, a younger model of Sir Gilbert.

"You do her an injustice," Kit remarked. I watched him butter his bread. Every movement he made was of interest to

137

me. "She has ten times the charm of your little Rose." He paused to eat, enjoying his food. My husband ate his bread and drank his ale as if it were an offence; as if the business of eating were beneath him. "Dorothy is a woman, Rose but a baby and of no interest to a man like Thomas."

"Thomas's tastes march with my husband's," I said, and my dislike for both men coloured my voice.

"You wrong my poor fellow, I think. Thomas is twice the man. My angel, the rain has stopped. This morning do we ride?"

At the stables we found Richard, following like Jess at Harrison's heels. He turned at once to us, begging mutely not to be left behind. We took him with us, rather than see his face fall, and in the event his candid worship added to our pleasure in each other's company.

"Today you may come," Kit said to him. "But not always, for sometimes Lady Fearnshawe and I will wish to ride alone that we may gallop. Truly you are a gallant horseman, but the pony, I think, not man enough to keep pace with us."

We rode along beside the cornfields, and then Richard said he must show Mr Selby where the gipsies had camped, going ahead of us till we came out at last on the common.

"This is the way I rode from London with Sir Gilbert," Kit remarked.

"How can you possibly know?" I exclaimed.

"I have a good eye for country. Even at night I doubt you could fault me."

"But Sir, you didn't know of the spring!" Kit shook his head, and Richard, satisfied, led the way into the hidden dell among the hawthorn trees, where the leaves were now a dull green, the fruit already turning yellow.

"This is where the gipsies came. It is our place not theirs, Mr Selby. But Lady Sarah! Mr Selby may share it too, mayn't he, if he will?"

"Indeed, I should be honoured," Kit answered gravely.

Under a cloudless sky we watered our horses at the spring. The sun fell hot on our backs, and the empty heath stretching away ahead held us isolated out of time.

Day followed day and I gave no thought to my husband's

return. Life, for us, burgeoned with the harvest. All that marked the passing of time was the change in the countryside. One day the wheat filled the field, waist high from hedge to hedge, the ears a smoky red-gold, the straw a bright brassy yellow, as if the sun had come down to earth and was itself growing from the ground; the next, the corn was falling to the flashing sickles.

We drew rein to watch, for it was a pretty sight, all bustle and yet all order; a sight moreover to turn the heart with pity for the corn and joy for man, that nature thus yielded up her store. The line of reapers went steadily forward, their feet and sickles moving as one, almost as in a dance; the women, following behind to bind the sheaves. Among the older boys helping to build the stooks I saw Richard's yellow head. The little ones were playing in the shade along the hedge, where the girls minded the babies and the jugs of ale and dinners for all.

"We should give largesse, I think," Kit said, and calling out, he tossed a handful of coins into the stubble.

The men and women did not pause. It was the children who scrambled after the pennies, and on a sudden I wished he had not done it, but that we had passed by unseen. To throw pennies distanced us, and I wished to feel at one with them. Deep in my being the child still lingered that would rather have been one among the others in the field, close to the earth, than the lady on horseback in her fine clothes. Yet would I then have had Kit?

I studied him as if I had thought myself invisible.

I can see myself now, gazing where he sat carelessly at ease, and wondering how I could wish anything different; seeking if there was any fault in his perfection, and finding none.

"You are dreaming, my Sarah," he said, with a straight face, but his eyes were teasing. "Come!"

I did not move, because I could not.

How dark his eyes were! brown — yet like the stream in the forest, pellucid. But the stream was shallow and they were deep, and I was sinking, to be drowned and altogether lost to myself.

His look became so particular that I blushed, and with a jerk rode Kitty forward.

The candles in the little parlour had been lit and supper cleared. We were tired from riding in the heat, and sat in that companionable silence which falls so comfortably between those who love. That I had a husband, other than Kit himself, had fled entirely from my mind. When Thomas came in with a letter, the picture we presented was, I fancy, indeed one of man and wife. On one side of the hearth, Kit, his lute abandoned, was occupied in stroking Jess's head; faithless Jess, who for the sake of crusts had transferred her devotion. On the other side I sat idle; my embroidery, as if but just put down, lying where it had done for weeks past, untouched on a stool. Caesar, at my feet, would have none of Kit. I was telling myself in some satisfaction, that being male, he was jealous.

Kit held out his hand for the letter, waiting till Thomas had left the room before he broke the seal.

"My father," and his face changed.

I had never seen anything written there that was not amiable; his mouth half smiling, his eyes lazy, except when they focussed on me, and then they expressed all manner of things, secret or otherwise. But now I could believe he killed a man. I would tremble for any who crossed him when he looked thus. And yet so swiftly all was smooth again that I wondered had my eyes played me false?

"He writes that all is forgiven and I can now return."

I cried out in protest.

"In truth I do not wish to." The letter dangled between forefinger and thumb.

"I never thought to be caught thus by any woman," and he said it in self-mockery. "But you have me fast, my Sarah. I would not live without you. Indeed I will not."

He crumpled up the letter.

"This paper never came, it was dropped on the way, never written, a puff of air," he lit the tight ball at the candle flame, and tossed it burning on the hearth.

In silence we watched it burn till the ink stood out black against the grey ash and then, the draught lifting it against the cold logs, it crumbled. A thread of fear crept round my heart. A father that writes once will write again, and what then?

He pulled me from my chair.

140

"Come my love, 'tis time for bed."

I should have taken heed. I had done well to reflect what manner of man I tangled with. But I was by then besotted, and when he kissed me I forgot all else.

That night, as if the letter had in truth been a bird of ill-omen, without warning, Sir Gilbert returned. We were resting from pleasure when his step fell heavy along the passage. I put my hand over Kit's mouth to prevent his exclaiming aloud. At once he snuffed the candle.

With my mouth to his ear I whispered "When he returns late he never comes to my bed. 'Tis one of his habits not to wake me. Wait and lie still. He sleeps at once and deeply."

We lay without moving, straining our ears to catch the smallest sound. I heard George run up the backstairs to his chamber. Then all was quiet. No board creaked, Sir Gilbert's door remained closed. Throughout the house nothing stirred, there was not a murmur.

"Now go," I said.

Moving in silence like a creature of the night, Kit slipped from my bed, put on his nightshirt and gown, and vanished from the room. The door opened and shut behind him without a sound; his bare feet made no noise on the boards. How at that moment I loved him!

CHAPTER TEN

Awakening

Life fell into a pattern. It was as if I had two husbands. When Sir Gilbert was at home Kit's behaviour to me was all that was correct. I acted the part of a virtuous wife, doing as I was bid, sitting in the evening, my head bent over that same vile embroidery, not venturing to interrupt while the two men discussed people I had never heard of and events of which I knew nothing; the stitching grew quite some inches that autumn. But whenever Sir Gilbert left for London, Kit and his lute and his cards took over.

Kit put me in such a condition, so constantly roused was I, that my fickle body took pleasure even from my husband. He did not remark on it, and such was his vanity that I fancy he would have taken the credit for my blossoming to himself. But whether he observed or not I shall never know; he was a silent man in bed, looking only to his own satisfaction.

Summer turned to autumn, and in these weeks I became practised in my deceits: I learned to cheat at cards and lie with two men and think nothing of it, nursing the fond belief that this happy state of affairs could last forever.

I did not see the second letter come. The autumn rain was falling, and one wet morning we were sitting at cards when Kit remarked:

"You are a pretty player, 'tis pity I cannot take you with me."

I sat like a stone, unable to believe my ears.

"You are going! And you tell me thus?"

He played his next card.

"My father insists. I did not wish to have to tell you."

I stared at the card. It was the Jack of spades. At this moment I knew not what it signified in the game.

142

"But I thought — I thought — you had other plans."

He looked not at me, but at the rain streaming down the window.

"I need his money. Besides, I cannot go on playing second fiddle to Sir Gilbert forever."

"You aren't second fiddle to me!" I cried.

"What a woman's remark!" He was waiting for me to play to his Jack. "You don't deny him your bed."

"What choice have I? You don't know him, he would have discovered me else and sent you away. And how could I bear it?"

He threw down his cards. "I do not choose to be a kept man longer."

At this I burst into tears. My cards scattered to the floor.

I wept and without shame begged him to take me with him. "I shall die if you leave me."

"Nay my Sal, I cannot have you die." He took me on his knees. "Don't cry, for pity's sake. I cannot stand it. I beg you, dry those tears. How can I think if you weep?"

"Then say you will take me with you!"

I think this course had not entered his head. He sat a moment, very still, then with his fine lace handkerchief began tenderly to mop my eyes.

"You don't know what you ask, my Sal. I cannot offer you the life you are used to here. Nor even the comforts of Bradstock. I intend to live by my wits."

"By your wits? But how?" I whispered.

"By cheating, if you want it plain. By sharping at cards. If you come with me you must help me and not be too nice, or we starve."

"What do I care for being nice?" I said. And in truth so consumed by passion was I, that I had lost all moral sense. There was nothing that he might choose to ask of me that I would not have done for him.

"My father will not help us, Sal, if I take you from Sir Gilbert. It will not be easy."

"I was not reared softly," I said with pride. "And do I not play as well as you?"

" 'Tis true we'd make a deft pair, and one that would take

143

the fancy of the town."

For a while he remained thoughtful. I listened to his heart beneath my ear beating steady in his chest. Then he smiled.

"Why not, my Sal?" and he kissed me, lightly indeed, but my body, my very bones, melted.

While yet in this languor I heard a cough outside the door. Footsteps moved away.

I stiffened, lifting my head. "Did you hear? Robbins, come to find me, oh Kit! What did he learn? What will he do?"

"Why nothing, the man loves you. 'Tis plain as the sun in the sky."

"He has a sweetheart in Gloucester," I protested, "and there is no sun."

At which Kit laughed.

I pulled myself together, and straightening my skirts, went to find out what it was that Robbins might want. He was not in his office, nor was there anyone anywhere to be seen.

So it was in silence, torn by uncertainty and apprehensions, that I sat down to dinner; I did but toy with my food. Kit attacked the hare and bacon pie as if nothing untoward had happened. Did it come, I wondered, of wars and privations? Must he eat, no matter how my fears choked me?

The sun was now beginning to filter through the rain, striking the drops on the windowpane and bouncing off as if they had been diamonds. The strange watery light showed off the beauty of Kit's skin and allowed me at last to read the unconcern in his eyes, somewhat comforting my dismay. In the company, under the protection, of such a man, surely fear was foolish?

He was still cracking nuts when Rose came in to take away the dishes.

The girl's face was flushed, her gaze full of a mute appeal.

"You would speak with me, Rose?" I said.

"Oh, my Lady!"

"I think the maid has something on her mind," Kit said, rising from the table. "You will find me in the withdrawing room when you are done," and he bowed and left us, closing the door behind him.

"Oh my Lady!" Rose said again, and I had never seen her so

disturbed; she made her little bob, then stood twisting her hands in her apron and glancing in apprehension over her shoulder as if at any minute the devil, no less, would appear. "I hope I'm not taking a liberty, but I think you ought to know."

"Yes, Rose?" I said. "Don't be afraid. I shan't be angry, nor shall I betray anything you may tell me."

" 'Tis Mrs Willis and Mr Robbins, my Lady. I was bringing up the clean linen and Mr Robbins was in the room so I didn't like to go in, but I couldn't help but hear. They was saying something about writing a letter to Sir Gilbert to fetch him back, and Mr Selby going away. And I hope I haven't done wrong my Lady, in telling, but I did think as first and last it was your business. And I would die for you, so I would!"

I smiled, though in truth with no smile in my heart.

"There is no need for that, Rose," I said. "But you did quite right in telling me. Mr Selby is indeed obliged to go back to London, for his father sends for him. No doubt Mr Robbins thinks Sir Gilbert should know, that he may return and make his farewells. Don't be troubled, Rose. It will be sad to lose such a visitor, he has been a merry guest. But should Sir Gilbert be delayed I must make his farewells for him."

Her face cleared.

"And now Rose, be a good girl and tell Mr Selby that since the rain has stopped, this afternoon I would ride. You may send Dorothy to me."

But in spite of my brave words I was cold all over; for all at once, in sudden illumination, I saw in what a fool's paradise I had been living. Robbins and Mrs Willis, and indeed all Marley, must have known of our indiscretions. If now they wrote to Sir Gilbert it was that Robbins had in truth overheard what we had said. And since they were my friends, they did so to save me from myself, that my husband, by his return, might prevent me from disgrace.

But I saw otherwise. Protest my innocence as I might, I was lost. Whether Sir Gilbert returned to find Kit here, or gone, it would be all the same. For time had made us careless, and Dorothy and Kit had met in the passage outside my chamber in the small hours more than once; as Kit had told me, laughing. And in truth, so long as Dorothy had Thomas her mouth was shut and nothing to be feared. But with Thomas taken from her? Hating me as she did, would she hold her tongue? My husband would lock me in my chamber and return me himself to my father. My ruin would be as nothing to him, an excuse indeed to rid himself of a barren wife and mine the blame. Even so guileless as I then was I could not help but wonder whether Kit's visit had been arranged a-purpose, and the outcome one for which my husband had most carefully planned.

How neatly had I fallen into his trap! I had laughed to myself at his legs while dreaming of Kit's; I would have been wiser to remember that at his most ridiculous Sir Gilbert could be at his most deadly — but this, in my excitement, I had forgot.

Now I had no choice but to leave Marley or spend the rest of my life a prisoner at Bradstock. Even had I not loved Kit to distraction I must insist he took me with him.

We must leave at once.

Meanwhile I must dissemble. Dorothy must see no change in my demeanour when she unfastened my gown. I exercised myself in a show of indifference as I crossed the hall to go to my chamber. Nonetheless I trusted that I was never to see Sir Gilbert again, and had I not been engaged in make believe, would have thumbed my nose at his picture as I passed up the stairs.

My heart missed a beat when I reached the stables to find Kit deep in conversation with Richard. The child's face lit up in the hopes of a ride.

"Not today, Richard," I said. "Mr Selby and I will be going too hard for you."

He looked so downcast that I added "Don't be sad, you shall come with us another time."

I stooped and kissed him, knowing that I lied, and wishing him to remember not my lie, but that I loved him.

"What's the trouble?" Kit asked as we left the yard.

"Wait. I'll tell you at the spring."

In the dell where none but the birds could overhear, I poured out my news.

"He will lock me up," I finished, "and challenge you to a duel. Oh Kit! He will kill you; we must fly!"

"Not a duel I think, my Sarah," he said drily. "The man is

146

too canny for that. But he would, I conjecture, make sure of my losing you, and the more I consider that prospect the less it invites me. We must indeed go." My spirits rose. "But my Sal, even should Robbins send his letter at once Sir Gilbert cannot be here overnight. Thomas shall go ahead tomorrow morning to prepare lodgings and we will follow when Marley sleeps."

I believe to this day that Kit was a stranger to fear. Indeed, when thought or courage was called for I never saw him anything but cool. What comfort, what joy it was to place my fate in his hands! I could have wished to throw myself into his arms then and there, but had to be content with looking my devotion. Though, in truth, I think he did not see, for he was staring into the distance across the heath, taking note already of the way we must go.

Sitting amongst the dripping hawthorn trees, the reins lying loose on our horses' necks, we planned our flight.

It was agreed that I was to ride Kitty, bringing with me no more than a change of clothes in a bundle that she could easily carry.

"The mare goes as well as my mount and you, my love, can outride most men." Kit smiled at me and I swelled with pride. "But mind, no feminine extravagances, we travel light. The journey should be easy, if it stays fine. 'Tis full moon, and we join the London road the other side of the common."

We were to leave at two in the morning, when the household and stables were like to be slumbering soundest; and that we might not wake the grooms as we crossed the yard, Kit said we should muffle the horses' hooves.

" 'Tis a trick I learned in France. Stockings stuffed with hay do very well."

"I will steal from Sir Gilbert," I said. "Four whole pairs. What matter if his legs go cold?" And we laughed at the jest.

Kit was to call me from my bedchamber when it was time to leave. "And I will not come to you tonight, for we must both get our sleep. And my Sal, with you in my arms I have better things than sleep to tempt me."

CHAPTER ELEVEN

Flight

PART I — MARLEY

Without Kit, I did not think I would sleep at all but I did; so soundly that on waking my first thought was not that I was leaving Marley but that the weather had changed. Even from my warm nest inside the bedcurtains I could feel the frost in the air. This was the first of that autumn, and in delight I jumped from my bed and pulled back the window curtains, to see how the rime lay white on the grass and picked out the spiders' webs strung in lacework between the dead leaves on the trees.

Tonight I must wear my cloak, for it would be cold travelling. In spite of the sun striking through the glass I shivered.

"My Lady will catch a chill," Dorothy said from behind me, and her voice was a frost in itself.

"Then make haste to dress me."

"Indeed, I'm not late, that I'm sure."

" 'Tis I that am early." I was too happy to scold her, for was not this the last day on which she could trouble me?

When I went downstairs to breakfast Kit remarked nonchalantly, as if it was the most ordinary thing in the world, that it was a perfect day and set fine. But I could barely speak; I feared the walls themselves heard every word and guessed our purpose.

"You are silent, my Sarah. No second thoughts?"

I shook my head.

Indeed, I was all impatience to accomplish the stealing of Sir Gilbert's stockings; but all that morning no opportunity came.

Mrs Willis and Robbins, each in turn, were full of business; and I must show no impatience; while the bedchambers were given over to sweepings and dustings and changing of linen. It

148

was not till afternoon, when the maid's tasks were done and the house was still, and I had with my own eyes seen Dorothy making her way across the Park, that I dared to venture.

Even so, I paused with my hand on the latch to look to right and to left down the passage, and it was with a palpitating heart that I closed the door behind me.

The odious purple and orange bed-hangings, the silver chamber pot enthroned on its polished stool, so conjured up the man that I was forced to tell myself that both he and George were at a safe distance in London, and that I had nothing to fear.

As courage returned, my indignation rose that I should thus be made to feel an intruder in my own husband's chamber. In what a predicament he had set me! How unnatural a condition for a wife, to be so ignorant of his habits: to be so little acquainted with his very linen! I should at once have been able to put my hand on what I wanted. Indeed, to reach his press I must go through into his closet, a sanctuary to which I had never so much as been admitted.

Here once more my husband's presence lay heavy; inhabiting the dressing-gown cast over the back of the chair, a ghost preening at the table on which a mirror and a set of hairbrushes and combs, with silver and enamel backs, were set out on a fine carpet overlaid with a silken cloth.

Two large presses and a chest with drawers completed the furnishing of this temple to his person. The first drawer I opened revealed the stockings, and snatching them up, I fled to my own chamber to hide them safely under the mattress.

I thought the day would never come to an end.

"Get some sleep if you can," Kit said, as we took our candles to go to bed.

But though I was yawning it was from the weariness of waiting, and I knew sleep would never come.

In my bedchamber Dorothy moved heavily about her duties, red-eyed and swollen in the face from weeping. Thomas was gone, ridden for London that morning. Her distress was such I wondered had she been left with child? Yet I could offer her no comfort. For though it was no secret between us how we had spent our nights while Sir Gilbert was absent, this was something about which neither could speak to the other. Our enmity was too great. Moreover, my mind was all on my coming flight. There was no place for Dorothy's anguish.

I submitted to the pantomime of being undressed and put to bed, and that she might have no smallest reason to suspect me I blew out the candle before she closed the door. I was glad to see her gone, to cry as she would for Thomas in her own chamber.

For what seemed like hours I lay in the darkness, listening while Dorothy's sobbing died away and little by little the household noises ceased. No matter how I closed my eyes sleep would not come. Nor could I rest. Assured now that in all Marley only Kit and myself were awake, I got from my bed, to pack and dress. The moon had risen, and I pulled back the window curtains to let in the moonlight that I might see to find my clothes and make my bundle without stumbling.

I was in the act of drawing forth Sir Gilbert's stockings from under the mattress when from below the window I heard the crunch of hooves on gravel. I was paralysed with fright. If Sir Gilbert came upon me now I was undone; I could not hide my guilt. While like a hare I crouched in panic beside my bed, his footsteps advanced along the passage. The thudding of my heart was so great that I could barely distinguish them as they drew nearer. Which door would he choose? When his own opened and closed again behind him I almost fainted in my relief.

Robbins's letter could not have reached him.

I was safe till morning.

What propelled me from my bedchamber that night was as much terror of my husband as love for Kit. I was in an agony for him to come that we might be away.

Kit called for me carrying his boots in his hand. Without word spoken he hooked me into my travelling habit, and we tiptoed down the stairs, keeping close to the bannisters that the treads might not creak.

When we reached the hall I breathed on a whisper, "He is returned."

Kit whispered back, "I know. What of it? He arrives too

150

soon to have had warning," and at this show of coolness all my terror vanished, blown away by passion. That he should have known of Sir Gilbert's presence and come for me nonetheless! What woman could resist such audacity?

We finished our dressing in the little parlour and left by the garden door.

The sky was clear, filled with stars; brilliant moonshine outlined the stables. The frost was already beginning to bite and I was glad of my cloak as we crossed to the yard.

Here nothing stirred. Harrison's little terrier, chained for the night in his kennel, recognising my step, didn't bark, merely lifting his head from his paws to watch me pass. From the lofts above the horses' stalls a groom's steady snoring never faltered as I drew back the bolt on Kitty's loosebox. She breathed softly into my hand, trusting my every move, though this was no usual hour for her to be called on.

It was familiar work to both of us to saddle and bridle our own horses, but it was Kit who secured my bundle behind and who came to muffle Kitty's hooves. She stood like an angel, showing no dismay at such strange footgear.

We led our animals out over the cobbles. Kitty trod delicately, her ears pricked, as if asking what this new play meant; Kit's mount, I fancied, had seen it all before. I would not have believed it possible for there to have been so little sound. We led cats not horses over the stones. Not a soul woke; no one heard us go. Behind us the groom's snores rent the air unabated.

As soon as we were through the archway and safely on to the grass at the edge of the drive we stopped to remove the muffles and throw them aside.

"We give back Sir Gilbert the stockings he so kindly lent us," remarked Kit.

"Yes," I said unsteadily, "they have served their turn," for though my heart was firm I was casting from me all that was familiar to venture into the unknown, and for a moment I trembled.

But then all at once we were mounted and away; the night air rushing past making the blood tingle. How I rejoiced to be taking my darling mare with me! — of the only two living creatures I loved at Marley, the one that was closest to my heart.

Feeling her moving under me I knew that she would carry me, not only to London, but, if need were, to the ends of the earth.

We had not gone more than a hundred yards when some unnameable feeling prompted me to look back.

A light was moving behind my bedchamber window where I had left the curtains undrawn.

"Kit!" I cried.

"What is it?"

"Dorothy is awake."

"What matter?"

He did not pause in the steady canter at which we were moving, our horses seeing their way as surely as owls. I was forced to keep up with him.

"She will wake Sir Gilbert."

"He cannot harm us now. He'll never catch us."

"Kit you don't know him. He rides like a demon. He has travelled the Forest in all weathers at all times when no one else would go. He will jump hedges and take secret ways."

We crossed the bounds of Marley estates, passing the circle of hawthorn trees round the spring without drawing rein: I put up a prayer for Richard, the one I loved and left behind. Then we were out on the common, a wild place in flat country high above the rest, swept by every wind that blew, the trees few and far between. I had never travelled its full extent and we were soon in ground unfamiliar to me, forced by rough going to slacken speed.

"Not much further to go till we come to an end of this," Kit said. "As I recollect, there's a gipsy encampment on the right and then on the left we hit the road. Such as it is. Meanwhile watch out for coney burrows."

It was as we picked our way, slowed to a walk, that in the distance I first heard the thunder of pursuing hooves.

"Don't panic, Sal," Kit said. "He must slow down here too or his horse will break a leg. There's better ground ahead."

We were moving again at a hack canter, but the thud of hooves was growing ever nearer.

"Oh Kit, what shall we do?" I asked.

"Keep our heads. I'm ready for him."

I could now distinguish the gipsy camp, the cluster of little carts and tents black in the moonlight, barely sheltered by a few straggling thorn trees. At our approach dogs began to bark and here and there a figure ran out to see what the disturbance might be. All colour was drained away by the moon, but I fancied I recognised among them, by her hair and by her gait, the crone who had so frightened me.

And now Sir Gilbert was upon us.

"Come back, villain!" he shouted. "Give me my wife!"

Kit pressed on. My teeth were clacking.

"Stop, Sarah, or I shoot him!"

I had heard that note in his voice before and I faltered.

"Go on," Kit said. "Keep out of my way, out of his line of fire, and wait for me."

I looked back. The cold light glinted on my husband's drawn pistol.

But Kit was too quick for him. He had drawn even as he pulled up and wheeled round to face his pursuer. Now he cocked his weapon. I can still hear the snick it made. I can feel Kitty trembling in sympathy under me where we halted; I who seldom prayed, praying wordlessly, fearing only for Kit, no thought else in my head but that he must live.

The two men fired at the same time. But as they took aim, the crone who I had spied, a shadow creeping from tree to tree, jumped shrieking out, waving her arms. Sir Gilbert's horse shied, unsteadying him so his shot flew wide. By the same token Kit's bullet took him full in the chest and he fell from the saddle, his horse careering off into the night towards home.

I cried out; then made to go to him.

"What are you doing?" Kit said roughly. "Now we must press on indeed."

"Kit, if he should be but wounded! I cannot leave him not knowing if he be alive or dead."

Yet in truth Sir Gilbert looked as still and dead as the man I found in the Forest.

"My bullet lodged in his chest. When I shoot I shoot to kill. He is cold mutton, I have seen enough dead men to know."

153

Still I hesitated. Every inch of my flesh objected to the body I had lain with being pillaged by the gipsy's filthy fingers.

"You must choose," Kit said. "Him or me. If you go back now it's the gallows for me. Do you wish to see me hang?"

We rode on in silence. I was telling myself that it must have been Dorothy in her jealousy who had sent Sir Gilbert to his death. It was on her head the blame lay, Kit was no murderer. Maybe a chink of moonlight shining beneath the door woke her, and with an instinct that the room was empty she went to look; maybe she was suspicious and in her misery sat with her ear to the keyhole, or heard the heavy curtain rings clinking on the rod. But wake she had done, and driven him forth; for once he knew of our flight, pride would not let him rest in bed.

I fancy now that it was no part of his design that he should follow us; he had rather we had got clean away. Nor did he dream that Kit would draw on him, or that his own horse would falter.

I looked back over my shoulder: the gipsy was already feeling inside my husband's coat.

" 'Tis cold," I said.

"You'll soon warm up, Sal, now we're going again."

But I shuddered. The gipsy's curse had found its mark at last. That it must find its mark in me also, I was too heedless then to know.

PART 2 — ABINGDON

Warm up I could not. Nor could I understand the lightness with which Kit rode ahead.

"Take care, Sal," he said, "keep two horses' lengths behind me, in case the going is bad," and then to my amazement, he began to sing.

Journeying through that wild and sleeping countryside, all my attention was at stretch to keep up with him over the uneven ground. My fear and horror did not leave me till we

154

came into Lechlade with the first cocks crowing and the wicked moonlight gone.

Here Kit insisted that we stop to rest both our horses and ourselves.

"I fancy they will not look for us on this road," he said. "If they follow us they will go rather by Oxford. But innkeepers are better with a story to pacify their curiosity. Ours shall be that you are my sister and we have been riding through the night to the bedside of our dying mother, but you can go no further and must sleep. And, my Sal, *that* is true enough."

"But I wear a wedding ring," I protested.

"Very well, if you like it better, I am a good brother taking my sister, Mrs Hargreaves, to her dying husband's bedside in London."

"Why Hargreaves?"

"Why not? 'Tis the first name that came to mind — now, remember, my dear sister, the worthy Mr Hargreaves, your spouse, is smitten with an ague and like to die."

In truth I was thankful that my husband was already dead. The relief was with me as we clattered under an archway to pull up in the inn courtyard.

"Kitty —" I said, able to think of her at last.

"You must go to bed, Sal. Once I'm assured of your comfort I'll see to the horses."

To be so cared for made my heart turn over.

The house was but just coming to life. An ostler still blinking with sleep took the bridles from us, while Kit shouted for the landlady. She came out in a flannel nightgown, her eyes full of suspicion. But what female could resist him? As he told his tale I saw her melt.

"Poor young thing!" Her tone was all compassion, and she led me upstairs.

She offered to bring me food and drink, but now we had halted I was almost asleep on my feet and wished for nothing but to lay my head on the pillow. A girl, only half dressed herself, unhooked my habit and I slid between the sheets.

The next thing I knew someone was shaking me awake.

"If you please, madam. Madam, if you please, your brother says 'tis time. Here is hot water, and dinner is ready."

I opened my eyes. Memory flooded back. I was afraid now of every minute's delay and my fingers were all thumbs as I washed and dressed.

I hurried downstairs to find Kit already calmly at table, as unconcerned as if this had been Marley. I had no stomach for food, in too great fear lest we be caught. Pushing my dinner about my plate, I asked Kit had he had any rest.

"Enough. Eat my Sal, there's time. Every good soldier stops for food. I shall sit here till you finish."

I obeyed, though I thought each mouthful would choke me. But it did not, and indeed when I had done I felt better.

The landlady came to see us leave, wishing us a safe journey, trusting that I would find my husband restored in health. "How pale you was, standing there in the lantern light! And not to be wondered at!" I was afraid she would never end. But once safely up on Kitty, I was able without blushing to thank her for her kindness, adding for good measure that she had earned my husband's gratitude.

In the October sunshine, last night's events faded like a dream. We rode out to be swept at once into the traffic of a great highway. Laden carts and a myriad travellers, both mounted and on foot, jostled about us as we made for the bridge out of the town.

"Father Thames," Kit remarked as we crossed over.

I was astonished. Here was a very different river from the Severn, and one much tamer. I was amazed to find on this gentle waterway the same traffic I had watched with such longing in the Forest: barges loading and unloading a multitude of goods at the wharves, gangs of men of the same rough sort hauling craft upstream against the current, while more fortunate vessels floated easily on the journey down.

Tame the river might be, but as Kitty, her ears pricked, stepped out on the further shore, my heart lifted. I knew from Nurse's tales that to cross water warded off evil. The gipsies, my dead husband, could not stretch over to harm me.

"Wake up, Sal, where are you?" Kit said, and I could tell he had been laughing at me these minutes past.

"At Bradstock, I think." Indeed, I had been wondering if any of these cargoes I saw had come from there or were going thither. But this fancy I kept to myself, for even I knew that Thames and Severn never met.

"I will not tease you, Sal, for you are too pretty a traveller. And I bow to your courage. To obey orders without asking questions and to see blood without fainting, and yet to remain all woman — 'tis beyond Nature. What a campaigner you would have made!"

On the instant I was a child again, seeing my father standing bloodstained in the candlelit hall. "I don't care for wars," I said.

"Few women do. And for that we love you the more," and he began to sing softly to himself, looking sideways at me, in the way he had.

I reflected what a travelling companion he was himself; in perfect cheerfulness denying his own needs to see first to my comfort and then to the welfare of the horses; rising fresh after sleeping in his clothes in a chair; so carrying himself that all loved him, from the landlord to the very pot-boy.

Now with every mile we journeyed my heart grew lighter, till I found myself laughing.

"Mrs Hargreaves," Kit said, "I think you are in too fine spirits to have a sick husband," and he laughed himself. He was about to speak again but stopped short, shaking his head; then, smiling to himself, spurred his horse on so that I was obliged to quicken pace.

"What is it?" I asked when I came up with him.

"Nothing, dear sister, nothing."

"I know it is not nothing. I will not be your sister," I said, nettled.

But he would not give over his teasing till we came into Faringdon: a dismal town that had suffered much in the late wars and was still all in decay, even the church not yet restored.

"Oliver Protector indeed!" he said. "This is his work. Small protection these folks had."

These events are far behind me. I see this was a piece of sympathy that cost Kit nothing. But at the time, in hearing him express concern for these poor people who were not in his charge, my confidence in his care for me multiplied, my love burned even stronger.

"Your thoughts are miles away again, my Sarah," and I blushed because they were of him.

"Aha!" he said. "I believe they run the same road as mine," and I knew we were both eager for our journey to be over that we might be alone together and in bed.

The heat was going out of the day and I could feel in the air that another frost was coming. I was wondering would it be as hard as last night's, and would I need the cloak from my bundle, when I saw in the distance ahead a delicate spire outlined in the sun's last rays.

"Take courage, Sal. Abingdon," Kit remarked. "We stay at the Antelope. 'Tis reputed the best inn and, better still, there they don't know me."

The Antelope proved a comfortable hostelry, standing in the market square. I was thrown utterly into a confusion when, on entering, Kit called loudly for lodgings for himself and his wife, at every turn addressing me as Mrs Selby.

So this was his "nothing"!

His behaviour to me was all that a new husband's should be, courting me openly as he had never done in public before, and I was obliged to swallow my surprise and play the part. Though my feelings towards him were indeed such as to make it only too welcome a game. Nonetheless I was put out that he should so tease me.

The landlady took my blushes to mean the name was new to me, as indeed it was, though not in the manner she imagined; supposing me, as she did, a virgin and this my wedding night. Her knowing winks and smiles made me blush the more. She went before me apologising all the way upstairs that had she known we were coming she would have had the fire lit already; but, to be sure, this was her best bedchamber, and fit for those of our quality.

It is plain to me now that Kit knew well what he was about. Not only the landlady, but all the persons of the inn, took us for a bridal pair; what's more, a runaway match, since we travelled so light and without servants. This fancy added to the excitement a wedding always rouses — every man and maid seeing themselves wed by proxy, their pleasure the keener that they believed our happiness stolen. Had we been enquired for, not one of them would have betrayed us.

We were served supper in a private parlour, but we had no privacy for the bustle of people coming and going to wait on us; every sort of indoor servant wishing to satisfy his or her curiosity as to how we looked and what we did. I could not speak; I could hardly meet Kit's eyes. I remember to this day the blue flowers on the dishes, but have no recollection of the meats we ate.

When at last nothing but the candles and our empty glasses remained, he pushed back his chair and held out his hand to me. "Come, Sarah. To bed."

A maid ran before us to light our way, but Kit dismissed her at our chamber door. "Tonight my wife needs no help," he said, and closing the door on her, turned and took me in his arms.

When I could draw breath I exclaimed, "Kit, why am I now Mrs Selby?"

"It is not a prettier name than Mrs Hargreaves?"

"But to spring it on me without warning! Leaving me no time to compose myself!"

"It pleased me to see you blush — Sal, your blushes would steal a man's soul. I find the word wife runs sweetly on the tongue, and I did not care that we should lie apart. True, I would have come to your chamber, but we have had enough of that. It was a throw not to be missed."

He began to unlace me and while he did so I leant back so that my hair covered his hands. I felt them tremble, and he fumbled with the fastenings.

I tossed my head and teased him. "You weren't so clumsy when you were doing me up."

"Hold still or I'll never be done."

At which I laughed.

He said nothing more. He was breathing heavily, as I could both hear and feel, hot on my skin.

I laughed again, but Love was already spreading his wings and I was lost before ever my shift fell to the ground.

What delight to stand naked at last together, ruddy in the firelight, and feast our eyes on each other without haste, without fear that we might be discovered! Shame, we had never had.

He took my hand and kissed the ring on my thumb.

"I could have wished to put this here myself, but I will steal it from him who did. But this comes between us." He undid the cross at my neck. "There," the chain dangled from his finger. " 'Tis safe. I lay it by your side. Now, my angel, you are all mine."

He picked me up as gently and with as much ease as if I had been a bird. "I'm a lost man, Sal. What have you done to me?" and he carried me to bed.

There had been no parson to bless us, no stockings thrown, no posset drunk, I was no virgin, no stranger to the man I lay with. But this, and none other, was my true wedding night, binding to all eternity.

Looking back, even now I catch my breath.

Lying in his arms I fell asleep in the fond belief that such bliss could last forever.

It was I who woke first, in the wainscoted inn bedchamber, with the fire cold ashes and grey morning light falling on Kit's sleeping head beside me. His hair was all in disarray, his eyes closed, the long lashes at rest. How innocent, how vulnerable he looked! Yet only one night since, and before my eyes, he had killed a man, and that man my husband. Once more I heard the thudding hooves as Sir Gilbert came up with us, I saw his arm raised as he took aim, and I shuddered for what might have been.

My hand went to my cross to give thanks in prayer, and finding it gone, for a second I trembled. But silver on ebony, its thread-like chain fallen in a coil about it, Nurse's talisman was still on the table by the bed. I told myself that with Kit to care for me I no longer needed such protection; but because I loved Nurse, and because in my heart I feared her visions, I fastened the clasp at my neck before bending to kiss his eyes awake.

The cross tickled his chin, and waking, he put his hand on the chain and smiled.

"It *is* a saint I've caught — I said so! Such a saint indeed that she doesn't know that she has sinned."

"You're teasing me," I said. "How have I sinned? Explain."

"My innocent! All the world knows that to kiss your lover's eyes promises infidelity. You tell me I shall lose you."

160

I protested. "What superstition! This is a fancy you learnt in France."

"Not so, 'tis an old wives' tale from our own England. But I forgive you in advance."

At this, had the chambermaid not been knocking on the door to say it was time we rose and breakfasted, we had fallen again to our lovemaking.

CHAPTER TWELVE

London at last

We rode out of Abingdon on a fine brisk morning and I thought that I could travel forever, but by the time we neared London I was mortally tired. Night was beginning to fall and now, two miles from our journey's end, the road passed Tyburn's empty gibbet. At the sight my terrors returned. I saw us taken, even in London, and Kit to be hanged here; I saw the cart and him standing, the noose about his neck, and for a moment closed my eyes.

I called out to him where he rode ahead and he drew rein that I might come up with him. But his countenance was so distant, so filled with thought, that I could not speak of my deadly fear, but asked instead was it much further?

"Not half an hour," he answered briefly.

I was glad to see the houses closing in about us and other people moving to and fro.

"Charing Cross," he said at last, breaking a silence that to me had grown to seem endless. "We shall soon arrive, and here there is no call for pretence. Mrs Goodchild knows you as Lady Fearnshawe."

It was as if a grain of sand had crept between my shift and my skin.

The house outside which we stopped had a mean face. The fitful light of passing links showed it to be tall and narrow, gabled, with leaded casements as at Bradstock. I wondered that in London this should be a gentleman's lodgings.

Kit banged on the door with his whip handle, and at once Thomas ran out to take the horses from us. I made him wait while I fondled Kitty, making much of her, for I was loth to leave her standing in the street and knowing nothing of where she was to be stabled, but I saw Kit grow impatient. I kissed her silken muzzle, my heart full as I wished her goodnight. She whinnied to me as I turned away.

"Take good care of her, Thomas," I said.

He touched his forelock and I followed Kit into the house.

I had to suppose that Kit knew what he was doing, for the place struck me as altogether inferior, and its mistress no better. Mrs Goodchild met us in the hall, carrying a candle in her left hand. She was a big, tall woman, encased in a black gown, stupid, I fancied even before she opened her mouth, and rigid with prejudice. She held up the candle not to light the way, which would have been better done by placing it on the table, but openly to inspect me.

"Welcome back, Mr Selby," she said. "I trust you had a pleasant journey. So this is Lady Fearnshawe. Very young!" — speaking as if to herself. "You are welcome, madam."

She touched the hand I held out to her as if it had been a contamination. My blood boiled at the insult. Candle or no candle it was her place to curtsey, for she was in every way my inferior.

"I have given her ladyship rooms on the first floor, with your own, Mr Selby," she said, and she ushered us upstairs.

As soon as her black skirts had disappeared round the door, before ever I glanced at the chamber we were in, I exploded.

"Mrs Goodchild looks at me as if I were no better than a whore!"

"The poor woman is behind the times. Pay no attention, Sal, there's no shame these days in being a man's mistress. I can't pretend you are my wife, for all the town knows otherwise."

When I had begged him to take me with him from Marley I knew it would be as his mistress, not his wife, and it had seemed of no account; indeed, high adventure. Only now did I begin to understand my situation and the slights that might be put upon me. Even so I could have laughed, but his tone was all impatience. My spirits fell like lead. Where was the man I had lain with last night at Abingdon? I clutched my bundle of possessions to me.

"My Sarah" — and he took the wretched bundle from me — "take no notice. She will come round."

I stamped my foot. I was convinced that she had ushered

other, light females, into these lodgings, and I did not at all care to be classed with their kind. But even as I flushed with anger and the tears rose in my eyes, I found myself in his arms.

"What does Mrs Goodchild matter, since I love you?" and he kissed me. "When she comes to know you she will have to respect you. Don't cry, Sal," he was kissing my tears, "I'm a wretch, I've tired you out." All the while he was speaking between kisses. "I forgot your sex's weakness and made you ride like a man; you are too good a trooper. How am I to be forgiven?"

But I was half melted already.

"Let me send a maid to you so you can go to bed and rest while I see to the horses. We'll take supper together in your chamber, and then you shall sleep."

So I had not mistaken him. This was, after all, the man I knew, he did love me. I forgave him everything: his past amours, and for bringing me to their scene; and while I was about it, for tiring me out, as indeed he had done.

The maid who came to me proved to be but a slummocky wench; but eager to please and, balm to my wounded pride, somewhat overawed at my being "my Lady".

"I'm Bess, if you please, my Lady," she said, dropping a curtsey, "and Mrs Goodchild says I'm to do as you bid, seeing as you have no waiting-woman with you."

She undid my bundle and helped me to undress, then washed my feet and brushed my hair well enough, doing her best to make me comfortable.

"I have warmed the bed for your ladyship," she said, taking out the warming-pan and turning back the bedclothes, "and they are the best sheets. Shall I bring my Lady supper now?" she asked when at last I was sat up against the pillows.

"Thank you, Bess, you are most kind," fatigued as I was I managed a smile. "But for supper I think I had best wait for Mr Selby."

The bed was comfortable; my eyes would keep closing. Kit was a long time gone and for very weariness I slept without waiting for food, or for his return.

It was a troubled sleep, full of dreams. I discovered myself back at Bradstock, in Nurse's room, but yet it was elsewhere;

though she was sitting where she always sat, mending a shift. I was asking her a question but she didn't answer me. When she did look up her face was grave and she was in tears. As my habit was when Nurse would give no comfort, I rushed out into the forest to find Old Sim. He was building a stack and stood with his back to me. I called out to him, and he wouldn't answer either. "Sim," I begged, "turn round and tell me." He turned round at last but he didn't speak. To my horror I saw that like Nurse he was in tears. At which I woke in panic, trembling with distress, to see my bedchamber door opened by a slippered foot.

Half awake, my dream fading, I saw the foot belonged to Bess.

She came in, shutting the door dextrously behind her with her heel, while at the same time carrying a scuttle in one hand and a shovel of hot coals in the other. Coals were new to me; their acrid smell, reminding me of singeing, drove the last vestige of my dream away as she hurried past the end of the bed to tip them into the grate, before proceeding to draw the curtains. Her white apron was smudged and I soon saw it must be from the coals, for without a word of good morning she began to make the fire, kneeling to pile sticks on hot coals, and coals on sticks again, wiping her hands on her apron and blowing with her mouth to make a flame. The hearth was without bellows.

Looking at her round bottom as she tended the fire, and at the indifferent furnishings, I thought what a strange setting this was for the foremost adventure of my life. The room was poky, and the hangings, in green dull as the grey sky outside, sorted ill with the tapestry cushion on the window-seat done all in dim purples and pinks. But the linen sheets I lay between were indeed fine, the bed clean and free from lice, which I had understood to be a particular hazard of inns and London lodgings, and even the flame from a smoky coal fire can improve one's spirits and animate the saddest hangings.

I watched the flames take hold, and as they did so Bess left the room as silently and hurriedly as she had come.

I was beginning to wonder what had become of Kit when Bess reappeared, in the same manner as before, foot first, this time carrying a breakfast tray. Even as she set the tray on the

165

table she was followed by Kit himself, gorgeous in a green and purple dressing-gown that was new to me. In such a presence it was impossible to consider furnishings: vividly alive, brilliant as a dragonfly hovering over a dull pond, he commanded attention to the exclusion of all else in the world beside.

"You can go, Bess," he said, holding the door open for her. "I will give Lady Fearnshawe her breakfast."

Poor Bess! From her stupidly bewildered look I surmised she had intended to set me in order; to brush my hair and see that I was comfortable before bringing the tray to my bed. She stared from Kit to me and back again before doing as she was bid.

"I don't intend that we should lie apart, but you were sleeping so sound last night I hadn't the heart to disturb you," he said, as he set the tray on my knee. "You must be half starving."

But now I was rested it was not food I wanted, but the man. I could think only of the body inside the shining gown. Had he not sat himself down on the bed and coaxed me to open my mouth like a bird in the nest, I doubt I could have eaten a single morsel, hungry though I was. I ate because he fed me, and in anticipation of what was to come. This, I fancy, he knew well and took pleasure in.

Once I had begun, I found I was ravenous and could not help myself. Kit laughed as he buttered bread and popped small pieces into my mouth, while I cut up pheasant pie, and that gone, dug my spoon into boiled eggs. How delicious the hot chocolate tasted after innkeepers' ale!

When the last crumb had vanished, my other appetites revived. But though I let my shift slip from my shoulders to show my breasts, though I knew he was as roused as myself — languish as I might, I saw he was not going to pleasure me. He remained standing with his back to me by the table where he had set the tray.

What was he at?

"You may go away now and send Bess to me," I said somewhat stiffly, "for I want to dress and say good morning to Kitty. I wish to satisfy myself that she has taken no harm from yesterday's journey."

166

To my surprise he came and sat down again on the bed.

"That, my love, I'm afraid you cannot do."

"And why, pray?"

"Kitty is sold."

"Sold? But she's mine! How can she be sold?"

"Of necessity."

I burst into tears of grief and rage, beating his chest with my fists, calling him thief, traitor, liar — anything and everything I could lay tongue to. He made no excuses, letting me rave on unanswered, merely at last restraining my fists by imprisoning them with his hands while I howled, roaring my abuse into his face. When my sobs turned dry and harsh he let go my wrists, dropped his gown and climbed into bed. He tried to take me in his arms and I fought him with all the force I had. I was still sobbing, half fighting with him, as he made love to me. But it was feeble force indeed, for my body was my enemy; passion conquered me, I could no other. Our pleasure was as never before.

At last I lay in his arms content, languid after love, exhausted by tears. And now I went back to my complaint: "Kitty! — You knew all along. You knew you were going to do this. She knew it herself, else why did she whinny to me? You have cozened me out of what I loved."

"*Touché*. But for your own good. I had to plan for our support. There was no other way. Don't think I enjoyed the doing of it. Or that I liked the thought of telling you, when it was done."

I remembered his silence as we were coming into London the evening before, and how it had troubled me. This was why! In truth, I loved him for wishing to spare me.

And yet, as I thought that I would never see Kitty again, I felt the tears pricking.

"Don't cry, Sal. 'Tis all for the best. You wouldn't have the mare rot in a London stable while we starve. No lady goes about these streets unless by coach. Moreover, we hadn't the money to keep her — or ourselves."

"I had rather she had stayed with Harrison," I said. "Had I known, I could have taken Sir Gilbert's own mount. I would have been glad to see that go."

"My love, what folly! For sure Kitty would have been sold, and how could you tell she would have found a good master? I got a fair price and I know my man. He wants her for country usage, for his wife to ride. She will be well cared for and lead the life she knows. After paying such a sum for her, for very pride he will not have her mistreated or seen to be neglected."

"You should have asked my permission," and I turned my head away from him on the pillow.

"Come now my sweet, acknowledge. Had I told you first you would have forbidden me, and we should have been lost."

"Nonetheless — nonetheless —" But his hand was caressing my breast, and I forgot poor Kitty.

"Now my Sarah, we have the money to make you fine, so that when men come to play they will lose their wits for looking at you. This morning I intend we shall go shopping, and first to the tailor to measure you for new gowns."

I put my hand on his and sat up in bed.

"Will you be safe?" I said.

"You insult me! Do you think I would take you otherwise? Be easy, Sarah, there may be a noise, but in London I have friends who will not let me hang for killing in self-defence. It would have been a different affair had we been taken in Sir Gilbert's own country."

My mind now all on the future I said, "Very well, if you promise me so, you may send Bess to me."

I made the poor girl run to and fro, fetching me hot water that I might wash all over; and then I required my one gown ironed and, when I was dressed, my hair done to the last curl. She was flustered, but I fancied flattered, to be called on to wait on one so nice in her requirements.

I saw nothing of London that morning, for a fine rain was falling and we went to and from the New Exchange by hackney coach. Here every sort of merchant was to be found, and on our return I sat down in Mrs Goodchild's parlour amongst a litter of shoes and gloves and shifts, quite drunk with shopping. I was eager now for my gowns to come from the tailor; not only for the love of new clothes, but because Kit refused to start on our venture till I was outfitted to his satisfaction.

"My Sal, as a country nymph you are bewitching, but will be

twice so much so when innocence is set off to its proper advantage. Tonight, I try my hand on my own."

"Kit! Take care!" I said.

"Come, Sarah. The town must know I'm back or we shall have no custom."

All my fears returned. I had visions of him apprehended and carried off and my never seeing him again. As I sat alone over my supper by the smoky coal fire I wondered in panic what would become of me: left on my own in these dismal lodgings, at the mercy of Mrs Goodchild, who, it was plain, had no kindness for me? I sent for Bess that I might undress and go to bed. Here I took comfort, telling myself that Kit understood danger and had cunning enough for ten men.

I was half asleep when he came in. He was singing softly to himself, and I heard the gold clinking as he emptied his pockets on to the table in front of the mirror. At the sight of the lace ruffles on his shirtsleeves falling over his hands as he moved my cares all dropped from me. I watched the light from the half burnt candle playing on his dark curls and wondered how I could for one moment have been afraid.

"Kit?" I said. "I'm awake."

He came and sat on the edge of the bed and took my hand; his form in his shirt outlined against the candlelight.

"Well, Sal, it seems we are famous already."

He told me news had reached London almost as soon as we had ourselves, that Sir Gilbert was dead.

That his body had been despoiled lent colour to the supposition of its being a highway robber, not Kit, who had shot him: "So, my sweet, you can put all thoughts of Tyburn out of your head. I didn't deny carrying you off, or Sir Gilbert's pursuit. But since none had heard of them, I didn't think necessary to mention the gipsies. They will have packed up and vanished, lock, stock and barrel. Without them, there's none to say what in truth happened, or to bear witness against me."

I had not believed I could feel such relief.

"I tell you, Sarah, we are made. 'Tis a fine tale — a great draw, it will pull men in, they'll come like larks to a mirror."

"To these drab surroundings?"

"They will come to look at you, my angel, not Mrs

169

Goodchild's furnishings. So innocent and so much a lady, 'tis all they'll see."

"Here the venture is without quality," I said, for even for Kit's sake I did not care to be a peepshow. "I wish to be seen a lady in a lady's setting."

"So you shall," and he yawned. "But we must make a start with what's to hand. I warned you, Sal, that to come with me would be hard."

We were sitting at breakfast next morning at ease in our dressing-gowns, without a care in the world except that I fretted because my gowns had not come, when George's voice sounded in the hall, asking for Mr Selby. I turned cold all over. For one dread moment I thought my husband must be still alive. I rose and fled to my bedchamber as footsteps mounted the stairs.

"What can I do for you?" and Kit sounded as if he were dying of boredom.

"I have a letter for Lady Fearnshawe. I would be much obliged if you could tell me where I can find her."

How I hated that voice! Yet I stood with my ear pressed to the crack of the door.

"You may give the letter to me. I will see it reaches her."

"I was particularly instructed by Mr Robbins to put the letter into Lady Fearnshawe's own hand."

On hearing the word "Robbins" I took courage and came out of my chamber, and looking George straight in the face, "You may tell Mr Robbins I have received his letter," I said, holding out my hand.

His manner as he let the packet go had all the politeness due to my rank, but the smile behind his eyes was full of evil pleasure. He inclined himself in a stiff bow and left the room.

"I wonder who pays the cur now?" Kit remarked.

I sat down, turning the letter over and over before me on the table, wondering what it could contain.

"Go on, open it," Kit said impatiently. "It can't bite you."

But bite me it did. I blanched as I read.

Robbins told me, apologising at every other word, that I was entirely unprovided for. Sir Gilbert in his will had left all he possessed to the legitimate heirs of his body, their mother to be

170

housed and fed and clad; but in the event of there being no legitimate heir, everything was to go to Richard, and Dorothy and the ironmaster were appointed guardians.

I had even lost Bradstock.

For I now learned for the first time just how unsatisfactory the terms of my marriage settlement had been. My father had in no way secured my future. Not only was Sir Gilbert under no obligation in this respect, he would even, on my father's death, acquire Bradstock as my marriage portion.

So my birthplace, too, would one day become Richard's. How right Old Sim had been! My father had indeed sold me.

Robbins concluded, "If there is anything whatsoever that I can do for your ladyship, you have only to call on me. My life is at your service."

I was speechless. I cared nothing that Richard should have Marley; and indeed, he would make a good heir for Bradstock. But that Dorothy should queen it in my old home and that I should be cast on the world with nothing, turned my stomach.

"Well?" Kit said.

"I'm afraid you have but a penniless wretch on your hands," I faltered. Unable to say more, I handed him the letter.

He read in silence, his eyebrows raised. "Beyond belief!" he said at last. Then his face cleared. "Cheer up, Sal. The case is no other than it would have been if Sir Gilbert had not died. Take courage," and he smiled — how I loved him for that smile — " 'tis no great matter. We can make our way without his money."

He tossed the letter on the table. "Poor Robbins. I told you the man loves you. He would marry you out of hand if he dared ask."

So besotted was I that I did not think to wonder at Kit's not asking me himself; still less, to wonder why he failed to do so. For in truth, in my own silly eyes, ring or no ring, I was wed to him already.

CHAPTER THIRTEEN

A golden time

I was now to discover what I had never troubled to foresee, that life with Kit in London was to be very different from our idle pleasures at Marley. He was back among his old pursuits while I had lost my occupations. He could no longer indulge himself in my company and I was to be much alone.

My terms were upon me. My new gowns had not yet come. I was sitting in my dressing-gown waiting for Bess to distract me with doing my hair, when he came into my bedchamber, dressed to go out, elegant in his black velvet suit and wearing his sword.

Taking my hand, "My sweet," he said, "I hate to leave you where everything is strange to you. But today I must go about the town to ordinaries and coffee houses, and they are no fit place for you."

"Gaming?" I said, barely hearing his words, for at the touch of his fingers my thoughts had strayed.

"We need the money, Sal, and I must bait our hooks. Mrs Goodchild will attend to your wants and Thomas has my orders to wait on you."

My eyes rested on the silver buckle at his belt. How I wished he would stay, and that I were in a condition to undo it!

He mistook my silence. "Only give me time, my love, and I will find you a waiting-woman, then you won't be tied to my comings and goings. In London I wouldn't have you walk abroad alone."

"Of course you must go," I said. "I don't wish to go out anywhere; I shall do very well."

As soon as he had left me I wondered how I was to pass the time once my hair was done. Then, remembering how mistaken I had been at first in Mrs Willis, I determined to try my

172

hand at friendship with Mrs Goodchild. I found her downstairs in a terrible parlour; small and wainscoted, the hangings
in the same sad green as everywhere else in the house, the only
ornament a large Bible.

She was engaged in the manufacture of another of the insipid
embroideries which covered the cushions in my bedchamber.
As I opened the door she treated me to a stare of such disapproval I could fancy my husband looking at me out of her
eyes.

"Well, Lady Fearnshawe, I trust you can find nothing
wrong?"

"No indeed," I said, hastily reordering my ideas. Feeling
foolish, I retreated upstairs again.

It now occurred to me that I might answer Robbins's letter. I
went downstairs once more to find Thomas where he was
idling in Mrs Goodchild's kitchen and sent him out for pen and
paper, ink and sandbox.

I was glad, now, that when looking at the piles of coins
emptied the night before on my table, I had insisted Kit put
some aside in my purse. Indeed, I was learning fast that I had a
better head for the daily use of money than himself; that it
would be prudent to take what was needed to pay Mrs Goodchild before he could put all back in his pockets for gaming
with. Nor did he once count up what he gave me: I could have
fleeced him had I so wished. How tender I felt towards him for
his weakness, proud that in one small way I could protect him!

My letter to Robbins was all too soon done: I thanked him
for his own and told him that I wanted for nothing. Then I was
at a loss. I left the paper for Kit to seal and, yawning, wondered
what to do next.

The entry of Bess with a tray put off my dilemma. Like a
prisoner in his cell or the sick confined to bed, I welcomed food
as a diversion. I spun out my dinner and then once more time
hung heavy.

My eyes now fell on the pack of cards left by Kit on the
parlour table till he should be at leisure to mark them. Comforting myself with his assurance that at play everybody
cheated, I sat down to practise all the sharping tricks he had
taught me, taking as much pains as I would have done over a

173

new piece for the virginals, so that when the time came to play I would be ready.

But a pack of cards is no defence against the phantom thoughts that come to a woman in solitude, especially when she is in the low state her terms can bring. I began to pity myself for my being so confined and, now that I no longer feared for Kit's life, to be jealous of his freedom. I grew angry. I was obliged to sit alone in contemplation of Mrs Goodchild's backyard; he could go about as he pleased. I fancied him laughing with his friends, at court in brilliant company, fawned on by beauties. Worse still, now that I had my terms and he could not come to me, I saw him in other beds. I pictured London peopled with willing females and the cards dropped from my fingers.

What of the She on whose account he had been banished from the town?

He returned to find me sitting with the candles unlit, staring at the growing dark outside the window.

"Sarah! What *is* the matter?" His voice shook with concern.

I lied swiftly. "Nothing. My terms pain me," though indeed they did not.

"Then you must go to bed and I will find you a hot brick to put on your belly. Come my love," and he shouted for Bess.

At once I was ashamed. I wondered how I ever could have doubted him.

"You shall have a hot posset, or would you like chocolate better? I'll go and set about Ma Goodchild."

I had to smile. "A posset, I think."

At last Bess appeared, flustered, to help me to bed, and he was gone to see to my needs.

He sat on the bed while I drank, and then, at ease, I cried on his shoulder, and when my tears were done he made me laugh at how he had chivvied Mrs Goodchild round her own kitchen.

I resolved on patience for, as I had learned already, all females are governed by men, and how was I, in my position, to change the whole lot of women? Was it hard to obey one I loved?

The next day being Sunday I attended church with Mrs Goodchild, hoping to subdue my rebellious thoughts; and

174

indeed the sermon proved so long-winded I fell asleep, much to her disgust.

At last the tailor called with my gowns; and as I look back, from that time forward it was as if the sun shone every day.

Kit insisted he oversee the trying on, turning me about this way and that while the tailor smirked: a pompous, mincing man, he walked round about his handiwork adjusting a fold here and another there.

"If I may be allowed to say so," he intoned, "both gowns become my Lady quite remarkably."

Behind his back Kit winked, so that I could hardly keep my countenance.

That same evening we entertained at cards. I chose to wear the blue, my favourite colour, and my glass told me I was *en beauté*.

A dozen persons, all men, crowded into our small parlour, and we were obliged to set up a second table in Kit's bed-chamber.

I soon perceived that it was myself, not the cards, they were come for. Men's eyes rested in surprise on Nurse's cross at my neck, travelling thence in open admiration to the cleft of my bosom, so that I was hard put to avoid blushing. I disguised my distaste, and maintaining my dignity played the hostess as I would have done at Marley, ignoring as best I could the coarser kind among them, who, in kissing my hand, made no secret of their appraisal of my body.

On this occasion I took no part at cards, but moved from one table to the other, watching the play. The stakes were high and Kit was winning heavily; being alone among them in attending fully to the cards.

The candles burnt till late into the night, and when the last of our visitors had gone I was yawning. Kit emptied his pockets.

"What did I tell you? We are made, Sal."

"But I do not care for this company." My shame was like a bad taste in my mouth. "They undress me with their looks."

"You have them all at your feet, my angel. 'Tis only they can't believe their eyes, such beauty and so innocent." He put his hand under my chin and kissed me softly. "You were raked with fire and did not flinch. What a partner for a man!

175

Tomorrow evening you shall take a hand and distract them further."

At such praise I glowed, resolving on the next occasion to be put out by nothing.

To our satisfaction the crush was even greater. Men had to take their turn to play, but indeed they were happy enough to stand conversing that they might eat me with their eyes; and to my chagrin I once more found myself confused.

I was put at my ease by an elderly man whose discreet attention supposed me as wellbred as himself. He was thin: I had never thought to see a man so thin. Moreover he wore a vast wig which made his face narrow as a wafer; all nose and chin. His tone was kind, and he spoke to me as if I were of interest not merely as a nine days' wonder, or a body to lie with. I was soon chattering to him of Bradstock and my childhood, and my misery on returning there to find all changed and Old Sim dead.

"Mr Selby is indeed a lucky man," he said, "to have found such a treasure." At which I coloured.

"Mr Fuller," Kit interrupted, "I must snatch Lady Fearnshawe from you. My love, Mr Roper here is dying to be presented."

Poor youth, he knew not where to look; the blood flew to his cheeks. I held out my hand and he kissed it, stammering that he hoped I found London to my liking.

"Well enough, Sir."

But in turning hastily from him to avoid Kit's silent laughter, I found myself trapped by one I cared for less.

"Lord Buckhurst, Sarah," Kit's easy manner told me he was pleased, "and he has brought his friend Sir Charles Sedley, who writes pretty verses. We are flattered."

To Lord Buckhurst I took an instant dislike. Dark pouches under his eyes betrayed his dissipation; the polite insolence of his manner told me he counted me a whore, the insult made the worse in that I perceived him to be no fool. To rid myself of him I sat down to play, but the move was in vain.

"Charles," he said, almost tipping his friend out of his chair, "give way. 'Tis my turn. I mean to try my hand against Lady Fearnshawe. Does her play, I wonder, match her looks?"

I felt myself flush with anger.

"As a *protégée* of Mr Selby's, madam, you are no doubt familiar with piquet?"

"I have played a little, my Lord," I answered, my eyes downcast to hide my rage.

Fury turned to excitement as I picked up my hand and sorted the cards. I was determined that at play, at least, I would subdue him, and feigning clumsiness and indecision I rejoiced, remembering each one of the lessons Kit had taught me. Nonetheless I played straight for there was no need to do otherwise, the luck being all with me. A heap of gold grew steadily in front of me, till at last my opponent threw down his hand.

"Who can win against beauty?" he said, rising from the table and bowing. "Charles, Lady Fearnshawe indeed ensures we return to play again."

I, coming out of the trance that winning brings, perceived that it was late and the company beginning to leave.

I was in triumph as I set up the coins in neat piles on the table. I had never seen so much gold in my life, and yet at that moment the round coins, stakes in a game, appeared to be not money but counters, so many tokens of success. Sitting at the empty table among the litter of cards, I moved the little stacks about like pieces on a chessboard till they fell into a pattern that pleased me, on a sudden believing that this would bring me luck.

"A splendid evening," Kit said, looking over my shoulder and rattling his pockets. "But I think your little fortifications too great a temptation for Thomas and Bess."

"It shall all go into a stocking," I said swiftly, "and we will hide it under the mattress."

Which, in fits of laughing, we proceeded to do. "So 'tis my stocking which is to be sacrificed now," Kit said, adding his winnings to mine, sweeping all together without counting our gains.

"What a pair we make!" he remarked as we stuffed the stocking deep under the bottom mattress where, shake the feathers as she might, Bess would never come on it, "you steal men's wits and I fleece them as I please."

177

Tucking the bedclothes into place, "How comfortable to sleep on our fortune!" I said and this set us instantly to pleasure.

As I was drifting into sleep I murmured, "Yet your Lord Buckhurst is an odious man, and his friend Charles no better."

"No matter, my sweet, they set the tone. Where they go others will follow."

Drugged by gambling and by love, I found no fault in what he said.

Next morning Bess surprised us with Kit still in my bed. She turned red as a turkey cock and nearly dropped her shovel of hot coals.

"You may light the fire," I said, yawning, "and set breakfast in the parlour. Then come back and see to me."

She stared in determination anywhere but at us; when she was done, banging the door after her in her hurry to be gone.

"Has the wench never seen a man and woman in bed together before, I wonder?" Kit stretched and kissed me. "I'd better be going before she comes upstairs again. If she encounters me in my nightshirt the sight of my bare shanks will give the poor girl a seizure."

We were still sitting at breakfast, not yet dressed, when there was a knock on the door and Mrs Goodchild, rigid as a poker, stepped inside.

"Well, Mrs Goodchild, and what can I do for you?" Kit enquired blandly.

"You can pack your bags and go."

In her black dress she was like a thing blanched, as if she had never eaten good food or taken enough fresh air. She drew in her breath and let fly.

"Turning my house into a den of vice! I would never have thought it of you, Mr Selby. Quiet female guests I have never objected to. But gambling at cards, that I cannot tolerate. If you wish to entertain your friends in this manner you must do so elsewhere. My husband was a godly man. He would turn in his grave to think of my being put to such nuisance and disgrace!" She cast a pitying eye on me. "If Lady Fearnshawe chooses to remain she is welcome to. Poor innocent creature!"

I was blushing to the roots of my hair.

"My dear Mrs Goodchild, I beg you not to distress your-self." Sitting back in his chair, his legs crossed, Kit, in his green and purple dressing-gown, had the whole air of a king among men. "If they trouble you, our parties shall cease, I would not dream of inconveniencing you." He smiled at the odious woman; I wondered how he could. "But it is hardly convenient for myself to move at such short notice, nor do I care to leave Lady Fearnshawe unprotected, even thought it be in your careful hands. You and I have had a long friendship. Come, don't let it be spoiled. If you will consider our remaining, I will ensure that you are subject to no further annoyance."

Slowly she unbent. A faint pink tinged her cheeks. "Well—" she said. "One week. And I shall be obliged to charge extra for candles."

"Her husband indeed!" Kit exclaimed when she had left the room. "A little timeserving presbyter who was carried off by an ague, to her great advantage. The old hypocrite!"

"One week!" I exclaimed. But in truth I was glad we were to be gone so soon.

" 'Tis enough. And just as well, we could never have advanced to great profit here, even had Mrs Goodchild been as complacent as we required. You were right, Sal, what we need is a setting where you can shine in the manner you wish, and none to question who comes or who goes," he smiled, "or my right to your bedchamber.'

Never had the business of dressing seemed so tedious as it did that morning. Bess was an age making the bed and tidying the room. She would pause to push heavy sighs and look at me piteously, as if she knew full well the sentence we were under and was rendered unhappy. I was too impatient to put my hand under the mattress and pull out the stocking to encourage her to speak. Poor Bess, hers was an unkind lot, and I fancy Kit and I and our noisy visitors opened windows into a more enviable world.

"My Lady," she said at last. "If you please, my Lady —" Then Mrs Goodchild called her from below.

At once the stocking was in my hand. How heavy it weighed as I ran to lay it on the parlour table!

"Kit!" I called, "Kit! Come!" waiting for him to join me

179

before pouring the coins out.

He strolled in and sat down in no haste at all, as if he were planning a campaign — as indeed he was.

"Buckhurst played deep," he said, as the coins rolled on to the cloth. "There's enough here to lay out a week's rent and engage servants, and upholsterers. We can start; the rest will follow."

We counted up three hundred guineas; a small fortune to one reared as I had been.

He was gone all day, and I in a fever of impatience. It was late afternoon when he returned. How eloquent is a man's footfall! I knew before he entered the parlour that he was content.

He was indeed triumphant. "My love, come and see our house," he commanded.

I leapt for the door.

"Wait, you will need your cloak, Sal. 'Tis but a step, but the day grows cold."

I had not known what to expect; perhaps another such as Mrs Goodchild's, but less mean. What I saw took me entirely by surprise. On a sudden London opened out, the city flowered. Instead of narrow streets here was a spacious piazza, and in the centre the green square of Covent Garden. Here was an artificial village green; on every side buildings of a novel refinement, in style all of one piece, and on the West, a strange church in brick. The house Kit led me to was on the North side; one of a row in the new Italian manner, built over a colonnade of brick arches, elegant, with light long windows as at Marley. I fell in love at once.

He took the key from his pocket and turning it in the lock, stood aside for me to enter.

"The rent is down," he said, " 'tis all yours."

Shallow stairs curved upwards from the hall: even as I looked I felt I had trod them all my life. I threw myself into his arms and kissed him.

We explored the house from top to bottom, planning what needed to be done.

The attics for the maidservants, and indeed the whole kitchen quarters, were well enough; and the housekeeper's room, somewhat dark on account of the colonnade, I saw no reason to alter, meaning to make use of it myself and be my own housekeeper.

There were two good bedchambers, and two smaller that would do well for Thomas and for a waiting-woman, though my eye at once told me that in my own bedchamber the hangings would have to be changed, for they were in turkey-work, and red.

In the great parlour, a gilt mirror reflected back the fading light from the tall windows across a polished floor in parquet. Along the walls rows of chairs stood ghostlike in their white dustcovers. Double doors opened into a withdrawing room, shrouded also, and beyond that we found a small parlour and a tiny closet, wainscoted.

In these rooms, with the addition of extra tables, there would be room enough to entertain three or four times what we had done so far, and in comfort.

I lifted the cover on the daybed in the withdrawing room, to find that like the hangings it was in rose colour. But in the great parlour all was in green; a quite tolerable watery green, but I saw at once it would not do.

"We cannot have green hangings in a room where men gamble," I said, "or it will sour their minds."

"Sal," Kit interrupted, "have what you like, spend what you like. No tradesman expects to be paid on the nail, and by the time they complain the money will roll in. But 'tis too dark to talk colours. We will come back tomorrow and decide with the upholsterers."

By the time the upholsterers arrived I had quite determined on the decorations for the great parlour. It was to be all in blue and gold and green. Watching for the workmen from one of the two long windows, I dreamed of how beautiful it was to be.

Kit said he cared nothing if his bedchamber were red or blue, or black for that matter, so long as there was a press for his clothes and a bed where he could lie if I were indisposed or he came home drunk, and the turkeywork would do very well as it was. But for myself, on seeing the patterns spread before me, I decided on one of the new chintzes for the hangings and wallpaper to match, with chaircovers and cushions in pale blue velvet.

"A true woman's choice," Kit remarked, "I shall hardly dare draw breath here." But I saw he was pleased.

I now had but one care: that I had as yet no waiting-woman. The women who came to see me were either too superior: sharp females, contemptuous of my ignorance of London and the fashionable world, who clearly intended to do as they pleased, so reminding me altogether too much of Dorothy. Or they were stupid. Or indeed they were genteel young persons fallen on hard times who had no wish to sully their hands with labour; and though I pitied these, they were of no use to me, for I was in no position to be anyone's nursemaid. I needed a faithful servant on whom I could depend.

With only one day left before we were to move I was at my wit's end. As Bess knelt to wash my feet that night, I exclaimed aloud in my despair, "How am I ever to find an honest girl in London?"

"Oh my Lady! There's me!"

It had never occurred to me to think of Bess. On her knees in front of me, the soap clasped between her hands, plump and untidy, not even very clean, she was in no way the waiting-woman I had imagined for myself.

"Please my Lady let me wait on you. I was brought up proper, indeed I was, and I can wash and mend linen, and there's nothing I wouldn't do for you. And here I cannot stay with you gone. Not for nobody."

So this was the reason for her sighs. This was what she had been trying to say and I never listening. I thought of the warm beds prepared for me without the asking, and the hot possets carried upstairs without complaint; the respect with which she handled my gowns, her growing skill at dressing hair. If she were taught to be clean and given a proper gown and not driven to do two women's work instead of one, she would be a different girl. And indeed I would never find a more honest face. Was she not a comfort to me already?

I remembered her blushes. "If you come, Bess, you must understand that Mr Selby is as a husband to me."

"Oh my Lady!" She reddened, and it was plain that any man in bed or dishabille would cause her tremors. "Oh my Lady, I wouldn't mind if you was to have twenty gentlemen to husband, do but let me serve you!"

Then and there I engaged her.

When I told Kit what I had done, he laughed.

"Old mother Goodchild is not going to like you any the better for it."

At which I was pleased.

I paid our reckoning with her and we parted with icy politeness on both sides, Thomas loading our belongings into a hackney coach. Bess fled without word said, on the pretext of shopping, leaving everything she possessed behind, so that I was obliged to equip her afresh from head to toe; which, in view of her slummocky state, I was only too eager to do. She was waiting on the doorstep when we arrived.

What delight to enter our own front door, to climb our own stairs, to walk round the freshly done rooms, now free of workmen, and, at last, to throw off my cloak in my own bedchamber!

"Oh my Lady!" Bess exclaimed, looking this way and that about her. "Oh my Lady! And to think, if Mrs Goodchild had had her way there would have been none of this! She was all for stopping you, saying you was going to your ruin and it was her duty to speak. But indeed," and turning to, she began to unpack, "for all her big words, it was only the kitchen sink to hear her."

Even though the household was still in confusion we dined well. Jane, our new cookmaid, worked marvels. We had not yet our full complement of servants, and those there were, bewildered, and finding their way about, needing a housekeeper's hand. I resolved to set about putting this to rights, but my first act as a housewife was to go shopping. I foresaw that before play started we must have a safer container than a stocking for our moneys. Attended by Bess I stepped out to the New Exchange, and in addition to outfitting her anew, bought a stout coffer with a key, for which on our return I found a snug hiding-place in a little cupboard over the chimneypiece in my bedchamber.

I was busy engaged in the transformation of Bess, involving as it did the washing of herself and her hair, when Kit returned, half opening the door.

"Go away!" I said.

"Why so?"

"Bess is in her shift and would not care for you to see her nakedness."

"Oh, la! And where am I to go?"

"You may wait for me in the withdrawing room. What is it for else?"

I had forgotten his lute. It had left Morley with Thomas, and in all this time of turmoil there had been no leisure in which Kit might play. Now the sound of its strings floated through the open withdrawing room door up the stairs to where I stood, dressing Bess's hair. He began to sing. It was as if, on the instant, the house came alive.

I fastened Bess into her new gown, and she gazed in round-eyed pleasure at her image in the glass.

For a moment, I relived my own astonishment at seeing myself in my first new gown, transformed at Nurse's hands in readiness for our celebration of the King's return; all eagerness to show my new self to Oliver.

"If you please, my Lady, may I go now?" she asked.

"Yes, Bess. I need nothing further."

The singing stopped as I entered the withdrawing room. Kit looked up from his lute, his eyes were naughty.

"At last Bess lets me see you!" he said.

"What a tease you are," I accused him. "What is it you are hiding from me now?"

"A present. I have taken Kitty from you, but I give you Joseph. I won him at play." He raised his voice. "You may come in now, Joseph, and meet your mistress. She won't hurt you, that I promise."

The child was coal black, dressed all in yellow satin with a turban on his head. He entered timidly from the great parlour, clutching to himself with both arms a bundle no bigger than the one I had fled with from Marley.

I saw at once that he was near to tears. My heart went out to him in pity. He could have been no more than ten years old.

"If you are wholly to stun the town, Sal, you need a page. Moreover, the boy was ill-treated where he was. He is to walk behind you when you go abroad."

"Come with me," I said. I took Joseph by the hand — how small it felt in mine! — and led him downstairs to the kitchen, where the maidservants made much of him.

That night Kit and I took supper alone together, as any man and wife. After, we went our separate ways to bed; he, like every prudent householder, remaining to see that all was secure while I climbed the stairs. A fire leapt in the grate. Bess, wholesome in her russet gown and white apron, was waiting for me. I touched the chintz of my bedcurtains, wondering at the texture, so different from any I had known before, only half listening to her all the while she was undressing me, her mind running on the little black boy and how he was black all over — as if she expected him to be piebald. Then, impatient, I dismissed her, and the door opened to let in Kit. Behind the bedcurtains our joy broke all bounds.

But now my pen moves with difficulty. Through the vista of the years I see too plainly that the home I had devised with such love for Kit's delight was indeed but a honey trap for victims; the intention debased from the start. What gives me shame now was then a source of pleasure.

Almost before he was awake Kit said, "I have put it about that today we shall be at home. Can you manage, Sal?"

I said, yawning, "Why not?"

Indeed, by the time the candles were lit we were ready.

After some deliberation I decided to wear that evening my apricot gown, and that Joseph should attend me to hand out comfits and coffee. For I saw thus I would be set off to best advantage against the blue and gold of the great parlour.

Robert, in chocolate and brown livery, our new man engaged for the purpose, stood ready to open the door. The bell tinkled and a babble of voices rose from the hall.

What a heady wine I drank that evening! No woman could have mistaken the astonishment and admiration in men's eyes as I received them. Even Lord Buckhurst, on appraising his surroundings, treated me with a new respect, requesting a return hand at piquet as if he were in truth asking a favour. Mistrusting his intelligence I again played straight and this time, the cards being against me, lost. Piqued, and Lord Buckhurst done with, I for the first time gave myself up to cheating, putting to use all I had practised.

Conscious of my own supposed innocence as a protection, I was by that token now well on the way to losing it altogether. But such self-knowledge I had still to learn.

The players' attention was all on myself; on the elegance of the rooms, the novelty of Joseph and of the coffee and comfits. We knew that nowhere else were gamblers so served.

Kit, all ease and suavity, once more made a killing.

As we walked round the empty rooms, snuffing the candles, he said, "Well done, Sal. You showed a pretty wit. Buckhurst went away content with himself. Now he will come back and you can take from him what you will, for he will never think to doubt you. 'Tis no good thing to win every time. Even *you* would not be forgiven."

What a gamble this venture was! We could have been altogether ruined: but Kit had calculated the odds to a nicety. From that moment we never looked back; our fortunes were assured.

The devil is a careful builder, raising up his victims before he casts them down. There was I, happy as never in my life before, yet sinking ever deeper into an oblivion where I could see no evil.

I had no scruple in taking money from those who came to play. Some of these young men were so corrupt already, at such a tender age, that it was no harm to take their money from them. For the gulls fresh from the country I felt a fleeting pity; but reflected that if they chose to ape the town they had only themselves to blame. In some sort, indeed, we did them a kindness; for otherwise they would only have lost their money in some ordinary, and their coats stolen too, and broken bones very like into the bargain. As for Lord Buckhurst and young Mr Roper who were among our most constant visitors, they, like the rest of the *ton*, were, I reckoned, well able to look after themselves. But in truth I began to esteem them, like Mr Fuller, old friends, and treated them kindly.

One gamester, a raffish army captain, came all too frequently and him I detested, for he was often drunk, and then when Kit's back was turned, would put his hand up my skirts. I decided to teach him a lesson, and sitting down to play with

186

him, proceeded to strip him of his last penny. I guessed the whole pantomime was noticed by Mr Fuller, for I saw him raise his eyebrows, and I fancied he well knew what I was at. At length, his pockets empty, the creature stumbled from the room, white faced.

Afterwards, Kit took me to task. I had never seen him angry before.

"What were you dreaming of? You ruined that fellow."

Leaving where they lay on the table the coins I had won, he began walking up and down. From his manner it was plain he was disturbed, and I perceived that part of his anger, for indeed he was in a rage, was caused by finding himself obliged to be so.

I answered in surprise, "Why are you cross? You laughed when I cleaned Lord Buckhurst out."

"Buckhurst never ventures more than he means to lose. If you ruin men you breed suspicion and drive others away. Never do it again. There's one already won't come back."

"So I should hope," I answered hotly. "That was my intention, I never wish to see the man again. I'll not tolerate drunks, nor lechers neither, in my withdrawing-room. That sot was both, he tried to fumble me."

Kit stopped dead. "You should have told me." His face was white and set, as I had seen it in the moonlight when he killed Sir Gilbert.

"I feared that had I done so you might have run him through," and indeed, such a thought had crossed my mind.

"It would have been a pleasure. Listen to me, Sal, I'll have no man lay a finger on you. If it happens again, leave the fellow to me and I'll settle his hash with cold steel." He came to me and took my hand in both his. "Say you forgive me if I distressed you. But, my sweet, if you don't tell me you are in trouble, how am I to know?"

At that moment I would have died for him.

Autumn turned to winter. The bills were all paid. Play in our rooms was deep, and in spite of the heavy expenses for firing and candles the coffer in my bedchamber began to overflow. It was of no use to ask Kit what was to be done, for his answer I knew would have been to spend.

So it was I thought to take advice of Mr Fuller; telling myself

187

that he being elderly, I could ask a favour without anything expected in return. I led him aside one evening into my closet.

"My dear lady," he said, and the lines in his narrow face crinkled as he smiled, "I am only too delighted to be of use. Your best course is to open an account with Mr Robert Blanchard, the goldsmith banker. He will look after your monies for you and see that they increase." I took my pen and he gave me an address in the City. "It might be wise," he added, "to invest in some merchant venture to the Indies. If I can put a good thing in your way I will do so."

He took a little turn about. "What a pleasure it is to see Mr Selby so devoted! 'Tis rumoured he has turned down a wealthy match." He rubbed his fingers together, then pulling them till the knuckles cracked. "A changed man indeed. One can only wish he had not left his regiment, for he has all the qualities to have made a first rate soldier." He hesitated, but thought better of what he had been about to say.

I thanked him warmly and looked no further.

I was now entertaining regularly, in my own house, men from the fashionable world, and they treating me as if I were a beauty and a prize for Kit to have won. But they did not bring their women, nor did I encounter them elsewhere, unless as distant visions driving in the Park. Kit never offered to take me to Court, nor did I press him to do so; having learnt from my brushes with Sir Gilbert that to press a man to give what he wishes to withhold is a recipe for disaster. Nor did I ask Kit what he did or where he went; content for him to tell me what he chose. How often he was at Court himself and who he saw there, I never knew. I was aware he frequented the Groom Porter's lodgings to gamble, though he seldom spoke of it. I also was convinced from his bearing that sometimes he had visited his father.

One evening that winter when there was to be no play, I was sitting in a low chair by the withdrawing-room fire watching the flames, when Kit burst in exclaiming:

"Old men do nothing but nag nag nag. Thank God for you, Sal, and my independence." He tossed his hat on the daybed, and throwing himself on the floor at my feet, put his head in my lap.

His hair ran cool like water through my fingers.

"What a home you make for a man! Here I have peace." Then as our fondness mounted, "How sweet to come home to such tranquility!"

What more could I wish for?

Since in these pages I am making confession, I must record that gaming is like a fever in the blood; the pleasure of winning — what is more wicked, the pleasure in a successful cheat — was second only to the pleasure I found in Kit's arms. Before the year was out I found myself living from one evening's play to the next, waiting for the candles to be lit, the sweetmeats and coffee to be laid out, and, at last, the moment when I spread out my skirts, sat down, and picked up the cards: as if picking up the cards of life itself, playing the game of my own destiny.

CHAPTER FOURTEEN

What to do now?

A cold November rain was falling. I had had big fires lit in all the rooms. Kit was out; I was afraid that he would be chilled to the skin. As I stood at the window of the great parlour, watching the passers-by bending in front of the rain, the water turned to fine snow. It was then that I saw him returning, even in his hurry avoiding, without checking, the puddles in the roadway.

Two years had passed since we first came to this house, and life never less than perfection.

I ran to meet him, eager to take his cloak and sit him down by the fire. But his mien was such that I stopped dead.

"What's the matter?" I cried.

Without taking off his cloak, he began to pace up and down. I watched the snow melt, feeling cold all the way down my throat and into my belly, into my very womb, as if the snow fell inside me.

"I must leave you, Sal."

"*Leave* me?"

"Today. I am to be married."

"*Married*? But I thought —"

"My father presses me. He needs an heir and estates to grace his name and these you cannot give me. He speaks soberly and with guile, but I know him well enough. He can make life hard for us if he chooses."

"I thought you loved me."

"So I do. But a man can't eat love or live on kisses. Our present fortune won't last forever, fashions change. He's right when he says I need a safe harbour for my middle years. The girl is heiress to a great fortune, and no encumbrances, her father dead. A man doesn't throw such a chance away."

190

"I have money saved."

"Not enough."

"Had Sir Gilbert left me Marley you would have married me."

"But he did not. What can you give me? Your father's lands go to Fearnshawe's heirs."

So my fate had been sealed even as he read Robbins's letter.

"What's to become of me?"

"You are young enough and fresh enough to find another protector. Young Roper is dying for you."

"Then I am to be a whore now!"

"I would hardly put it so. Would you call Lady Castlemaine a whore? You are no worse without me than with me. You have another trade should you so wish and, you tell me, money saved."

"Kit, I shall die without you! If you must make this marriage at least let me see you, come sometimes to my bed."

He was still walking up and down. I could not touch him or reach him in word or fact.

"It's all very well for a man to sow his wild oats, but enough is enough. I can't see you and not live with you."

"If you leave me altogether it will kill me. *Why*, Kit," I begged. "Why must you do this to me?"

"In truth my father requires an heir of me and this it seems is beyond you. A match between us could never have been in question. Sal, don't make it difficult for me. No man in his right senses could do otherwise. Besides, I have given my word."

At this I fainted clean away.

I came to my senses at the smell of burning feathers, held by Joseph under my nose. My head rested in Bess's lap. As I opened my eyes she said:

"Oh my Lady, Mr Selby is gone and Thomas with him and Jane too. What are we all to do?"

"First help me to my feet."

It is strange how panic in others helps wonderfully to deaden pain and prevent the giving way to grief. In a false calm, moving like someone numbed, I went down to the kitchen where I found the servants in idle disarray. I ordered Robert to take over Thomas's duties and, in addition, to make himself responsible for seeing we were secure at night. "And, Robert," I concluded, "until I instruct you otherwise, I am at home to nobody, nobody at all — unless it should be Mr Selby." Then I turned to Catherine, our chambermaid, and enquired of her whether she was able to cook.

She nodded her head, whispering that she had often done so "when Jane was courting with Thomas," and she blushed.

So it was arranged, and our maid of all work now to be chambermaid.

"Catherine, you will come to me for orders in the morning to my housekeeping room, as Jane did," I said, and I mounted the stairs.

Now indeed I was in pain, unable to believe that Kit could be gone. Yet the house felt empty of his presence. I looked in the withdrawing room. His lute was no longer in its place beside my virginals. With heavy feet I climbed the next flight. Outside his bedchamber door, with my hand on the latch I hesitated, in dread of venturing inside.

All sign of him had vanished: no brushes and combs on the table, no bright dressing-gown, no clothes cast aside for Thomas to set in order.

I opened the press: empty. Then in wild haste I went from drawer to drawer, all empty, not a pin, not a scrap of paper. The bedchamber was without life, left as it had been when I first set foot there.

He had never given me any present, not so much as a trinket. Now there was nothing of him in the house.

I stared at the hateful turkeywork.

"I should never have allowed it to be so red."

I had spoken aloud.

Last night he had lain beside me falsely, while even as I slept in innocence, Thomas did his work. How could he so deceive me? Had all our pleasures from the first been lies?

Grief is a sharp knife that will not leave its wound; a move, and it pains again.

"My Lady!" Bess, following like a dog behind me, put her hand on my arm.

"I will go to bed, Bess, make haste to undo my gown." Her

kindness was suffocating, I was in agony for her to be gone. But this she would not. Her troubled eyes were telling me how strange I must seem, and that she feared to leave me.

"I want for nothing," I said with impatience as she laid my hairbrush down. "Do but draw the bedcurtains and let me be."

But neither the darkness, nor my soft bed, nor solitude, brought me any solace. The front door bell tinkling incessantly as callers were turned away, pulled me back to be tormented by Kit's words. I fancy now that for a while a fever was upon me, for I remember my hair clinging damp to my brow. Tossing to and fro on my pillow, I became confused: I must get up and dress, the candles must be lit, the cards laid out — where was Kit — why did he so delay?

The bell stopped, the house lay silent. I heard the bolts shot on the front door and the key turned in the lock. I held my breath to listen.

The footsteps died away. It was Robert, going to the kitchen and his own quarters. No steps came running upstairs. In the unearthly quiet my ears beat with the sound of my own heart thudding in terror. There was to be no escape in sleep or anywhere else: the heavy news was borne in upon me that Kit would never come back.

I fell into wild weeping. I know not for how long I cried for I was out of my mind. I was surprised to hear my sobs diminish and turn to dry groans.

I was startled out of the black nightmare I was in by the curtain rings rattling and a light shining in my eyes. Joseph stared in at me, wide-eyed. He wore only a nightshirt and the candle in his hand trembled and flared, for he was shivering. I smelled burnt wick; my own bedchamber candle was nothing but a pool of wax.

"Joseph!" I said, sitting up, "What is the matter? You are cold!"

At that he put the candle down and shot into my arms. I took him into my bed that he might warm himself against me. His feet were two blocks of ice. He laid his cheek against mine and putting his arms round me held me tight, as if to prevent the soul from leaving my body.

"Mistress you are not to die! I won't let you!" And he held

me all the tighter. I shall never forget his springy curls rough against my skin.

The little world made by drawn bed curtains is designed for the pleasures of love and is but a cruel prison for despair. By breaking in upon me Joseph did indeed fetch me back to life. In this black child's arms slowly I took comfort, wondering to find myself amongst the living.

"I am not going to die, I promise you," I said at last. "But why are you out of your bed? What brought you here?"

"I was afraid. Mistress, you was making the same noise my mother did when she was beaten."

"Poor Joseph. But where were you to hear me?"

"Bess came to me and said Robert and Catherine was gone to bed and what was we to do and what was to become of us all? She could do nothing with you, for you wasn't yourself, Mistress, for you had drove her from you with words that made no sense. Then she threw her apron over her head and cried like a booby, and I saw that no good would come out of her till she had slept. So I led her to her bed. And when I promised her that I would lay outside your door she said she would undress. And I have been here ever since."

Joseph had been caring for all of us in his own fashion, carrying the weight of my troubles on his small shoulders. Overcome by shame and gratitude I held him close, and so fell asleep.

When I woke he was gone and Bess was clattering the fire irons.

I was no city lady, but a healthy young woman and country bred, and after being fed meals on trays for two days, my physical body had recovered from the shock it had received. On the third day, presented with a particularly fine dish of pheasant followed by black hothouse grapes, I thought to compliment Catherine on her housekeeping, for I had given her no orders.

At which Bess hummed and haaed, and when at last she let fall that these delicacies were the gift of Mr Roper who called daily at the house, I almost leapt from my bed.

I did not intend to be beholden to Mr Roper or any other of the gentlemen who came to play. I would tolerate no *protector*

— at the memory of Kit's words I bled inwardly, and blushed outwardly with rage. Indeed I was resolved that no man should have knowledge of me again. I was done with London. I would go back to Bradstock and begin my life afresh.

Sitting on the edge of my bed while Bess, in a flurry, went for hot water that I might wash, I determined on taking her and Joseph with me. I had savings enough to settle the bills and pay off the servants and, moreover, that we should travel in comfort and for a while at least be no burden on my parents. Beyond that I gave no thought, fancying Joseph taking his part in the household and Bess in due course getting wed. As for myself, was I not the daughter of the house?

A breath of unease crept upon me. I had heard no word from Bradstock for two years; I had written no letters and received none. Could I be sure that the house still stood, that my father was still alive; that he, not the ironmaster, or worse still, Dorothy, was its head?

I decided that I would write of my predicament before taking to the road. And as soon as I was washed and dressed, I repaired to my closet and my pen.

I wrote begging my father to look on me with pity, for I had been abandoned in London with no one to turn to: that I knew I had done wrong in leaving my husband, though as I wrote this I feared that it would choke me, for I did not in the least believe it. However, I had repented of my folly. This again was untrue, I regretted only that Kit was gone — and I wished to return home to live a sober life in widowed penitence.

"God forgive me!" I prayed. But in truth I did long for the Forest and its undefiled peace, seeking, like any other of its wounded creatures, to hide in its depths. Nor, after Kit, could I bear the thought of another man, husband or no, in his place.

I sighed as I put down my pen. Every fibre of my body was pulling me back to the Forest. But was it not lost to me already? When my father died, were I at Bradstock, would I not then be left Dorothy's pensioner? How she would enjoy to see me suffer!

Nonetheless, I folded the paper. My father was not dead that I knew of. And before he did die much could happen. By that time I would be healed and able to see my way.

It remained to find a messenger. The posts were of no use to me, for I must know that my letter was received; I wished for an answer swiftly, and news of Bradstock by word of mouth if by any evil chance my worse fears were realised and I was now fatherless. Robert I could not part with, for I needed a man in the house as a protection against unwelcome callers. Bess I doubted could be forced from my side and, if she were, could not be trusted to arrive, and if she did so, to return, without mishap. There was left only Joseph. He indeed had both resource and devotion enough, as the last days had proved; but I felt it cruel to send one so young, and a stranger to the land, on such a journey. I hesitated before summoning him to my cabinet; not only for his sake but, in the emptiness of my life, unwilling to part with his affection even for a short time.

"Joseph," I said, and then I faltered. "Joseph, I need one I can trust, to take a letter to my father."

He looked me straight in the eyes understanding at once all my misgivings.

"I will go for you, Mistress." He held out his hand.

" 'Tis a long journey, and I know not what you will find at the other end."

"Mistress, no harm will come to me. I am not afraid. I have made great voyages, with bad men. And I am here!"

I gave him directions and made him repeat them. He was word perfect at the first telling. I put monies for the journey into his hand, and then, at last, the letter, bidding him God-speed.

"Bess," I said when he was gone. "I think to return to the country and to my father."

"What, my Lady! And are we to leave all this?"

"I am sure, Bess, that you would like Bradstock."

"I will like anywhere so long as it be with you. But oh, my Lady! And all the gentlemen!"

"Bess, I want no more gentlemen. And you are to say nothing of this to anyone, for indeed till Joseph's return, I know not if my father be alive or dead."

It was plain as the days passed that we waited for Joseph with very different hopes: Bess, puffing heavy sighs the while, gazing on all about her as if she were seeing it for the last time, and would, if she could, take it with her; myself, sighing to be gone.

In the long hours of waiting I saw as if it were written in the pages of a book that my marriage to Sir Gilbert was the root of all my misfortunes; and this marriage had been my own wilful choice. My husband had laid his finger across the whole of my life. Though he was dead, it was through him that I was now ruined. There had been but a phantom escape from Marley. My new enemy, Kit's father, would not have been one had he not been Sir Gilbert's friend and myself Sir Gilbert's widow.

And yet, without Sir Gilbert, there would have been no Kit. The pain and the infinite joy weighed in opposite scales.

I asked myself over and over again why Kit had left me, and in so cruel a manner. But I was too much in love and too hurt to understand.

In calmer times I have been able to see that it was inevitable from the first meeting. No woman without lands, and barren at that, could have held him.

True love takes no account of man's sins, but lasts no matter how great a hurt it receives. Hardly a day has passed since that I have not thought of him. Now, years later, I still believe that in his own fashion he loved me, and it was this that made him deliberately cruel. Because he suffered himself at parting from me, he blamed me for making him do so: if he suffered, then I must suffer too. In his making me out of no account, I became not worth his suffering for; it was no matter if he hurt me. Thus he could stop suffering. And to crown all, he wished to see me suffering, and to prove to himself in watching me that he felt no hurt.

I was sitting in the withdrawing room on a fine clear afternoon and very cold, looking at my virginals, but with no heart to play, when Joseph returned. Bess ushered him in to me, protesting all the while that he must be hungry, that he might have caught a chill and should be downstairs by the kitchen fire, that *she* could hand me letters. But he would have none of this. Without a word he gave me the letter, addressed in my father's hand, telling me with his eyes that he brought bad news.

There was but one sheet of paper and few words, with no

endearment or even my name at the start.

"There is no place for you here. As you have made your bed, so you must lie on it. This ironmaster sends me to an early grave."

He signed his name in full, no more. I might have been another man's child. I sat stupefied.

"What of my mother?" I asked at last.

"The lady would not speak with me."

"And Nurse?" I cried. "Nurse cannot have been unkind!"

"That one took me in and fed me and asked me questions how you did. She cried some tears and said to me: 'Tell my child to keep faith with her old nurse,' and bade me give you this." He handed me a sprig of rosemary. "She is a very old lady."

Not knowing what I did, I thanked Joseph and sent him to the kitchen, wondering at how upstanding he looked, and indeed, well.

I turned to Bess who had been waiting by, big with unspoken questions. "We shall not now be going to the country, Bess. You may tell Robert that if Mr Roper calls I will see him."

As soon as she was gone I tore the letter across and across, letting the pieces lie where they fell. Then, fearing they might yet be read, collected them up and put them on the fire. The rosemary I carried upstairs and laid under my pillow that in the nights to come it might bless my sleep.

CHAPTER FIFTEEN

Young Roper

Nurse had sent me rosemary for remembrance and bade me keep faith with her. But this I could not do, I was too hurt and angry. That my progenitor should turn against me when I most needed him was more than I could bear. As I lay in my bed I thought how as a child I had sat by his side, spelling out my letters, confident of his love. Did he now care nothing that he forced me into whoredom?

The rosemary was safe under my pillow, but during the night I slept hardly at all. I thought not of Nurse, nor of virtue, but that I had been betrayed. Husband, lover and now father, had cast me aside. My answer was to take revenge. And so, as the church bell tolled the passing hours, I resolved it was to be war between myself and the whole sex.

I dismissed almost as I thought of it, the idea of virtuous employment; for even to find it, with no one to recommend me, would have required more firmness and humility than I possessed. I must continue in the trade I knew, of gaming, and for comfort in this I needed a protector.

"Fresh enough" I might be — Kit's words burned in my head — to take one from the fashionable world and in this way reach the Court itself; but my whole being revolted against such traffic.

Mr Roper was another matter: "dying of love" for me, and here I raged again.

He was a youth for whom I had no inclination. But he was not unpleasant to look at, well-built if somewhat heavy in his limbs and, which was a virtue in my eyes, seeming not quite a man, almost a boy. I could bear to let him touch me for he was in no way debauched, without a man's vices as he was without a man's charms. His manner led me to suppose that he could confess to little knowledge of women, and of this I was now wise enough in the ways of the world to know the advantage: he was unlikely to give me a disease. Moreover, he was generous, and the son of a noble and wealthy father.

And yet, when, as I could not help, I pictured him standing beside Kit, I blushed that I should join myself with one so inferior.

The London sparrows began their early chirping. I told myself that what I was about to do was the first step in my revenge. It was certain to come to Kit's ears, and if, as he said, he loved me, it would hurt him.

At this I wept a little into my pillow, and then, confirmed in my purpose, at last slept.

It was late morning when I woke. Bess brought me my breakfast on a tray.

"You was sleeping so sound I wouldn't disturb you, my Lady, but I am to tell you Mr Fuller called. Robert turned him away, but the gentleman asked particular that you should be let know."

I had no thought to send for him, for to what end? My mind was all on young Roper.

"If he calls again I daresay I will be at home to him," I said absently. "Bess, since we must go on as we are, I am obliged to take a protector. If Mr Roper calls, I fear I must receive him."

"But my Lady," and Bess was blushing. "Mr Roper is a very proper man! He does truly love you, that I know. When he heard you was in bed and could see no one and I feared for your life the tears ran down his face. Why, he would give his right arm for you, let alone pheasant." She fiddled with the dishes on my tray, straightening those that were straight already. "And, my Lady! His yellow curls!"

It was indeed those curls and his pink and white complexion that I found distasteful.

"You had best put sheets on the bed in the red bedchamber," I said. For I did not choose that any man should sleep the night beside me.

Bess looked at Mr Roper with a female's eyes, and silly at that. I dreaded to tell Joseph of my decision, for I valued his good opinion. Nonetheless I sent for him before I dressed. I justified myself: "We must survive, but Joseph, I like not at all what I am about to do, I am ashamed to enter my own kitchen."

"But Mistress," he said, "Mr Roper is in great favour. He has given presents to everyone. Mr Selby was loved, but now he is gone he is forgotten. He gave nothing."

So my servants conspired in my wrongdoing. Comforted by their support I told myself that since it was but one, to lie with a man and not love him was no worse prostitution than had been my lying with Sir Gilbert.

In this I was mistaken. Sir Gilbert I had been in no position to refuse.

For the first time since my abandonment I dressed with care, taking an age at my mirror, studying each curl.

"Oh my Lady!" Bess exclaimed when at last I was satisfied. "I don't know when you has looked better!"

Joseph knocked. "Mr Roper has come, Mistress. I have shown him into the withdrawing room."

The colour rose in my cheeks. I went downstairs with the same determination, the same lack of feeling, as when I had gone to my marriage.

I entered the withdrawing room to find Mr Roper blushing too. Anyone coming upon us would have wondered to see two young people so covered in confusion.

I held out my hand to him, and when he kissed it I let my fingers lie where they were in his; while he stammered that he hoped he found me well again.

"I hear you have been kind," I said, "and I must thank you for not deserting me in my distress. It is to you, is it not, that I am beholden for the delicacies that helped in my recovery?"

"Lady Fearnshawe — madam — it was nothing — there is nothing, nothing, that I would not do for you."

His eyes told me that he meant what he said. He was still holding my hand, as if he had forgotten what he did, and I led him gently to the rose-coloured daybed.

And so we sat down together side by side; babes of an age, but I was twice his age in sin.

I put my head on his shoulder and murmured how I was so alone and unhappy. Whereat he could not contain himself any

201

longer but covered my face with kisses. His hand was at my breast, I made no protest; strayed to my thigh. I lifted my skirts and let him have his way with me. He was somewhat clumsy and I had but a tepid satisfaction, but not unpleasant, as I had feared.

Now he was all apologies, red in the face and once more stammering: "But, Lady Fearnshawe, you are too much for me. Will you ever forgive me?"

"Sir, there is nothing to forgive," I kissed him gently. "But if you are to be my friend, Lady Fearnshawe is too formal. Let it be Sarah."

"And you will let me care for you?" It was as if he could not believe his good fortune.

"Indeed Sir, I am too alone in the world." Whereat he kissed me again.

"Not Sir," he said at last, "not Sir; Edward." And now the poor youth was rosy with happiness.

I bade him stay and dine with me; and after, he asked me did I play on the virginals and did I perhaps sing? I answered yes, and he begged that I would oblige him.

"I have no music myself, I can neither sing nor play, but Sarah, if you would sing it would give me joy to hear you."

This proved to be true; when I sang sad songs the tears came into his eyes. He was a young man easily moved in his emotions; as I could make him cry, so I found I could make him laugh as I chose, and then he would be like a puppy gambolling at my feet.

When at last I dismissed him, pleading fatigue, and in truth I began to feel my lack of sleep, I said: "Tomorrow you shall take supper with me if you will, and we need not be disturbed."

At which he thanked me profusely, blushing again, which I wished he would not, for blushes go ill with yellow hair.

In triumph at my success I did not pause to consider that as once I had been sold by my father, so now I had indeed sold myself.

Mr Roper took supper with me the following day; but not before calling to inquire how I did, and to leave sweetmeats and the new delicacy, tay, for my delight. It set Bess in a great flurry of excitement that I entertained him in my bedchamber, and after, between the sheets of my own bed; this to revenge myself on Kit. But I would not have him sleep beside me, banishing him to the barrenness of the red bedchamber, where he had undressed; and he in the seventh heaven that I should allocate a bedchamber in my house for his own use. Yawning, I had to confess to myself that his legs, though not to be compared with Kit's, were yet tolerable.

Nor would I see him in the morning, but threw him out fasting that I might enjoy my breakfast chocolate alone.

"Poor gentleman!" Bess scolded me. "And the morning so cold!"

"Nonetheless I do not care to receive before I am dressed."

She shook her head, murmuring, for once in disapproval of what I did.

As soon as the young man was confident that he alone enjoyed my favours, he showered gifts upon me: rings, bracelets, necklaces in precious stones. I complained that at London I did not get enough fresh air, that I was bored at being so confined to the house. At once he took the fault upon himself, calling next day to take me driving in the Park; and then, the morning following, taking my hand: "Sarah, please forgive me, but I cannot bear that you should lack for anything," and he led me out into the Piazza. "For you, if you will."

My own coach and pair! With two incomparably matched black carriage horses, my own coachman!

"Edward," and I fear the name came grudgingly to my tongue, "I can refuse you nothing! How can I thank you enough?"

He wished to take me everywhere; for my pleasure and, it was plain, that men might envy him: driving in the Park, into the City, out into the countryside, in every public place. He would have taken me to Court, but this I would not allow, knowing too well the slights I might receive. Nor was I grateful to one who counted it a virtue to be so giving to a woman, to be so obedient to her wishes. I blushed to be seen in my carriage with him. I did not care for his appearance when dressed to go abroad.

I have never thought a sword a pretty accompaniment to a

man's dress; either it will be used, in which case it is barbarous, or it will not, when it is no more than a silly ornament. On Kit it had been truly dreadful and yet in a strange way it became him. On Edward Roper it appeared to me the trappings of a booby.

I protested. "Swords frighten me."

" 'Tis not done for a man to go about London without hat, cloak and sword," he said, surprised. "He is no gentleman else. Don't be alarmed, Sarah, for I would never draw."

It was of this indeed that I was most afraid.

Now for the first time I went to the theatre, a pleasure I had long wished for but which Kit had never permitted. We were to see Mr Betterton in Shakespeare's *Hamlet*, and for this Edward had taken a box, that we might enjoy the play and at the same time he might show me off and I in my turn might inspect the company.

But I heard not a word Edward said, for the first sight my eyes fell on, in the box opposite, was Oliver. He was dressed in russet velvet that set off his ruddy complexion, and was now become a very pretty man: twice the man my companion was; of an age, but years more mature. His young wife was very fair, with pale silken curls drawn back from a high forehead. She was dressed in blue, of the shade I had always thought particularly my own, and was, I noticed at once, big with child.

I stared so, that Oliver turned to look at me. He showed no flicker of recognition; and then, slowly, turned his back.

I thought I would fall to the ground. I no longer heard the play, I could not tell after what it was about. I thought only of the insult I had been offered, and how fate had cheated me. My mind was all on not bursting into tears. At that moment I hated my companion, piling on his head the fault of my present situation. Why had he brought me to this place? Why was he not Kit, of whom at least I need not have been ashamed? I thought of my home and of the past, of Oliver sharing my childhood bedchamber and our watching together the pictures on the wall, and the pain was nigh unendurable.

"Sarah, are you not well? Does your head ache?" Edward asked.

"A little but 'tis nothing."

"Let me take you home."

"We will see the play out," I said, for I would not give Oliver the satisfaction of knowing he upset me.

Nonetheless we left as the play ended, even before the actors could take their bows; I saying that after all, I would be glad to go quickly.

As soon as I was confident that nothing would shake Edward's need of me, I began once more to hold evenings at cards. For not only did I long for the excitement to relieve the tedium of my life, but I had no intention to be dependant for my subsistence on the goodwill of one young man.

I sent to Lord Buckhurst and to Mr Fuller to inform them, knowing that these two men between them would bring the others flocking.

"Edward," I said, as we sat over our wine, "tomorrow I intend to receive at cards."

The colour rose in his cheeks. "Please, Sarah, I beg of you not. I beg that you will allow me to provide anything you need. I thought," and he looked at me piteously, "I was all in all to you."

"There is no other man, nor will there be. But indeed Edward I love play and where else that is respectable am I to find it?" I put my hand on his where he trifled with his glass on the table. "Please let it make no difference between us. Come and support me, for I need your presence to protect me; and I shall expect you to stay after if you wish. But if it distresses you that I amuse myself at cards," and I sighed, "I will not dream of continuing."

I gambled that he could not bring himself to deny me: nor could he. The following evening all the rooms on the first floor were full. I saw to it that the stakes were high, for I was playing to hurt; every man with whom I sat down was either Kit or my father. Sir Gilbert counted for nothing; I saw him a villain, not a traitor, and beneath my concern.

I had just risen from the card-table when Mr Fuller approached me. He bowed over my hand.

"I am delighted, Madam, to see you looking so *en beauté*. I need not enquire whether you are recovered." He led me to the window where we could speak privately. " '*Nimium ne crede colori'* — 'Do not trust your complexion too far' — fashions come and go. One day there will be a new star. I am in hopes that my advice has been useful to you and that you invest your monies?"

I flushed and thanked him. "Indeed I do, Sir, and my ventures prosper. I am in hopes to be dependant on no man." Then I took him up, not to seem learned, but to keep hold of the position I had been born to, "Virgil was indeed wise."

"Aha! A scholar! How that pleases me! I am delighted that you make your dispositions." He looked at me sideways, hesitating, and then continued, "Mr Selby is retired to the country but he takes care to keep himself informed. I fancy that he finds his wife a little dull. In truth, she is no beauty." And here he smiled at me. "How men suffer for their worldly advantage! I have it on good authority that she is a strong-willed lady."

In spite of myself I coloured to the roots of my hair. The news was balm to me, but a bitter balm; for I knew not where I was going, and sometimes, in panic, felt myself to be as a riderless horse, galloping to destruction.

Meanwhile, everything I touched turned to gold. I won heavily at cards, but I cared not whom I broke in so doing. The ships in whose voyages I had invested came home laden, escaping the attacks of the Dutch as if under some miraculous protection. Indeed, so successful was I in my trading that Edward decided to try his hand.

Merchant ventures were now a hazard since the Dutch were bold, and we were soon to be at war. Nonetheless Edward was at first successful, and so was encouraged to plunge again. He was lavishing gifts and love upon me, and I accepted what he gave as if it were my right.

The year began very cold, and my mind was all on keeping up big fires and making money as salve to my constant hurt. I cared nothing for the Dutch. I was gambling with cargoes as with cards, growing ever more reckless. Rumours passed from mouth to mouth of encounters between our ships and theirs, but I heeded only my card tables and my balance with Mr Blanchard.

No one believed the Dutch could stand against us, and men

206

were too given over to a fever of patriotism to be troubled when the plague broke out in a scattered few of the out parishes. Only Joseph was uneasy. A comet had traversed the skies at Christmas, and now, at the beginning of April, it was seen again.

He pulled at my gown, his black face grey with fear. "Mistress, 'tis bad luck! What will befall us? I think all should pray."

" 'Tis but a star," I said. "It can do no harm."

But, fed in the crowded warrens, the sickness was creeping ever nearer. Once more Joseph sounded the alarm. He came to find me where I sat in my bedchamber, dressing for the evening's play.

"Madam — Mistress — you wouldn't listen to the comet, but he was right, and the plague is now in the City! Catherine is come back from her sister crying. She says the house is shut up and no one allowed to come out and she not to go in. There is a red cross so big," he made a gesture with his hands, "painted on the door." He nodded his head. "It will come."

My wounded state had set me apart, rendering me indifferent to the public troubles. Nonetheless I could not but see that like Joseph, Bess was afraid. Her hand trembled as she dressed my hair. Now she burst out: "My Lady!" 'Tis not only Catherine in a taking, indeed so are we all. Mr Roper can compass anything. Will he not carry us out of this to the country? Robert says wagonloads is going, folk and all their goods."

One part of me was indifferent as to whether the plague came or no, for what was my life? But I answered as in truth I believed.

"Oh Bess! I'm sorry indeed for Catherine, but for us here 'tis fear for nothing. We have no need to remove. Covent Garden is as airy as any country town, and the houses new."

The pestilence spread fast; and now, suddenly, two houses in Drury Lane were shut up. But in Whitehall there was as yet no general alarm, and Edward's mind was, as I could plainly see, all on his latest venture and the Dutch peril. Their ships were in the Channel, indeed the war was come so close that the cannon of both navies could be heard even in the city itself. The

207

weather was uncommon hot for June, and along with many others Edward took a barge on the Thames, both that we might refresh ourselves and listen to the battle. As Mr Dryden, a greater pen than mine, has writ with such perfection, the sound came to our ears "like the noise of distant thunder, or of swallows in a chimney."

All the town was still rejoicing at our victory when three days later, Edward, having left me that morning in the best of spirits, returned at a run, stumbling up the stairs in his haste.

It was mid afternoon, a time I preferred to spend alone, gathering myself together before I made ready for the evening's gaming. Often, I played the virginals, and so I was doing today. As Edward burst in I turned from the keyboard but did not rise.

A dreadful foreboding came over me, for he was a creature all gone to pieces, his face milk-white and his mouth trembling. He cried out piteously, "I am a ruined man, Sarah — marry me, save me! Oh, help me!" at which he fell on his knees, dropped his head in my lap and burst into tears.

Has ever a female received a stranger offer of marriage?

When a woman loves a man his tears will move her to utmost compassion; they do but swell indifference. His weakness disgusted me.

"How ruined?" I said. "Stop weeping and explain."

"My ship is taken by the Dutch."

"And was your whole fortune on board?"

He clutched my knees.

"Oh Edward!" I said. "How could you be so foolish?"

"It was a last throw, to pay my debts. I am too deep in. Now they dun me for what I have not."

"No other revenues at all?" I asked. A chill had crept over me — for myself; not, it shames me to admit, for him.

"They are gone. My father — oh Sarah!" He broke out weeping afresh.

His father! My heart sank at the word.

Edward continued between sobs. "My father — says he will pay all and set me straight — but only if I will leave London! — I'm to go back to the country — I'm to learn to manage the estates — under his steward's eyes!" He clasped my hand. His

own was sweating but held mine like iron. "I can't leave you —
I would die! Sarah, marry me, come with me — then all will be
well. If we are man and wife my father will forgive me — he'll
have to, he never denies me anything, I am his only child.
Sarah, I am his heir."

He was more than ever like a puppy, pawing at my skirts,
asking to be thrown a ball.

For a moment I could say nothing; his offer came as a shock.
Prudence dictated that I should at once accept, and so acquire
title, wealth, and a husband pliant to my will. But I could not. I
was appalled at the prospect of spending the rest of my life in
his company; even to secure my future such a course was
unthinkable. I envisaged Edward in old age: still pink and
white and baby-faced, with gooseberry eyes popping, a little
round belly, his soft limbs, their youthful charm gone, mere
fat; and not a thought in his head; an elderly male Jess.

Concealing my distaste, for the young man was after all in
distress, I said: "I have no such faith in fathers. If you wish for
money and support from yours you would do better to leave
me altogether. Go home, Edward, do as he bids you."

"But I love you!" He raised his eyes to mine. "I would live
with you in a garret!"

I began to grow impatient.

"No, Edward. I married once without love; I could not
honestly wed again unless I loved with my whole heart."

"But I believed you did love me." His voice was hollow. "I
thought you had forgot Mr Selby."

A strange sound escaped me. It was no laugh nor yet no cry.

"Did you really expect that I would forget the passion of a
lifetime in a matter of weeks?"

It was as if I had whipped him. His grip loosened on my
hands, and scrambling to his feet he rushed from the room.

I left my virginals and going into the great parlour began
walking up and down. With what joy I had first looked from
these windows; with what high hopes for the future! What was
I to do now? In truth I was afraid, for I had no idea.

By now the cards were laid out ready for the evening's play
and new candles set in the sconces. Daylight was beginning to
fade and I was still pacing to and fro, when the door flew open

to admit an Edward unknown to me, wild-eyed, a pistol shaking in his hand.

He levelled the weapon at my heart.

"Will you change your mind?"

"I cannot." My hands took hold on Nurse's cross as I waited for death.

A terrible despair came into his eyes, a final understanding. He put the pistol to his own head. Behind him the mirror became a thousand crisscrossed lines. My senses stunned by the explosion, I watched him fall.

His body lay at my feet, half his face blown away, the rest a mess of blood. Blood and brains and fragments of bone splashed the floor, the wall, even the ceiling.

My stomach turned, I wished to vomit. But for Edward himself I could feel nothing, and this turned my bones to water with fear.

At the sound of the shot my household came running. All was confusion: Bess screamed and went into hysterics, the tears running down her face; Catherine turned chalk white and hustling Bess with her, fled the room; Joseph held tight to my skirts. Only Robert kept his head. "I will fetch the Watch, my Lady," he said, and on the instant went.

I stood where I was, staring at the pistol where it lay by Edward's corpse. My ears still rang with the noise. Smoke hung in the air, and a fusty smell that I remembered only too vividly from the moonlight night of my flight from Marley. Blood pursued me: blood on my father's clothes, blood on the dead man in the Forest, blood on my husband's body; now, blood at my feet.

Joseph pulled at my gown. "You should come away I think."

I allowed him to lead me upstairs. I had never imagined Edward had it in him to love with such folly or to act so desperately. Had I thought it was himself he meant to destroy I would have made some shift to stop him.

"Mistress you are cold," Joseph said.

I found to my surprise that I was holding Nurse's cross, its silver chain dangling. My neck was sore. The chain had cut me as I tugged when Edward fired.

"Tell Catherine I would have a hot drink. I must see the Watch. There is play tonight."

Not knowing what I did, I put the cross on its broken chain away in the drawer of the table by my bed.

CHAPTER SIXTEEN

A whore indeed

The Watch were come and gone again, bearing Edward's corpse away. I sent for Robert and ordered the floor to be washed and the doors locked and the keys given into my own hands before the company could arrive.

"Tomorrow the soiled hangings are to be taken down and the room properly cleaned; and then the shutters closed and the doors locked, for it will not be used again."

I found Robert to have a stouter heart than I had known, for he would not allow the women in, but saw to all himself, prudently removing the cards and the candles; without my knowledge, for I would have left them standing.

That night my remaining rooms were crowded. I played like a fiend, like one possessed, using gaming as another might laudanum.

"I see, Madam, that you have a nerve of steel," Lord Buckhurst remarked.

"Of necessity," I replied, and I took his stake from him.

Not one man present dared question me as to what had passed. There was that about me that closed their mouths.

Bess's eyes were red with weeping, and she still shook with little bursts of tears as she undressed me for bed. My own eyes were dry, and I slept like a log as soon as my head touched the pillow.

I woke before dawn, before the sparrows began to chatter: long before Bess would come to rake the ashes from the fire.

My bed was warm, my body refreshed, but I was as one turned to stone inside. Over and over again I asked myself *Why?* "Edward," I said half aloud, but could not even feel pity. I could only see one answer: it was men who had damaged me thus. I loved Kit, and he left me half destroyed; I allowed

Edward my favours, and because I would not live a lie he shot himself at my feet. The charm I had for men was fatal to myself. Men were a trap; my body's need for them, which had indeed been strong, was to be mistrusted and overcome. To this dusty prospect I saw myself condemned for life.

How I welcomed it when at last my bedchamber door opened and I heard the window curtains pulled back!

But every hour of that day Bess's red-rimmed eyes reproached me that I neither wept nor took to my bed. To her, Edward's death was more deserving of grief than Kit's departure, and I to blame. Poor wench! I fancy that indeed she loved him.

Nonetheless I rebelled at being blamed for what was not my fault. It was a weakness in Edward's own nature that undid him; another man would have faced such disappointment. Nor could I respect a passion content to feed on shadows.

As I write, in what bitter regret, I perceive that I wronged the young man doubly. Already, at that age, I should have known from my own misery that love can be wilfully blind in respect of its object; I should have seen his weakness and let him be to sigh unsatisfied. His love was true; it was a crime in me to allow him my person without loving in return.

I had now to look to the cost of my household amd, having discovered that Robert was to be depended upon, I entrusted to him the selling of my coach and horses; I not wanting to be burdened with their charges, which had always fallen on Edward.

"If I might be allowed to say so, my Lady, is it not foolish to get rid of them in these times, when you may wish to have the means of leaving London easily to hand?"

"I have no intention of removing," I answered.

Even without Edward's help I was now in comfortable circumstances and, had I chosen to leave London and live modestly on my revenues I could have done so; but for this I had no appetite. I had no wish to be buried in some country place where even the pleasures of gaming would be lost to me. Moreover I knew too well the curiosity that my arrival would arouse, and that I would before long find myself both talked about and ignored, a target for every virtuous tongue. I

213

thought how one such as Lady Cobleigh would advantage herself at my expense; at once publicly condemning my life and satisfying her prurience.

Yet in London my life had become empty. I had loved Edward not at all, but I had liked him; I found I missed his company. Almost for the first time I was entirely on my own, with no loving companionship except for that of Joseph and Bess, who were in every way my inferiors. The gentlemen who came to gamble eyed my person with interest but for me as a fellow creature cared nothing.

In desperation, heedless of the pestilence daily gathering strength, I distracted myself in gaming. Up till this moment I had made sure of not cheating too often. Now I threw caution to the winds, careless of the future, thinking only to take all I could from a sex I held to be my enemies. Moreover, in a desire to feel some emotion were it only of fear, I increased the stakes I played for: on occasion laying my body against vast sums. Driven by the recklessness that comes to men and women alike when destruction lies on every hand, I allowed myself to lose to men I hoped might prove to me that I could yet be moved.

The first of these gentlemen, a handsome blade with dark curls that somewhat reminded me of Kit, after play was done and the company gone, took me on the daybed in my with-drawing room with no more ceremony that he might have used to relieve his bowels, leaving me with no sensation but of shame. The second, a ruddy man I had often taken money from, I allowed into the red bedchamber, hoping by this means to fare better. Thinking he was to have his night's lodging with me — of which I had no intention — he threw off his clothes; but then removed his wig, and when I saw his cropped poll all inclination fled.

"Madam," he said when he was done, "I think you hardly know your trade."

At which I slapped his face. "Perhaps, Sir," I answered, "you do not know yours."

I make no mention of those other men, for they passed like moths through my life, leaving no trace, and the memory of such idiot commerce still makes me blush. Wig or no wig, it was all one. My flesh turned against this false usage.

I craved for Kit. Why did he not return, that I might know myself a woman again? Had he so chosen he could have seduced me to rise from the grave.

The plague was now all about us and those who could, departed from the town. My customers were beginning to fall off, my servants to get restless at my not removing, and I could see they were afraid. But my resolve was unchanged. I buried myself even deeper in play.

One evening when there had been few at the tables, Mr Fuller remained behind.

"*Ma chère*," he said. "I advise you to be careful. One of these days someone is going to rumble you. I fancy Buckhurst is no longer deceived." He took my hand. "This pretty little hand is not suited to its trade. I am not a young man, but I can give you a home, in the country, safe from the pestilence. Give this wild life up and marry me. I will do my best to make you happy."

"I am honoured," I said, "indeed, touched. But you are too good and too kind a friend for me to cheat you so. You would be marrying an image not a woman, and that I would not wish on any man."

His kindness took me by surprise, and what I answered was the truth. For a moment I considered that he was old and I might soon be a widow; but I could not have stomached those spindle shanks between the sheets, even though my life were to depend on it.

"Think twice," he said. "I leave London in two days time."

I shook my head; for the first time since Kit left me, feeling tears rise.

Two days later wagons stood outside Somerset House: the Queen Mother was gone to France. Mr Fuller went to his country seat. The Court itself left town, and, after one miserable evening when only two came, my card tables stood idle. I could no longer ignore what was happening in the city, for there was nothing else to occupy my mind. By day the bell tolled almost without ceasing for those dead of the pestilence; at night, I found myself waking to listen for the plague cart creaking through the streets. Less than a week later the plague was in the Piazza itself. Two houses were shut up and red crosses painted on the doors; at which the last of my servants fled, of them all only Robert coming to me to say that he and Catherine intended to retreat to the country and there get wed. I gave them money to help them on their way, and thanked them for their services.

On a sudden how empty the house had become! I walked through the deserted rooms listening for some sound of life; pausing outside the great parlour, but thinking better of unlocking the door. The fire still burned on the kitchen hearth, as Catherine had left it.

I checked the stores in the larder as if preparing for a siege.

I had mounted again to my bedchamber, and was considering with Bess how, in our straitened circumstances, we were to arrange ourselves, when through the open window drifted the song of a woman crying lavender, her chant coming nearer all the while. As one, we stopped to listen.

"Who'll buy my sweet lavender?
Fourteen branches for one penny.
Who'll buy . . ."

Together we went to the window, and I knew we were thinking the same: it was the country come to London, a strange sight at such a time. The woman was already crossing the Piazza, and at once I was reminded of the gipsies, I knew not why, for I could see that she was not of their kind. I bade Bess stay where she was and ran down. It seemed to me that the town stank of fear, and I was overcome with longing for the clean smell of the herb.

The heat from the paving stones rose up in my face as I opened the door.

It was three o'clock in the afternoon of a burning day; the countenance I looked into was tired. These eyes were not black, but grey; a countrywoman's; her clothes, though old and travel-stained with dust, tidy and well kept. I stared in fascination at her basket. It was of osier, such as my mother used for picking flowers, and it was still half full, the bunches of lavender braided in and out with ribbon.

216

"I will take all," I said, and I put a guinea into her hand. Under their brown her cheeks reddened. "I have no change for so much money."

"Keep it," I said, "perhaps you have children."

"I have indeed, and that is what brought me here, for living is hard without a man. May God forever bless you, lady! — and sure the blessings of my own poor family will rest on your head. Now I can go back to them out of this pestilent town. I have been walking all day."

It was the first time anyone had blessed me since I last saw Nurse, almost three long years ago. I felt my heart stir.

Passionate desire for the countryside I had forfeited, no matter whether it were Bradstock, or even Marley, swept over me. London, so craved after, was like to prove my coffin.

Nonetheless I suffered all that came to me as if I had been a sleepwalker. I knew that my heart was moved, but I knew it from a distance. I knew I must dismiss Bess and that this would pain me.

I carried the lavender upstairs and stood the branches upright in a jar in my bedchamber, Bess protesting all the while that it should go among the linen. I watched myself performing like the actors on a stage.

"Yes, Bess, I know. But I wish to have the sight and smell of it about me. And, Bess, you are to leave me. Now, at once, while you can take a boat down the river by day." Her mouth fell open in dismay. "You should be in the country, finding yourself a husband, having babies, not waiting here in London to die of the plague. I can see from the way you mother Joseph that you need children."

"But my Lady, I could never stomach a man! Indeed I could not!"

"What nonsense! You don't know what you speak of."

"Well my Lady, I cannot do it. How could I leave you? After all you has done for me! Taking me when I knew no better how to be clean! Seeing to me with your own hands! Fastening my dress!" She began to cry. "And you said my hair shone like a lady's!" At which her sobs burst out unbridled, and plumping herself into a chair, she threw her apron over her head. I thought she would never stop.

217

At length, when she began to be a little quieter, I took the apron from her face.

"Bess, dear, it is with your mother in Woolwich you should be now. I have nowhere safe that I can take you, I will not have it on my conscience to keep you here longer. Joseph is in the same case as myself; we will sit this evil time out together."

She stared at me in disbelief. Then, reading in my looks that I meant what I said, cried afresh. I trembled for my resolution; for in truth I was fond of her and had no wish to part from her. At last, impatient to have done, I ordered her to go and pack.

Directly I was alone I took the coffer out of its hiding-place over the mantelpiece. The whole of my winnings from the last evening of play still lay there, for I wished to have money by me without the need to go into the City. I divided the coins in two, putting back half for my housekeeping and tipping the rest into a handkerchief for Bess.

I carried them to her bedchamber, to find her sitting on her bed, staring at the wall, her hands folded.

"To think of leaving all this!" she said, and I saw her eyes fill once more.

Hastily I poured the coins into her lap.

"This is to be for a dowry," I said. "It will get you a good man."

"Oh my Lady!" she exclaimed. "Oh, my Lady!"

The sight of so much gold and the idea of arriving home rich, effected a transformation. She began at once, though with sighs, to pack, showing a surprising prudence in hiding the coins about her person, only keeping in her purse what she would need for the journey.

When she was finished, she gave a last look round the room; then flung her arms round me and we embraced like sisters. I picked up her bundle and went with her downstairs, pushing her from me out of the door lest either of us should change her mind, and locking it behind her. When I dared look after her from the withdrawing-room window the Piazza was empty.

Where, I now wondered, was Joseph? I found him in his attic, perched crosslegged on his bed and laying out cards on the coverlet.

"Joseph," I said, "I would send you away to the country if I

218

thought you had anywhere to go, but I believe you have not. Bess and all the others are gone. We are alone, you and I, and must make out as we can."

His face beamed with smiles. "I heard them, they ran away. I never will."

The spread of cards on the bed was nothing I had seen before.

"Tell me, Joseph, what are you doing? 'Tis surely not practising gaming?"

"Mistress, I ask them questions."

Overcome by the conviction that Joseph had the gift, and clutching at straws, I asked eagerly, "What do they say?"

But he would not answer. Pretending I had not spoken, he swept the cards up and jumped from the bed.

"Now I am to look after you," he said.

Protest as I might, he insisted on taking over all the household duties; and indeed it was as well, for in these I had no skills. He occupied himself with the shopping, the cooking, and even with the fastening and unfastening of my gown. In the kitchen Joseph was master. I, my skirts tucked up, assisted him as best I could in washing dishes and sweeping floors. We were two innocents, keeping house together.

We lived in the present; I not speaking of my past life and he, though ready enough to chatter about the doings in my own kitchen, telling me nothing either of his travels or of his native Africa. Seldom can two human beings have been in such close company and yet known so little the one of the other.

To pass the time while waiting for I knew not what, I taught him all the card games that two can play; but without the cheating tricks, playing for stakes made from little bits of kindling wood and pieces of torn paper, as children do. Thus, when the day's work was done and the cloth spread and the candles lit in my bedchamber, I made for myself a make believe of gaming.

We had lived in this manner, from day to day, almost from minute to minute, when after a week's silence the front door bell rang.

CHAPTER SEVENTEEN

I reap as I have sown

At once my dreams rose up and assumed the shape of a wild fancy that this was Kit come to rescue me, and before I could stop to reason my heart began to race.

I ordered Joseph to see who was there.

He returned quickly up the stairs. Heavier footsteps followed, and hastily I swept our cards and our childish stakes out of sight under the bed.

"A gentleman. He wishes to play. I do not like him," said Joseph rapidly. "I smell that he intends wrong. I saw him in the cards but I would not tell you."

My visitor knocked on the bedchamber door.

"Come in," I said.

The man who presented himself to my gaze was somewhat heavily built, of middle age, wearing an auburn wig and well cut clothes, his linen fine. My eye was caught by the mourning ring on his finger. His face, not unhandsome, was grave but in no way evil. He cut a distinguished figure and I was sure I had never seen him before.

"I understand there is play here, Madam," he said. He looked round my bedchamber, his eyebrows raised.

"In these days there is little amusement to be had in town. Will you play tonight?"

How my spirits rose! "With pleasure, Sir, if you will forgive my receiving you so meanly. I have been obliged to close my withdrawing room; the pestilence has driven my servants away, or I would entertain you better. Joseph, if you please, fetch the cards."

But before Joseph could move: "Let us play with mine." He put his hand into his pocket.

"Provided they be new ones, Sir."

"A wise precaution." He laid two packs on the table that I might see for myself; they were quite new, the paper unbroken.

So confident had I become of my skill that I was content to forego my own marked pack and, all eagerness, set out my store of coins and sat down to the table. Joseph stationed himself behind my chair, like a footman in waiting.

"Will you cut the cards, Madam, since we play with mine?"

At which I was happy, for here was my first opening to cheat. Even as I began to deal I determined that in due course I would stake my person, for he was not unpleasing to me and I wished to wring from this surprise encounter all the pleasure and excitement that I could.

My opponent played in silence, losing heavily at first, and then beginning to win. As time went by I noticed his presence to be increasingly filling my bedchamber. A strange feeling came over me that he had been there before — though I knew he had not — that even my bed was familiar to him.

This idea distracted me into playing a wrong card, and to steady myself, I sent Joseph to the kitchen for coffee and sweetmeats.

Coffee done, all my coins stood in neat heaps before my adversary.

"They tell me you play for your person," he said.

To this I made no demur; but to my chagrin, in spite of my cheating, I once more lost.

"The evening is young, Madam. Will you continue?"

I nodded. Determined to repair my losses, I staked my savings with Mr Blanchard, sending Joseph for pen and ink, writing a paper and laying it triumphantly on the table.

The hazards of play went now for me, now against; little piles of coins, my written paper, passed to and fro across the table. A kind of madness seized me. The excitement that only gamblers know, the drug I had been so missing, whose fatal nature cannot be conveyed to those who have never tasted it, possessed me wholly. My vision closed in upon my adversary's expressionless face, the cards in my hand and those he placed for me to counter, as if all else had vanished. The stakes I played for, my own body, my savings in the bank, my goods at sea, in themselves had no value; they were but a means to my sole end, which was to win; on this my whole mind was bent, and every artifice, cheat or no, permissible. I was in the grip of those same evil forces which had driven more than one young man to ruin at my hands; galloping headlong from game to game, hoping at each deal to retrieve my fortunes; till at last even the contents of my household and the clothes on my back were gone: nothing remained but Joseph.

"We play for your boy?" by opponent asked. I heard Joseph from behind my chair draw in his breath; but I was too proud and, by now, too fevered with play to stop while a single chance remained to me. Once more I shuffled the cards.

When I lost I could not believe my eyes.

"You cheated!" I cried, "You could not have won else! The cards were marked!"

He looked at me with contempt.

"Cheat has but tricked cheat and I fancy, Madam, your cheating was the heavier." He threw his cards down on the table. "Now, out!"

"Sir," I said stiffly, "I beg you will make yourself plain."

"You will allow, Madam, as the keeper of a gaming house, that by your rules all you have is mine. Your body I do not want, you may take that and peddle it on the streets, where it belongs. Nor will I deprive you of the clothes you stand up in. The rest I will keep. So will you please away?"

Trembling in disbelief I said, "You may send men to take away my goods, but you cannot turn me from my own house."

At this for the first time he smiled; but it was a smile without mercy, vanishing to leave his face stony and unbending.

"It is no longer your house, Madam. You are mistaken. I have been your landlord now these past two weeks. I became its owner to give myself the pleasure of putting you out of doors."

I was cold to my very bowels at the prospect dawning in front of me. "What, you would do so *now*?" I faltered.

" 'Tis what I said."

"But where am I to go?"

"Where you please."

"Why, Sir? But why so inhuman? Why do you do this to

222

me? You send me to my death."

"Edward Roper was my son."

The look in his eyes was one I hope never to see again. He meant that I should die; though he did not choose it should be at his actual hands. His was a carefully engineered revenge, designed to this very end. He had achieved what he set out to do, and nothing I could say would move him.

My hand flew to Nurse's cross, but to my horror my neck was bare. I remembered with shame that the precious talisman still lay in the drawer by my bed, the chain left unmended.

I rose from the table, and brushing past Joseph, hurried to the drawer. The cross was there; I took it, with its chain, in my hand.

"My Lord," I said, "this one thing I would have with me. I think you can hardly deny me."

No muscle of his face changed. "I would not withhold that symbol from anyone, even from such a creature as yourself."

I turned to Joseph. "Goodbye, Joseph," I said. "And forgive me if you can."

The tears were running down his face.

"Don't snivel, boy." Lord Roper had not even risen from his chair. "You go to a better mistress; from a bad woman to a good one."

Alone, I walked down the stairs and out of the front door. It was two o'clock in the morning and the rain pouring down. For a moment I blazed with anger. I was the victim of a most unjust revenge for an imagined crime; a revenge cunningly devised by a man insane as a wounded bull, and all the more dangerous because so controlled. Whore and gamester he might think me, but I had not killed his son.

With no idea where I was to turn, I left the shelter of the arcade and stepped out. Before I had gone five yards I was soaked to the skin.

I was already exhausted; the emotions of the evening's play, the shock of my present plight, the lateness of the hour, had taken their toll. There was nothing in my head now but how to put one foot in front of the other. The night was extraordinarily hot, but the rain cold; I was soon chilled through and shivering, my wet clothes clinging to me and dragging round my legs. With no idea of my direction I wandered up and down through black streets and narrow alleys, my feet carrying me I knew not how down to the river; guessing its presence only by its evil smelling mud, so that I turned back in terror lest I fall into its filth.

The plague cart went by me, heaped with corpses, their limbs dangling. To see a lantern carried by a living human form for a moment raised me from despair. I wondered should I speak.

"Bring out your dead!"

At his dreadful shout I flattened myself against the wall, in panic once more, my teeth chattering as well with cold. Even as I strove to avoid the contagion I was feeling ill, and knew it was too late.

From a house nearby came the sound of loud lamentations. "I too am dying," I thought, "and none to know or lament my passing."

I stumbled on in the rain and darkness, for there was nothing else I could do. I was no longer cold but burning hot, my head in agony. I fancied the houses about me to be changing size, now swelling vast, now shrinking to nothing; I heard bursts of voices, but whether in my head or out I could not tell; however hard I strained my ears I could make nothing of what they said.

I was becoming lightheaded, so that it seemed to me I was stripped from my body. From outside I observed my feet moving with difficulty one in front of the other; till at last my legs gave way under me and I pitched forward to lie in a doorway, my head on the step.

On a sudden my wits cleared. I saw the rain-soaked street and my dreadful condition. I knew that I had the plague, and would be cast naked into a common grave. The Lord had visited me with retribution worse than any man could inflict. I asked myself, why? and answered as my mind began once more to leave me, that I had run from my husband to enjoy pleasure with Kit that was too great for any mortal woman: greater than the gods allow, too great for them to pardon. Prometheus stole fire from heaven. I stole from Venus, and now she punished me.

At no point did I think to blame myself.

I felt the water running cold between my shift and my skin, and as my wits slipped from me my last thought was a wicked one: a hope that Edward's father had caught the contagion from my breath.

CHAPTER EIGHTEEN

Francis

I opened my eyes to find myself perfectly clear in the head; in bed, but with no idea where I was.

I remembered the stone step and the rain pouring down.

How delicious the pillow was!

This must be the pest-house. I tried to raise myself to look about me, but could do no more than turn my head.

A female figure in a white apron was sitting at my side. I took her for one of the rough women who nursed the sick that they might rob their bodies.

I was content to lie and look at her white apron. By little and little it came to me that she was not rough. Her apron was too white; the gown beneath, of silk. The sheets I lay between were soft to my skin; and no pest-house bed was ever hung with tapestries such as curtained mine.

I coughed; I felt as if it would tear my chest apart. At once the woman rose.

She smiled at me:

"You have had a severe fever, my Lady," she said, "but the crisis is passed."

"Not the plague?" I asked in trepidation.

"No, but your chest is affected, and now you must let us nurse you."

She handed me a potion to drink, and having drunk, I sank back on the pillow and slept again, content to know that I was cared for.

When next I woke it was to feel my face and hands sponged. How gentle my nurse was! And how refreshing the warm water on my skin! My hands lay languid on the towel in front of me. I was surprised to find myself too weak to raise them. There was something wrong with them. I thought hard what it

226

could be. My cross was gone. Nurse's words came back to me: "Lose it, and who knows what depths of evil you will fall into."

"My cross!" and my voice was no more than a hoarse whisper.

She smiled again. " 'Tis at your neck, my Lady." She took my hand and closed my fingers round Nurse's sacred talisman. "The Master had the chain mended and we put the cross back where we knew it belonged. We thought you would never let go of it from your hand."

Before I knew it I was crying.

"Come, come, you must not agitate yourself. 'Tis sufficient you should rest and take nourishment."

She cleared the towel and basin away, and I was now able to observe that she was indeed no common servant who attended upon me, but one of some authority; greyhaired but upright, spare in build, wearing a cap, but no wedding ring. She left the room to return with a tray and, sitting once more by my side, fed me with broth.

When I was done, "Where am I?" I asked. "How did I come here? What manner of man is your master that he would risk taking the plague into his house?"

She took the tray from the room and composed herself in her chair before speaking.

"These are the town lodgings of Sir Francis Page. His man found you on the step at dawn and called the Master to you."

I was overcome with gratitude that I should have been so preserved.

"He would not have let a dog lie there in the condition you was in. Nor does he fear the plague for himself, indeed he has waited in town a-purpose to do what he could for its victims, in the setting up of a pest-house at Spitalfields."

"And yourself," I asked, "who are so good to me?"

"His housekeeper, my Lady. Now I would have you rest; you have talked for long enough for the present."

So I slept and woke and slept again, to wake at last and ask what had happened to my clothes, for now I could recognise that it was not my own shift in which I lay.

My nurse laid her hand on mine. "My Lady, you must not

227

distress yourself, but we was obliged to destroy them, for you had fallen in who knows what filth and infection."

I wondered that I cared so little for their loss. In the matter of possessions I was as naked as the day I was born; naked in mind too, for with my possessions I had shed the life that went with them, and in this comfort I rested.

No doctor came near me, but with such good nursing as I received, my chest treated with herbal remedies, my appetite tempted by delicious foods, I soon found my cough begin to abate. Life flowed slowly back into my veins; yet I had no desire to move from my bed. I lay, without thought for past or future, content to exist in the knowledge I was alive.

As my mind revived I began to grow curious as to my host, and my nurse, whose name I now understood to be Mrs Finch, beguiled the time by singing his praises, little by little, that I might not get tired. I learnt that he was the last of a long line of country gentlemen, with a seat and lands in Sussex; that he had travelled widely, that he was the perfect master but, to the distress of his sister, who was all his family, still unmarried.

"Today," she concluded, "I have told him he may visit you." And when a knock came at the door, "There! This will be Sir Francis himself!"

She propped me up on pillows as the door opened.

Now at last my eyes rested on my benefactor, standing at my bedside. He was neither tall nor short, his hair neither fair nor dark, his eyes somewhat of blue, somewhat of grey; neither plain nor handsome; an altogether middling man to look at, and yet distinguished, perhaps by an air of intelligence and compassion, so that once having been seen he could never have been mistaken.

I guessed him to be older than Kit, but younger than Sir Gilbert, and it was with an odd sensation of relief that I saw he wore his own hair. The gaze he levelled on me was kind but dispassionate, full of interest but asking nothing of me. He impressed me as being so much at ease that he distilled peace about him.

"I am glad to see you better, Lady Fearnshawe," he said.

On being addressed thus I gasped.

"Please don't distress yourself. I know who you are and

what has happened to you and must apologise for the inhumanity of my sex. I will do my best to make amends for us."

I was shaking under the bedclothes. "How do you know who I am?"

"You talked in your delirium. But don't be agitated, nothing you said will go beyond Hannah and myself. Who is this Joseph about whom you were so troubled? I will enquire after him."

I closed my eyes, for the tears began to trickle and I too weak to stop them. In my horror at how I had betrayed Joseph, using a fellow-creature as coin, I groaned aloud.

"He was my blackamoor," I managed to whisper at last. In that instant I vowed I would never touch a card again. And that vow I have kept.

"My Lady has had enough, Sir Francis, and should sleep."

"We had better do as Hannah tells us. As a nurse she hasn't her equal." He smiled on me and withdrew.

My body grew calm once more and I drifted into sleep, comforted by the astounding certainty that I was known yet not cast out, and had no cause to be afraid.

I looked forward with impatience to my host's next visit. Nor had I long to wait, for the following afternoon he came to me again. He asked at once how I did, and then said:

"I have good news for you. You need have no concern for your little black boy. He has gone to the country to wait on Lady Roper — a virtuous woman with the reputation of keeping her servants. I fancy he will be well cared for."

Here I sighed, both in relief for Joseph's well-being and in sorrow at losing him.

"You tangled with the wrong cub," Sir Francis added, and I perceived with surprise that there was no condemnation in his voice; indeed, he smiled. "Lord Roper was a doting father, he could not admit of any imperfection in his child. Myself, I have no use for such men: neither father nor son."

He turned to my nurse. "Hannah, how soon will you allow Lady Fearnshawe to travel? My business here is done and I wish to remove us all to the country at the first opportunity."

"She makes very good progress, if the journey is taken in

229

easy stages there is no reason why she should not be moved. Country air will do her good."

"Then we can leave for Morbury the day after tomorrow?"

At the thought of movement I began to tremble. In my extremity the sickroom had become a refuge that shut out the rest of the world. The pest-ridden streets, London itself, what was to become of me, were all unreal. In my distress the colour flooded into my cheeks.

"But Sir," I protested before Hannah could speak, "I have no clothes to wear and nothing with which to buy new."

My host smiled. "If I am to be forgiven for my sex, you must let me provide and finish what I have begun."

"She should wait till we reach Morbury to be outfitted afresh," Hannah said firmly. "The country tailor will be uncontaminated by the plague."

I could only comply.

As I was carried out of the house, still in my nightgown and wrapped in blankets, I shook with dread. But once settled against the pillows in the company of Hannah and her familiar impedimenta I could accept that I was safe enough, and that in coming out of my sickroom into the coach, had taken my first step toward good health. When we rolled over London Bridge and on uphill till at last the air blew fresh through the coach window, I felt my first timid pleasure, for what lay ahead must be better than what lay behind.

The coach, as even in my fear I had taken note, was drawn by four handsome bays, and we were unencumbered by all but personal luggage, since the household effects and the servants followed by wagon. Sir Francis himself accompanied us on horseback. As we journeyed Hannah explained to me that he did not care to be away from the country for long, seldom going to London except to attend the meetings of the new Royal Society, of which he was a fellow. He could, she intimated, well afford to leave everything at Morbury in the hands of his steward, Mr Bradley, who had been steward in his father's day. But it had long been the custom for the Master to oversee the harvest, and it was one that Sir Francis liked to keep.

That Sir Francis was a fellow of the Royal Society and so must know not only the King, but all the virtuosi of the age, occupied my mind for some miles in wondering at my good fortune at being rescued by such a man.

It came as a shock when towards midday, leaning from his saddle to speak through the coach window, he announced that we were coming into Dorking and were to spend the night here with his sister.

"Poor woman, she has no idea yet that she is to expect us, so I am riding on ahead."

I was at once frightened, for I had grown to feel quite safe in the coach and must now get out of it and, worse, must encounter strangers. I watched in disquiet as Hannah began to pack up her hamper.

After five minutes he returned. "Elizabeth says she has been waiting for me this last week." Perhaps he saw my agitation, for he hastened to reassure me. "We go to a clerical household; but don't be alarmed; my brother-in-law is a worldly parson, given to chasing the fox; nonetheless well thought of. My sister is on the way to becoming a bishop's wife: I find it hard to see her in the part."

He had only succeeded in making matters worse. For now the fancy took me that because our host was in holy orders he would have a special power to see my shame.

The coach was turning on to gravel, and from my pillows I glimpsed tall wrought iron gates and through them, yew trees and a black and white house in the style of Nuttley. And now I was in added confusion at the thought of appearing in such company without luggage of my own, dressed in a borrowed nightgown and wrapped in blankets. I wished I could sink through the floor of the coach and into the ground and never be seen again. I closed my eyes, feigning even greater fatigue than was in truth the case.

It was in this state that I heard the friendliest voice in the world, and at that, a female of my own age, exclaiming, "Welcome, Lady Fearnshawe. My dear, you must be exhausted."

Somewhat sheepishly, I smiled. My hostess's face was merry, her eyes dancing with interest. In relief, I reflected that

231

with such a wife her husband could not be too holy. She herself directed my removal from the coach, walking beside me into the hall.

"I will not stop to talk now," she said, "or Hannah will scold me, that I know." I wondered that she dared tease Hannah, but saw that it gave pleasure. "I will visit you when you are comfortable in bed. I have put Lady Fearnshawe in the blue bedchamber, Hannah, and yourself in the green beside her," and I was carried upstairs.

I came out of a deep sleep to see my bedchamber door opening and my hostess tiptoe in.

"Ah! So you are awake," she said. "I trust dinner was to your liking and that you find yourself restored." She came to my bedside. "Indeed, you look less pale already. I see you are to be a monument to my brother's skill in herbs."

She began to move about the room, going at last to the window. "I trust the boys haven't disturbed you."

"I don't know when I have slept so sound," I said, "or found myself so comfortable," and here I sighed, for the low window and the smell of mignonette drifting in upon me, the green treetops I could see beyond, reminded me of Bradstock. "I am indeed grateful for all the kindness Sir Francis and yourself have shown me."

"Francis is only too pleased to have a victim to practise upon. Our mother came from Wales and was learned in the healing arts. As a female, it was for me to take after her, but it is Francis who has inherited her love of medicine. The doctors do not care for him for he will not be bled. I warrant he allowed none near you."

"No," and I had wondered why before. "No indeed, I saw none."

" 'Tis always a treat for us to see Francis, and today 'tis an added pleasure that he should bring me a female acquaintance of my own age. Nor do I intend to allow him to carry you off too soon. He wished to make for Morbury tomorrow, but I say you must rest three nights at least. I say, too, that you must have somewhat to wear more to your taste to travel in. Indeed, I think nothing of Francis's ideas, nor Hannah's neither, on this matter."

232

As she chattered she was measuring me with her eyes where I lay in bed.

"We are of a height, I would say; I am a trifle stouter, but with three boys, what would you expect? And you having suffered so! My waiting-woman is a splendid hand with a needle, we can manage something, I'm convinced. I'm red and you are brown," and in truth her hair was pure copper in hue, "but blue is kind to us both. I have one such to spare. Now do hurry up and grow strong so that we can play gowns."

How is it that two persons can know so swiftly that they are of one mind? So much at home was I in her company that I can fancy Elizabeth my sister; in her I recognised my mental twin. I stared speechless, lost in wonder, and then, both at once, we laughed.

That night Hannah saw to me herself, attending to all my wants and at last brushing my hair.

"You should not be doing this for me," I said. "If I am well enough to travel any little maid could see to me."

"You are in my charge, my Lady. You are to be good and do as I bid."

"I am not good, Hannah," I said wistfully, forgetting for the first time to call her Mrs Finch.

At this she drew herself up. "What nonsense you talk! You are goodness itself. You have been a very sick young woman, yet never a word of complaint have I heard from you."

I sighed, for that had not been my meaning. But before I could speak again:

"I know a good heart when I find one," and the matter was closed.

How secure she made me feel!

I was to learn later that she had been my ally from the first, piecing together all my history and, having strong feelings as to a parent's duties, laid the blame for my misfortunes and misdeeds firmly at my father's door.

At Dorking, for the first time in my life since leaving Bradstock I felt myself to be among my own kind, and they my friends; it was as if I had come out of the darkness into sunlight. The past fell away from me like the skin a dragonfly sheds when it crawls from the water and takes to the air for the first time. I let myself forget I had ever been bad. Lighthearted, content to let time drift, I lay in bed washed clean of sin as a new-born babe.

We set out on our travels four days later. I already felt restored in the mere fact of being once more properly dressed. Nonetheless I grew tired, for the roads were all the way bad, and our journeying slow.

It was early afternoon when the coach turned in at the gates of Morbury House. Ahead of us, as far as I could see, a gravel drive wound gently uphill among oak trees scattered here and there in parkland where fallow deer were grazing. Their spotted coats in the dappled shade took me back to my Forest childhood.

As the coach rolled on I called out to Sir Francis in amazement: "How long is this drive? It would seem a mile."

"From lodge to house is a mile and a furlong exact." There was no boasting in his voice and I could not but think what my late husband would have made of such a feature.

Now at last, at the top of a rise, Morbury House itself came into view. I had thought to see a building in the manner of Marley. But what a difference was here! The house, set about by trees, was twice the size, the stone mature. Two turrets, one at each end, flanked the long south front, which was pierced to the left of the doorway by tall mullioned windows. I gasped aloud in pleasure.

"Welcome home," Sir Francis said.

So busy were my eyes and such was my excitement that his meaning went over my head.

"When you are well again you shall see my improvements; I am building in the stable courtyard."

Mr Bradley himself, and two menservants in white stockings and scarlet and black livery, the identical colours of the coach, were waiting in readiness on the steps. I was lifted from my pillows to a carrying chair and in this manner entered a magnificent hall, its furnishings softened by time and living, the whole blazing with light from windows I now saw to be three times the height of a man and reaching from the ceiling almost to the floor.

Here Sir Francis took his leave, holding aside the tapestry

curtain before an archway through which we were to pass. Escorted by Hannah, I was carried up shallow stairs to a bedchamber where a maidservant was in waiting and the bed turned back.

"Sir Francis wished you to have this room. It was Mrs Elizabeth's favourite. It opens into a cabinet in the turret where there are fine views over the garden. There you may be private. And this is Emily, who is to attend upon you." Emily dropped a curtsey. "She is well acquainted with her duties."

Never had I been housed in such grandeur; not the false kind so dear to Sir Gilbert, but that comfortable grandeur that arises from noble proportions and elegant hangings, fine carpets and embroideries, the chairs and chest all good. Two needlework pictures took my eye even in my tired state; the spotted leopards walking with lambs, and all of a size, filled me with delight.

As Hannah disposed her potions about the room where she thought fit, it was plain to see from Emily's bearing what a great personage it was who nursed me.

I was compelled to rest in bed all the next day, though in a fever of impatience to explore my surroundings. But how quickly youth mends when eager to begin life afresh! Before long I was able to come downstairs on Hannah's arm and was then made free of all about me.

Summer moved slowly into autumn; and I all the while in a haze as golden as the year, living in the present moment, with no thought of what was to become of me.

Now, in late October, I had quite regained my strength. One bright day, suddenly thick hoar frost lay on the grass; the air was chill and I took my morning walk in the long gallery. I was running my fingers along the blond oak panelling, thinking how much I loved this house, when my eyes fell on Sir Francis's gloves. They were lying on an Italian chest, the front carved and painted with an ill-made Venus riding on her scallop-shell, which he had acquired on his travels. He had taken them off that he might lift the lid to show me the fine key which he kept inside, and which was the work of a master.

I measured my hand palm to palm against a glove. The hand that wore it was much bigger than mine, and what a good hand!

How, in fondness, the clothes speak of their owner!

As I touched the leather that held the imprint of his fingers I blushed, and was flooded with passion. I had rested on his strength as a nurseling on its nurse; but now I was all female. Love and desire had risen within me unbeknownst, like the Venus rising from the sea. In the false innocence of sickness I had been taken unawares.

I recoiled from the knowledge, my pulse racing. I had not wished ever to have to feel again. I had wanted no more of the joy and agony of knowing my heart, my very life, bound to another. Now I was trapped. I had thought love only came at sight, as I had known it with Kit, and so I had been deceived: this time it had crept up on me by little and little, and all the more fatal for being of the mind first.

I held the glove against my cheek. Then I trembled, for the man I loved was out of my reach.

I began an agitated walking up and down. One after another, in vivid pictures, I relived the stages of my downfall.

I saw myself coming downstairs for the first time unaccompanied and finding my way to the great parlour, where, to my joy, I discovered a spinet. I had lifted the lid to try the notes and as they sounded, added my voice to theirs. It was the songs from my mother's songbook that I sang; not the lovesongs I had learnt with Kit.

Sir Francis had entered silently, and when I became aware of him standing behind me I at once took my fingers from the keys. He put his hands on my shoulders. "Go on," he said, "you have a sweet voice." But it had been a friend's or a brother's touch, not a lover's.

I saw long mornings spent in the library and Sir Francis teaching me to play chess; at which I learnt fast. I watched his hand move across the board to take my queen: "You are done for, I fancy," he said in satisfaction.

In that same library, under his guidance, I had rediscovered my delight in the Latin tongue. I saw us at the table, our heads together over a text.

"You are a better scholar than Elizabeth. Poor girl, she has no patience."

I saw him escort me for my first walk across the park; to view the quarry whence the stone had come for his new building.

"Take care, for the sides are sheer." He held me back when I would have leant to look over.

I wondered now how it was that I had felt no tremor at his touch.

So near was I to loving him that it had been easy for him to get from me all the story of my marriage and of my life with Kit; understanding my wilder self though he had no kinship with it. He would never have stolen me from my husband, or killed a man, or galloped through the night to an uncertain future; but nor would he lightly have accepted the last favours from a woman, or had he done so, have abandoned her; and that I could put myself in such straits he deplored.

At this, my past life, which I had so conveniently hidden away, came surging back, and my steps grew faster.

My wickedness rose up to mock me. I saw the young men I had ruined at cards. I thought of the men I had lain with for gain; worse than a whore, for I gave them nothing and had no honest need. I saw Edward, lying dead, his head a mess of blood; and myself, filthy in the gutter to which my sins had driven me. I was not fit to be any man's wife.

And what of Sir Francis? For so I must call him, since he had never addressed me as other than Lady Fearnshawe.

I searched my memory for any sign of tenderness towards me, but could find none. I had never seen in his eyes the affection I now longed for, nor even the open desire which in other men I had learnt to recognise so easily. I was no more than an object of his benevolence, to be pitied and cared for in kindness, a stray; and now that I was recovered, what did he intend?

The blackness of no hope out of which I had crawled when rescued from the gutter, wrapped round me once more. I saw no future. I loved Sir Francis so that I could not live without him. But he did not love me. Penniless, outcast, barren, I could never be the wife of such a man. Must I peddle my body in the streets as Lord Roper had decreed?

I saw then what I must do and where I must go. I dropped the glove and I ran.

I was eager to make an end while my courage held.

I stood on the brink of the quarry. I heard the wings of the angel of death, and I was afraid. Never in my life have they come so close.

An evil spirit whispered to me that this was the home for which I had been destined, on these stones below I could rest. In that moment of madness, what unseen presence stayed my feet?

The strange sound of my thudding heart distracted me. I found myself counting the beats. They made no sense, they were too loud; they grew louder, drumming as no heart ever could. While I still wondered, gazing down, I was held firm round the waist and snatched back, my feet dragging. Francis's arms were round me and his voice shook with terror as he called my name. He was covering my face with kisses.

I burst into tears, with my head on his chest, unable to stop, nor wanting to.

"Sarah, my love, what were you doing? What possessed you?"

But I could not speak. The horror of what I had so nearly done was still upon me.

"Speak, Sarah, I order you to explain."

I stifled my sobs enough to whisper, "I thought you could not love me."

He groaned. "Not love you?" and his voice broke. "I loved you too much to dare breathe a word. I was afraid."

"Afraid, Francis? Of what?"

"I feared you thought so ill of men that if I behaved to you as a man you would hate me."

I let out a sigh from my very heart.

"I had to be sure you would not run away if I asked you to be my wife. What a fool I have been! I ought to have seen you might misread me. I gave you no chance. Sarah, will you ever forgive me?"

"How could I not?"

He put me a little from him that he might see my face. "But Sarah, my angel! Why did you imagine that I brought you here to keep you by me, if not that you were dear to me?"

"From goodness. Francis, I cannot marry you." Though in my guilt I must refuse him, what joy it was to speak his name!

"Not marry me? Why?"

I could not meet his eyes. "Francis," and my voice failed me.

"Yes, Sarah?"

I could not hide what I had been, and yet, even to Francis who knew so much of my history, I could not call myself a whore. I put it otherwise. "I have led a wicked life. I am not fit."

In perplexity he protested, "Do you tell me you have a disease?"

At which I exclaimed in horror, denying hotly.

"Well, then! I won't have you making us both wretched; it is the Sarah of today I wish to marry, not her of yesterday. Do you not suppose there have been other women in my life? They are past and I am not going to tell you of them; nor do I wish to know of the men you have loved — or hated!" and now he smiled.

My resolution began to crumble. But I could not cheat him; again my voice sank, "I doubt I can ever bear you a child. I fear that I am barren."

"What is an heir? I have nephews a-plenty. I will admit to some relief there is no bastard to be rescued." It was the nearest he ever came to a reproach. "My charity would hardly run to welcoming Selby's get into my house, for I fancy you would be too fond for my comfort."

To this I said nothing, for I could not lie to him.

"I will allow, too, that I have some jealousy on account of that man, for I fear you will never forget him."

And this also, I could not answer.

"Well, Sarah, is it to be yes or no?"

"Yes," I said simply; and at last I could look him full in the face and smile.

All this while his horse had been cropping the grass.

"How did you come upon me when you did?" I now thought to ask.

"I had gone to the town to confer on business with my brother magistrates, and I had just entered the park on my return when I saw you in the distance. I did not like the way you ran." He held me very tight. "Now let us forget it."

In spite of his embrace I shivered. I was at last feeling the sharp air, for I had no cloak; moreover, though happy beyond belief, I was cold from shock.

He reproached himself bitterly, "My child, I don't know how to look after you." He tore off his riding coat and forced me to push my arms through the sleeves.

"I have not won you only to lose you to another illness," he said, wrapping the garment round me and turning up the collar. He searched for my hand in the dangling sleeve and held it fast in his, while with ihs other he led his horse. And so we walked back to the house.

Now Francis showed me every attention and at this my agitation grew. That morning I had been half out of my mind at reading no desire in his eyes; but now, as the day passed, I saw too much. All my experience told me that he would come to my bedchamber that night. I was in blind panic: I feared that my body, which had since Edward's death been left unstirred, would now refuse me the ultimate pleasure, and Francis satisfaction. Outside the marriage bond I dared not put it to the trial, lest he or I should go to the altar wretched.

As that night Emily made me ready for bed, I saw from her admiring looks that I was *en beauté*. How fast my heart beat! What was I to do?

Francis did indeed come to my bedchamber and in his dressing-gown.

Sitting up, "Francis," I said hurriedly, "you may kiss me, but you are not to come to me till we are man and wife."

At which he sat down abruptly on the bed.

"Sarah! I fail to understand you. You give yourself outside wedlock to a man who means you no good, but me, whom you say you love, who love you in return and intend to wed you, you refuse. 'Tis past belief."

Tenderly he began to lay siege to me; and at his kissing me I knew my danger, for indeed he possessed all the arts and meant to have his way. Before I could melt I pushed him from me, but I could not explain; I could not bring myself to tell him what my fear was, or that I needed the security of wedlock in which to face it.

"Francis," I said, "I beg of you, if you care for me, humour me in this. 'Tis not in lack of love that I ask you."

240

In a huff he got from my bed. "Then there is only one thing to do about it. That is to get wed tomorrow. I had thought to wait until Elizabeth could be at Morbury; but you must make do with Hannah." He pulled the ring from my thumb. "And I will have this. Since you are to come to me virginal."

I saw his condition plain: indeed, I was roused myself. But I could not relent, and he left me without so much as bidding me goodnight. Never before had I seen him in anger.

That he should be so moved by his passion stirred my heart.

But when he left me I could not lie still. My heart spoke to me as if it had woken from a long sleep, demanding to be heard, so that I was driven to rise from my bed and take refuge in my turret room. The embers of the fire still burned on the hearth; I sat at the window staring out over the dark garden. There was no moon, but the sky was brilliant with a million stars; here, looking on such immensity, I could listen.

Only by God's mercy was I alive. But for His intervention I would not tomorrow be a happy wife, but lying in my coffin. As I gazed at the heavens, I understood that I was answerable to Him for my life.

I saw how time after time, for the wrong reasons, I had wilfully taken the wrong turning and brought ruin on my own head. From the moment I chose to be "My Lady" to the moment when I stood on the edge of the quarry, I had been at fault. My blood ran cold as it came home to me how lightly I had dared fate; gambling with my very life, running headlong on destruction heedless of virtue, or indeed sense: I had had no need to play with Lord Roper; had I but had the courage to consider virtuous employment I would have discovered Francis loved me. That I could have done these things still frightened me for the future. How I needed his protection from myself!

Twice Francis's timely action had preserved me from death. To what end? Not that I should burden him with my remorse. Nor yet that I should forget.

Another woman might have been driven to take the veil and so purge her soul, but for me this would have been as self-destructive as to throw myself from the cliff. Nor could I confess to a priest; for priests, though useful for their simple

241

duties, are but ordinary men, too many of them without calling and having an eye only to their tithes.

I must acknowledge my sins to my Maker. I went on my knees and prayed to God to forgive me. But even as I did so, I knew that for this to happen, I must first forgive myself.

It has taken long years to achieve.

Before I was dressed the next morning Hannah came to me and said, "I hear we are to congratulate you, my Lady. I am deeply touched that I am to be allowed to accompany you to the church this afternoon."

I wondered that Francis had told me nothing of the arrangements he had made, nor yet been to see me. But in truth he had had good reason to mistrust my resolution.

I said, "Oh Hannah! I am glad it is to be you with me. And I am further glad that you are here to continue the management of this great house, for I fear it would take long years for me to see my way round it."

"What nonsense, my Lady! But 'tis not fit you should. Sir Francis would not be suited by a maker of jams, nor yet an earnest housewife jealous of her pretensions. If I may say so, he needs a spirited young wife, and one who will be a companion in his interests."

"Hannah," I said, "it is very comfortable that you are my friend."

Francis did not make his appearance until dinner, by which time I had begun to fear every imaginable disaster. In his absence I found it hard to believe in my good fortune, and that at some moment it would not be snatched from me. He sat down still in his riding clothes, offering no explanation, but laughing.

"Where have you been and what have you been doing?" I asked hotly.

He only teased. "Madam, you will soon see," and with that I had to be content.

The very lack of ceremony made the proceedings impossible to credit. I had no bridesmaids to dress me for my wedding, I walked to church in my everyday gown and Francis no finer, our only attendants Hannah and Mr Bradley. As we crossed the park I had a vision of my yesterday's self, flying in the opposite direction across this same park in certainty of death, terrified nonetheless. Now, here I was, walking towards a new life in equal certainty, yet trembling also, for the prospect of great happiness fills the human heart with awe. I held tight to Francis's arm, and knowing my trouble, he placed his hand on mine. It came over me suddenly that he was as masterful as Sir Gilbert, only kind instead of cruel, and that once more I was to be obliged to do as I was bid. It has proved no great penance.

When I stood at his side and our hands were joined by the priest, I meant every word I spoke at his bidding. When Francis put his ring upon my thumb — and now I knew what he had been at all morning — I began to believe what was happening to me. But as we knelt at the alter my prayers were by no means the holy ones enjoined on my by the priest; my prayer was only that my wedding night might go as I wished.

"Those whom God hath joined let no man put asunder."

I was hearing the words for the second time in my life. I wondered now, had I the first time, with my mind all on garters, heard them at all?

We stepped out of the porch into sunshine.

"Happy the bride the sun shines on," the parson said, and I could not help but dislike the unction in his voice. But I was indeed overcome with joy as Francis kissed me and called me wife.

We returned to find the household assembled in the hall to wish us happiness. Francis presented me to them as their mistress, and then I thanked them.

"There will be no changes," I said, "for Mrs Finch will be beside me to manage everything as before."

They were to have a grand supper that they might celebrate, but at Francis's orders, no stockings were to be thrown, and we took our own supper quietly together in the dining-room before going unattended upstairs.

I was to sleep from now on in the bedchamber where the ladies of the house had lain since it was new built. It is a gracious room, with two windows looking south over the park, wainscoted, with blue silk damask hangings and a tapestry of Daphnis and Chloe in a country scene, all in pinks and blues. Yet, happy as I was, while Emily was making me ready for bed my tremors returned.

When Francis entered in his dressing-gown and pulled his nightshirt over his head and dropped it on the floor, I had a last moment of terror. But once in his arms my body came to life, and I knew pleasure such as I had forgotten possible. I laughed and wept, both at once.

"Sarah," he said, "what is it?"

And now I was able to explain.

"My poor love! I could have saved you your distress."

Our kissing began again. Love and passion went hand in hand, and after we were done we lay the both of us amazed. Before we slept he said: " 'Tis as well I have you safe to wife and you can run into no more follies."

How strange to wake and find my head lying in the crook of an arm that was not Kit's! Raising myself softly I saw to my surprise that it was freckled. This sleeping man was all new to me; this hair, neither fair nor dark, tangled on the pillow, this face even in sleep marked by the lines of experience. I gazed in fond ownership.

Now I had a great curiosity as to his legs, for the night before I had had no leisure to observe anything. They proved to be well enough; as in my happy state I was able to see when he got from bed. My husband's was a strong body and altogether pleasing, well knit, so that when he was in his clothes his strength remained hid. My eyes followed him in desire as he moved. When, in his dressing-gown, he kissed me, I wished him back beside me.

Emily, a gentle, brown girl, had always hitherto been sweet and respectful, but this morning there was a new deference in her manner, as if conscious that she was waiting on the lady of the house and I, by lying with Francis as his wife, altogether changed. So indeed I was. Now in security and happiness I felt myself once more begin to blossom.

I took an age debating this way and that what I should wear to go down to breakfast; deciding at last on my dressing-gown, for Francis had never seen me thus and I knew that it became me particularly. Besides, since I was his wife, it was correct.

We had breakfasted together every morning since I was well

enough to come downstairs. I was now to meet him anew in all the pleasant confusion lying with a man can bring. As we sat opposite each other at table, partaking of chocolate and fresh white bread, I was conscious all the time of his nakedness under his clothes, and my own newborn wish to be alluring, so that I hardly dared raise my eyes to his face.

When we were done breakfast Francis gave me back my old ring, setting it before me on the table.

"The ring is yours and I would not take it from you." Then lifting my hand and studying his own ring on my thumb, "But though your thumb would hold them both, I would rather you did not wear it."

I left the ring where it lay before me, and letting my hand lie in his, smiled on him, and he smiled back.

But I couldn't throw that ring away, for Kit had said he stole it from Sir Gilbert and to me it was Kit's ring. When I went upstairs to dress I took it with me and shutting it into a comfit box, put it away in a drawer I discovered in the cabinet in my new bedchamber; reflecting naughtily as I did so that I was now the wife of a better man than he who gave it me, and himself wedded to a shrew.

Now that I was in fortunate circumstances I was in hopes that I might make my peace with my parents, and in truth I wished to show off my happiness. I begged Francis to take me to Bradstock. But this he refused to do, saying that at this time of year it was not suitable for me to travel. He would go himself. "I wish to see your Bradstock," he said, "and before taking you there, need to satisfy myself that you will be properly received."

At once I was concerned as to his own travelling; but he assured me that he would manage very well, he had friends all over England at whose houses he could put up, and he would take his man.

He was gone a whole fortnight and never in my life has time passed so slowly. I sat in the library in an attempt to distract myself with reading; but my mind was absent, following every mile of his way, fretting lest the Severn flooded or the Forest was already deep in snow. I watched the weather and held my breath as day after day it remained mild.

I sensed his return long before I heard horses' hooves on the gravel outside. I was waiting for him in the hall and threw myself into his arms.

"Francis!" I said when his kissing was done. "Never go away from me again."

Without even taking off his boots he led me into the Great Parlour, and now I saw from his manner that he brought bad news. Taking me by the hand he told me that my father was dead, the ironmaster in possession of Bradstock already, and my mother removed in permanence to Nuttley.

"I rode over to offer her a home here, but she refused to see me, sending word that she had no daughter."

"She blames me!" I cried. "And with some justice," and I burst into tears; not the comforting tears of sorrow, but an uncomfortable mixture of rage and hurt.

He put an arm round me. "You must allow for other's faults, Sarah," he said gently. "For my part I am grateful that we are to be by ourselves.

"Your old friend Oliver is a very polite young man. He was full of apologies for her and we shook hands very amicable at parting."

"But Nurse!" I lifted my head from his shoulder, "What of Nurse?"

"She has gone to her rest."

My tears flowed again, in grief.

"Don't cry so, Sarah. Her end was peaceful. She was at Nuttley and well cared for, and I'm told that when she died, which was but ten days before, she was smiling."

Nonetheless I wept because I could not kiss her once more and tell her that I had seen evil as she foretold, but that I wore her cross and by its intervention had been preserved.

But Francis would have no more of regrets: "Now Sarah, you must put the past behind you; and I must take off my boots."

And so I dried my eyes; filled with remorse that on my account he was tired.

But I could not lose my sorrow all at once. That evening I gave myself up to our joy together; but next morning, when Francis rode out to see the men, my sadness returned.

I had taken up again my Marley habit of visiting my house-keeper's room every morning after breakfast, though I was on terms with Hannah altogether different from those I had sustained with Mrs Willis; for during my sickness Hannah had become more of a mother to me than my mother.

On a sudden, as we sat together to decide what Francis would fancy for supper, I poured out to her all he had told me the night before.

"And yet indeed it is not my mother's unkindness that I grieve for, Hannah, it is Nurse."

Hannah put her hand on my knee. "She gave you her cross. You have told me before, my Lady, that she saw the future. If she died happy, it is because she knows you safe."

At which my troubles left me.

"How strange fate is, Hannah," I continued as soon as we had settled the question of supper. "Once I mourned Bradstock and reproached myself with thinking that if only I had been good I might have married Oliver. But now I tremble to think that in that event I would not be married to Francis. In truth, though Oliver was a good enough companion in my tender years, I see now that I did not love him. And how could I have endured life at Nuttley, with those two mothers prattling to each other and all the time watching my belly?"

"No, indeed!"

Now that Francis was returned we were to have visitors. I had been longing to see Elizabeth again and at last, two days later, she was to come to us with her husband and all her family. Standing beside Francis I waited for them in the Great Hall, whose walls were hung with the portraits of his ancestors, of whom he was taking no notice; fleetingly, I could not but think of Sir Gilbert and his pride in the new solitary likeness of himself.

We had been forewarned by an outrider; now the coach arrived and the hall door burst open, and while Francis and his brother-in-law greeted each other and the little boys, escaping from their nurse, ran like beads about the floor, Elizabeth and I embraced.

"Sarah, how matrimony becomes you!"

She put me from her to look the better. "I so wanted to see

247

you before winter set in and the men could pretend the roads were too bad, there is so much to tell."

How overjoyed I was! — knowing I had been right, and that we were to be friends, indeed for life.

Converse all that day was general and Elizabeth and I could have no word alone. But the following morning was fine and we walked together in the park, the boys running on ahead, playing at catching the falling leaves, shouting to each other.

"I am so glad, dear sister," she said, as their voices rose, "that you are of our family. It is a great solace to me. I have so long wished to see Francis happy. He confessed to me when you stopped with us at Dorking that he had loved you from the day he took you into his house, even, he swears, from the moment he saw you."

" 'Tis past comprehension!" I said at last, when I could fetch my breath again, "I must have been no better than a drowned rat."

To which she answered in some satisfaction, "Francis sees straight, have you not found it so?" Before I could speak she continued, "I am expecting again, alas. I could wish sometimes that John were not so uxorious. I haven't told him of this one yet for fear he would forbid me to travel, and I did so wish that we should talk."

"I fear I shall never conceive," I said, for by now I had lost all hope.

She sighed, " 'Tis better none than too many."

But in truth since Francis cared nothing that I gave him no heir, nor has ever reproached me with my barren state, my happiness has been unclouded. He likes to lie with me, and thus has been able to do so without fear, he says, of spoiling my flat belly. "As well," he adds, " 'tis you, not a babe, I wish to hold in my arms."

What female could repine?

The security of his love has enabled me to look back at the past and, in confessing, to understand and put it behind me, as once he bade me do.

Below my window I can hear his voice in conversation with the nephew who is to succeed him. I lay down my pen with an

248

overflowing heart, and give thanks on my knees to my Creator for bringing me safe into harbour.

The autumn of my daies is sweet
My springtime hours
All stormes and showres
You who pass by
Let them lie
Wrapped in obscuritie.

Inscription on a tomb in a Sussex churchyard.